Toxic Torte

by

Lori Pollard-Johnson

A Just Desserts Mystery

Cover Art by *The Wild Rose Press, Inc.*

The Wild Rose Press, Inc.
PO Box 708
Adams Basin, NY 14410-0708
Visit us at www.thewildrosepress.com

Publishing History
First Edition, 2024
Trade Paperback ISBN 978-1-5092-5583-2
Digital ISBN 978-1-5092-5584-9

A Just Desserts Mystery
Published in the United States of America

Dedication

For Gloria, who loved good desserts, sassy girls and a great story,
and for Harley, whose perseverance I luckily inherited;

And for Brian, whose support is as rich and deep as the purest chocolate;

And for Kacea, Scott, Rhiannon, Juneau, Grady and Melissa
for sharing space in their lives with a fairly eccentric old woman who spins stories for fun.

Special thanks to the good folks at The Wild Rose Press for believing in my stories enough to send me Dianne Rich, Editor Extraordinaire, whose ideas always make my words shine and me a better writer. As always, thanks again to my Tiny Rhino friends who have supported, encouraged, critiqued and reviewed this story. I couldn't have done it without you!

Chapter One

Crashing funerals sucks.

Especially when the reason for crashing said funeral is to write an obituary for a dumb weekly no one ever reads. And especially when I had to wake up to the nasal undertones of Rodman, my *Seattle Sun* editor, who called at six a.m. on this dark and rainy February morning to inform me of the story he forgot to mention before I'd left work Friday night. But most especially when I had to skip showering and dig through a smelly hamper for something clean and dark, because this girl doesn't own a little black dress.

Another fabulous day in the life of Jess Harriet. Lifetime television should be calling for an interview any minute.

I parked on the street and stared at the oversized, dark wooden doors of Bellevue Mortuary and sighed. It didn't seem right to heap more bad vibes onto the good folks attending the funeral. I'd need to shake off the bad mood before entering. I practiced smiling in the rearview mirror and rubbed my right knee. Said knee still ached from tripping over a box of lotions and gels labeled "Fruity and Flirty" that my younger sister Jenna sent at Christmas time. I'd opened, but never unpacked, any of it, let alone used it. Each pink, glittery bottle reminded me of how little she and I had in common. She had married at eighteen against our parents' wishes, had her first child about nine months later and her second a year after that. I had taken a semester off from the University of Washington's Journalism program to help Jenna and never got around to returning.

That was four years ago. Now I was twenty-five, back in Seattle, and determined to maintain my unmarried and childless status. No, my goal was to become an investigative reporter for the *Seattle Daily Log,* Seattle's biggest, most widely-read newspaper. At a year shy of a journalism degree and without a savings account to re-enroll, though, I had to bide my time at the *Sun* until I got my big break.

I shook off the pang in my heart, exited the car, and headed for the front door. Once there, I squinted through the stained-glass inserts and focused on the fuzzy shadows inside. After reminding myself it was only a memorial—I wouldn't have to see any actual dead people—I grasped the cold brass handle and walked in.

The pastel foyer was warm and inviting, and I felt my guard letting down. I scanned the small group of people gathered in little knots of color. Only one woman wore black. I deduced she was the widow. Pulling off one rain-soaked mitten, I walked over to her.

"I'm Jess Harriet," I said, holding out my hand.

The woman frowned, worry lines appearing at the corners of her mouth and between her eyebrows. Pegging her at fifty-five and easily startled, I smiled slow and friendly, but respectful of my surroundings. She cocked her bottle-blonde head, her chin-length curls never moving, but she didn't respond.

"From the *Seattle Sun*," I explained, paw still extended.

Her dull blue eyes registered something minuscule, something nearly insignificant. That something could have been me or the *Sun*. Both qualified.

I shifted my weight off my bum knee and tried again. "Rod Henneman, my editor, spoke with you."

Her gaze traveled from my curly mop of still wet brown hair down to my black T-shirt and faded black pants, making me feel smaller than my five feet, two inches and a hundred forty pounds. No doubt she wondered what I was doing there. It was a question we shared.

It wasn't that her husband's death was unimportant. It was. As a talk radio restaurant critic, Perry Lowell could be called a minor Seattle celebrity. But the *Sun* rarely gets to report anything heavier than a neighborhood bake sale or the after-school activity roster of a kids' club. Occasionally, we run an overly polite and punny restaurant review. But we didn't have to. People weren't subscribing to the *Sun* for the articles.

The naked and not-so-pretty truth of the *Sun*'s success exists on its "back page," actually a six-page spread of personal ads. We have the biggest, messiest selection of girls wanting boys, boys wanting girls, girls wanting girls, and boys wanting boys of any Pacific Northwest newspaper. There's even a separate section entitled non-binary seeking same. People like it because everyone's local and there are far fewer scammers than there are on online hook-up sites.

Pasting on a smile, I waited for the widow to respond.

3

After staring a moment at my jagged nails and overgrown cuticles, her face relaxed. The motion sent a ripple of wrinkles across both cheeks as the corners of her mouth turned up. She reached out a French-manicured hand toward me. Perfect little white crescent moons tipped each finger.

"Calendra Lowell," she said. "Perry is, I mean *was*, my husband."

We shook. Her skin was warm, soft, and dry despite the weather. Mine was undoubtedly cold and clammy. She jerked her hand away, wiped it on one ample thigh, and shivered.

"Sorry." I rubbed my palm against my pants. "Rain started up again." Gripping the other mitten between my teeth, I wiggled it off, then pocketed both mittens in my brown tweed blazer.

"Seattle." Calendra motioned her head toward the rain pattering at the stained-glass window, and then finger-combed a lock of hair behind one ear, revealing a large diamond-stud earring. "Whatcha gonna do?"

I shrugged. Short of moving to Florida when I retired in forty years, nada.

She ran her hands over her black beaded top, adjusting the edge so that the design met its match on the skirt. The beads repeated the vine-like pattern at the arm holes and again just below the knees, guarding the hemline. Her bare calves were the color of old snow. On her feet she wore black Birkenstocks. No socks.

Her attire reflected a curious mix of eastside elite meets University District Bohemian and seemed more appropriate for an aging hippie than a widow. But what did I know? I was just a hack writer for a two-bit newspaper. And when I say two-bit, I mean we recently changed the cost of the paper from twenty-five cents to fifty cents for the damn rag. As much as a gumball. For my money, I'd buy the gumball.

"If you don't mind, Mrs. Lowell, I'll just mingle, maybe collect some quotes for the profile." I stared at her forehead to avoid her eyes. As insensitive as I may seem, I could tell that her eyes were sad in a way anyone would recognize. It hurt to look into them too long.

"Call me Callie." She took a deep breath before continuing and brushed back her hair once more. "Thank you for coming at this ungodly hour. We're having a family gathering later today, but restaurant folks have to come early. Chefs have to be in their kitchens by nine to start stocks, receive baked goods—you know." She made a rolling motion with one hand.

I nodded, despite my ignorance. I spent most lunches holed up in my office cave, leaning over a microwaveable carton of take-out from the 24-hour teriyaki place that had moved into the other half of the *Sun* building last summer.

Callie continued. "You know, this is more of an open house. There won't be any formal presentation. Nobody will speak. It's just a time for people to get together and acknowledge my husband's death." She shook her head, and two blonde curls sprang out from behind her ears. "And life, I suppose."

"I understand," I said.

"My husband will love the write-up you're going to do." Callie squeezed her eyes tight, the wrinkles fanning. She swallowed, nudged the curls back into place, then spoke again. "I mean, he would have loved it. Perry loved the written word. He was a writer, too, you know."

I pulled my notepad and pen from the striped beach bag I call a purse. "The profile will go on our 'Bistro Banter' page."

Callie's eyebrows furrowed.

"The 'Bistro Banter' page is where we report all kinds of, uh, food-related news," I explained.

Callie nodded, her face solemn. "Follow me." She turned and bypassed the cordoned-off room to the right and the cream-colored, wrought-iron staircase directly ahead. She headed down a short, mint-green hallway on the left toward an open space.

I trailed her, casting glances as we entered a large, overly warm parlor. About twenty people, including the caterers, stood in the room. Some held plates of food and paper cups of what I assumed was dark brewed coffee. I wriggled my nose in appreciation as its heady scent filled my nostrils. Just behind the warm java bouquet mingled the aromas of fresh baked bread and fried breakfast foods. My stomach woke up and rumbled.

Callie stopped in front of a fireplace, complete with fake wood bundle and gas flame. Above it, a large photo had been projected onto a screen over the white mantel. She peered at it a moment, then up at the ceiling, as if lost. When she faced me, she leaned in and whispered, "You want sunshine in the Northwest?" She pointed up. "You gotta get it indoors."

I followed her finger's trajectory. The ceiling had been painted a brilliant yellow, and in the middle, flush with the ceiling, hovered a brassy, three-foot-diameter sun. Complete with smiling face and wiggling arm rays, it beamed down at us without any warmth. Maybe it was a reminder of better days to come, but it felt inappropriate as hell for a gathering of this nature.

Callie rolled her eyes. She then motioned toward the photo, staring as she spoke. "That's my Perry." Her voice cracked. She swallowed hard. When she continued, her words were softer than before. "I have copies of this photo if you need one for your story. It was his favorite." An uncomfortable silence stretched between us before she continued. "Just let me know."

I nodded and flipped open my notepad. I scribbled the word *photo* and circled it.

Callie swung her gaze round the room, then said, "I need to see to my other guests. But feel free to speak to anyone you like. Everyone loved Perry. Everyone."

Callie turned, took a step, then swiveled back. "Be sure to have something to eat, too." She waved a hand toward a buffet that ran along the far wall. "There's plenty."

I watched her weave a retreat to the foyer again, then took a good look at my surroundings. The guests stood in clumps of twos, threes, and fours. No one stood alone. A few were dressed in variations of chefs' whites; others were dressed in hospital scrub outfits. One pair, a man and a woman, wore matching tiger-striped scrubs and tan canvas shoes, their twin blond ponytails hanging at the back of their necks like manes. The rest sported dressy street clothing. I buttoned my blazer, pulled it as low as possible, and focused on the décor.

The walls had been painted the same soothing mint-green as the hallway leading into it. Dark wood bordered each wall and continued onto the hardwood floor. Stenciling in a climbing ivy pattern wound along the walls to the end, then down the sides. Clumps of synthetic greenery dripped from planters niched into the walls at the corners. Raised, flocked wallpaper covered the lower third of the wall, and lacy tablecloths draped small tables. A lone, faded rug in various shades of green appeared dusted with a fine layer of white flocking, presumably from the wallpaper.

My gaze rested on the photo. I frowned. Perry could have been the love child of Frankenstein and Dracula. He had a broad, round forehead, short, straight bangs, and wide-set brown eyes atop a slender, fragile frame. But the grooming and expression told the story of the man behind the mask. A pencil-width moustache above thin lips suggested practical accountant, but his tapered eyebrows, one permanently raised, screamed high maintenance artist. That's Artist with a capital A. The lit cigarette in his right hand released a curl of smoke. Habit or affect, I had to wonder.

I jotted *creative* and *detail-oriented* on my notepad. Those were safe words. I took a deep breath and caught the scent of buttery maple and cinnamon rolls. My stomach gurgled a response. I'd skipped breakfast and began to regret it. I knew what I had to do, though: collect some first-person statements, scribble some notes, and get out of there. I could write the article from press releases and a few quotes, so it wouldn't take long.

But, then again, Callie did invite me to eat. Nay, she encouraged me.

I inhaled again in indecision. Some new spice had joined the scent fest. This time, the swirling, zesty tang of bacon and sausages embraced me like an old lover. My knees went weak as my mouth anticipated the twin flavors.

I moved toward the table. Maybe I'd eat a little something—something that wouldn't be taking from the real guests. A sprig of plump purple grapes or a handful of crusty country fries. Then I could concentrate on getting the story and vamoosing. I headed the buffet table's way. I knew I was weak. I'd never make it on one of those survival shows where contestants eat foot-long worms and bathe in salt water, but I didn't care. I got in line at the end of the buffet behind three women. They spoke in hushed tones, which to me was an invitation to eavesdrop.

A bleached-blonde, broad-shouldered woman with big teeth and diamond earrings the size of a small island spoke first. "She woke up, looked 'round, and he was dead." Her Texas drawl felt vaguely disconnected from the pale-pink suit she wore. She touched one of the chunky pink stones circling her black hat, lowered her eyes, and shook her head.

A shorter woman, also impossibly blonde, nodded several times, then added, "It was after midnight." She wasn't nearly as flashy as either of her companions, but her eyes spoke of her excitement. They were blue and wide, even with minimal makeup. She wore a deep navy-blue suit with a white camisole blouse underneath. A tennis bracelet with stones so large I wondered if they could be real glittered at her wrist. My mother would have called her handsome, which meant she could have passed for a man in the right light.

"I saw him the night before," said the third blonde. She bobbed her pointy chin and pulled her mouth tight. Lines radiated out from the edges, suggesting a tendency to pucker. Probably a smoker. She wore four-inch stilettos, which put her eye-to-eye with one of her companions, a head below the other. And she was puffy. Puffy hair, puffy lips. Her upswept hairdo, teased to terror, created a kind of hectic halo over her narrow shoulders. Below the neck, she was beyond thin. Except for her boobs. A solid D cup, they stood at attention under a red sweater dress like armored guards.

"Where, Trish?" the shorter one asked.

"Chocoholic Ball. At the Space Needle," replied Trish. "It was for charity, you know."

"Oh," the other two chorused, bowing their heads.

A self-satisfied smile settled on Trish's face. "Only forty-five years old," she said, pulling way ahead in their how-much-do-you-know game.

Trish and her companions stepped forward in line. I wrote down *Chocoholic Ball* and *Space Needle* in my notepad, then closed the distance before someone could cut between us. I'm cagey about free food.

Peering around the trio, I did a quick scan of the spread. First up was a cold pink salmon cut into diamonds and sprinkled with green, grass-like blades. Wedges of juicy oranges, lemons, and limes surrounded it. Next were two platters. On the first rested a heap of crisp, pepper-crusted bacon. On the second, neat lengths of sausage lay side-by-side, their ends tied in bows reminiscent of gifts. Beyond the sausages, a silver rectangle of fluffy yellow eggs dotted with onions and assorted bell peppers awaited.

I wiped drool from my chin and forgave Rod for the early morning call. Even if it wasn't a plum story, at least I got a free meal. Most of the time Rod assigned cat shows to me, while Cherrie Belle, the other *Sun* reporter, picked up the mayoral misquotes and the restaurant openings. I ended up sprayed by finicky felines, and she met powerful people who could advance her career. Rod always told me Cherrie got the best leads because she had a degree, but I happen to know the degree is in Physical Education, a far cry from my three years of journalism. Personally, I thought it had more to do with her short skirts and tight sweaters, and the fact that she's a Seattle Seahawks cheerleader on the weekend, than journalistic ability. Who can compete with that?

Not that I'd want to. Rod is the most arrogant man I'd ever known, and so long as I can keep my job, I didn't care if he liked me or not. I'd always thought his arrogance was due to his George Clooney good looks, but it didn't hurt that he drove a fancy sports car, too. Anyway, any illusion of him favoring me in any way dissipated when Cherrie walked through the *Sun* doors six months ago.

The group ahead gathered plates and forks and began a slow process of choosing foods. I watched carefully, particularly interested in knowing what Trish would choose. Never having been a thin woman with large breasts, I was curious to see how she got that way. My money rode on a radish with leaf lettuce garnish and a side of silicone.

"Hey."

I heard the male voice but didn't respond. Who'd be talking to me at a memorial of someone I didn't even know? I continued my surveillance, observing as hurried hands behind the table combined platters so everything looked full and fresh again while Trish and the others piled salmon and a trio of citrus slices onto their plates.

Hunh. Fish and fruit.

"Hey." A tap on my shoulder accompanied the greeting this time.

I swung round. Before me stood Dream Dude. Mid- to late-twenties, thick brown hair, big brown eyes, slightly Latin-looking. He was the kind of man that made me forget I'd sworn off men just last Friday.

"Hey," I replied, pulling my chestnut strands straight to frame my round face. My sister Jenna, a self-proclaimed fashion and grooming maven with a decent Instagram following, often told me that set off my eyes. To be honest, I wasn't exactly sure what that meant, but I knew it was a good thing.

I smiled and snapped a mental picture of the guy's attire. He wore a relaxed blazer in tones of gray and black, cuffs rolled up. Below was a snug pair of black jeans with a black and white shirt tucked inside. Everything was held in place by a smooth black leather belt. On his feet were black loafers. Between the hem and the shoe, a glimpse of bare skin winked. His shirt was black with white polka dots, the material looking suspiciously like silk and the sleeves decidedly puffy.

"I'm Will." He held out a tanned hand.

"Jess Harriet." I took his hand. It was soft and warm.

"You're the reporter, right?"

"Yeah," I said. Evidently, news traveled fast at memorials. "From the *Sun*."

Will's eyes brightened. "I know the *Sun*. Read it all the time."

I hoped he wasn't referring to the back page but had a hunch he was.

"I'm Perry's little brother," Will said. "And his

best friend. I'm Callie's best friend, too."

I made a note on my pad, then noticed the gossipy trio had pulled forward. Dropping pad and pen into my bag, I said, "Great. I could use some quotes from people who knew him well. It will help me tell the readers who Perry really was." I closed the gap and picked up a black plastic fork, spoon, and knife, and set them on a matching plate.

"Sure," Will said. "Ask me anything. I know everything about him." His face grew long, and his mouth twitched. "I mean, I knew everything about him. Or maybe I know everything there was to know about him." He shook his head and sniffled.

I grabbed a black napkin and held it out to him. He took it, dabbed gently at the corners of his eyes, then tucked it into his front pocket. He gazed at the buffet, then said, "Perry would want me to eat." He collected a set of plastic utensils, wrapped them in a napkin, and wedged the package into his other front pocket.

I nodded in agreement, then speared two sausage links and three pieces of bacon. I arranged them in a quasi-triangle that served as an embankment for the syrup I puddled in the middle. Next, I scooped a mini-mountain of eggs onto my plate. Will followed suit, and together we made our way down the line. I bypassed the low-calorie fruit platter with pink yogurt cups, opting for the pastry and bagel tier of a three-level lazy susan. Already holes had appeared in the piles that were big enough to drive a hearse through. If I didn't snag a few goodies, they'd be long gone by the time I returned.

At the end of the line, Will poured us each a cup of coffee. "Cream and sugar?"

"Black." I had to cut calories somewhere.

He grimaced and said, "Like a man," then handed the little white cup to me. "Let's sit over there." He motioned with his head toward a window seat next to the mantel, separated from the rest of the group. Without waiting for my reply, he headed that way.

I followed, my footsteps heavy next to his. At the window, Will sat, balanced the plate on his legs, and unrolled his napkin. The fork, knife, and spoon fell into his palm.

"Quite a spread," he said, laying the napkin between the plate and his torso. Using the black plasticware, he sliced a tiny portion from the salmon and inserted it into his mouth.

I didn't wait to unroll my utensil package. Using my fingers, I grabbed a slice of bacon and folded it inside my mouth. As I chewed, my tongue bathed in salty maple sweetness, I unwrapped the napkin and debated my next bite.

A moment of pure contentment passed before Will spoke.

"You know," he said after swallowing, "I don't get it."

"Don't get what?" I asked, my mouth full of a second slice of bacon.

Will pointed his fork toward the room of people. "Why they're here."

I stopped mid-chomp. "What do you mean?" I sipped my coffee to cut through the grease.

"I mean they hated him," he said. "And he hated them. It was a mutual hate affair." He continued to scrutinize the group.

"Really?" I rested my plate in one hand while I dug in my bag for my pen and notepad. I didn't see how that info could be worked into an obituary—not without the writer getting fired. But I wanted Will to know he'd been heard. Plus, I was curious.

Will scowled, then turned to me. "And people don't just die at forty-five," he said, his words catching in his throat. "Not when they're healthy."

Will's expression went wistful, then drooped into melancholy. He set his plate on a nearby table and blew his nose into his napkin. "I don't believe it was a heart attack," he said finally. Tears spilled over the rims of his eyes and coursed along both sides of his nose. "And I'm going to prove it."

Chapter Two

"What do you mean you don't believe it was a heart attack?" The sniff of scandal raised the hair on the back of my neck.

Will took a bite out of a mini-quiche topped with a swirl of cream and glared at the crowd before responding. He chewed, swallowed, wiped both corners of his mouth, then eyed me.

"I think someone did something to Perry." He raised one eyebrow. "He was in excellent health. He ate right. He exercised. He had a positive mental attitude. These things matter, you know."

I nodded but wondered if Will just needed to blame someone for his brother's unexpected death. Wasn't that one of the stages of grief?

Or did he have good reason to believe Perry's death had been planned? My curiosity piqued, I began to imagine writing front page copy for the *Sun*. Heck, why stop there? This story could go straight to the *Daily Log*.

A shiver raced down my limbs. It ended in a distinct prickling of my fingers and toes. I stamped my feet and bit into the obvious question. "Who'd want to kill Perry?"

Will lifted his finger and swung it round the room, jabbing as he spoke. "Him. Her. Him. Him. Him. Her. Him and her."

I grabbed his hand and pulled it down, setting the offending digits on his leg and holding them there. Besides being rude, his actions could tip off a murderer.

I looked around. A few people had noticed Will's finger zeroing in on them. Their stares confirmed it. I shoveled a spoonful of fluffy yellow eggs into my mouth, took a swig of coffee, and focused on my plate. When I raised my head again, the mourners had returned to their polite, hushed conversations, their eyes averted.

"Be careful," I said, hushing him with the tone my mother taught me in the back row of our strict Lutheran church when I was eight years old. "Someone might hear you."

"I don't care." Will's glare intensified, his eyes shifting back and forth. He pounded his fist on his knee. "I hate them all."

I ignored the venom and took in the scene. The people he'd pointed out didn't look like killers. Not to me, anyway. To my left, a dude wearing chefs' whites looked like an over-risen biscuit, his cheeks ruddy circles. I half expected him to giggle and clutch his protruding belly, then offer cookies all round. The flame-haired woman next to him looked more like a runway model than a murderer. She wore a red knee-length tunic jacket over matching slacks. The crease pointed to shoes the color of blood, their toes resembling medieval weaponry with their severe points.

As I watched, the two spoke, then separated. Quietly, they left the room without bidding the hostess adieu. Rude? Yes. But it didn't make them murderers.

I continued my surveillance. To the right stood the couple in twin tiger-striped outfits, their faces scrubbed clean. They both appeared tame, domesticated even. And the caterer busily building a donut hole pyramid was a Denzel Washington look-alike. I watched him a moment. His attention to detail suggested a logical, sane mind, one given more to crullers than cruelty. Callie's sharp-tongued friends had nothing to gain, and the rest of the crowd looked like anyone else you'd see strolling a Seattle sidewalk. Regular folks.

I swung my gaze back to Will. "I understand your pain, Will. Really, I do. But these people look pretty tame. Are you sure these aren't your emotions talking?"

He shook his head. "No."

"Then why are all these people here?" I asked. "If they, you know, hated him."

"Probably to bask in the glory of his death." His scowl dissolved a moment later. He held his face in his hands as a tear escaped the corner of his left eye.

"I'm sorry, Will," I said, more compassionately. "Grief screws with our emotions. It makes us believe things when we can't accept what's happened." I paused, surprised at myself. All of a sudden I'd become an armchair psychologist.

Will swung toward me, nearly upsetting his plate. "Look, you can believe me or not. I don't care. But I know someone killed Perry. I bet he, or she, is standing in this room right now. And I'm going to find out who it is." He folded the plastic utensils inside the half-full paper plate like a big taco, then sailed the entire mess into a nearby garbage can. It thunked against the far side and slid down.

The room silenced. The occupants stared at Will, and by association, me. I spent the next few moments inspecting the various foods on my plate and sampling them in an attempt to avoid eye contact.

After an awkward span of time, people began speaking in low tones again. I looked up. Several eased plates and cups into nearby trash cans and began a nonchalant scurry toward the door. A few spoke briefly to Callie, offering their hand for a parting squeeze. Others high-tailed it without a wave good-bye.

When I met Will's eyes, he was staring at me, tears brimming, pain creasing his brow.

I frowned. "Will," I said. "I'm really sorry."

He shook his head and said, "Help me. People will listen to you. You're a writer. A small-time writer, but a writer, nonetheless."

He had me there.

"And you have access to information and resources I don't." He faced me, eyes pleading, before continuing in low tones. "Besides, they all know me. I can't ask any questions without people clamming up. You can, though. You can ask anything, and people will talk."

"I don't know about that," I said. "What makes you think people will answer my questions?"

"Because." Will rolled his eyes as though talking to me was like teaching a kindergartener algebra. "You can make it seem like they're getting free publicity."

Touché. Why hadn't I thought of that?

Will cocked his head. "And after you find out who killed Perry, you can write about it for any paper in the world, even your silly little *Sun*. Everyone will listen. Everyone will care. Most importantly, the person who hurt Perry will get his...or her..." He closed his eyes and waved his hands in the air.

Just deserts? I wanted to ask, but didn't.

Despite my cool exterior, my insides rocked. First,

I didn't like hearing the *Sun* dissed. If anyone was going to do that, it was going to be me.

Second, there was something in Will's voice—a tremor. A conviction. It was in the tilt of his chin. I wanted to believe him. Call me a softie, but the sadness in the room permeated even my hardened shell, and I wanted to help Will and Callie. Closure, I think, is what folks call it nowadays.

Will sighed and spoke, his attention on the buffet table. "I'm sorry. I didn't mean to offend you. Or the *Sun*. I'm just so upset."

"Okay. Say you're right." I lowered my voice. "Say someone here killed Perry."

Will brushed nonexistent crumbs off his thighs before responding. "Okay."

"Why?" I paused a moment, letting the question settle. "What's the point? What'd he do to make someone that mad at him?"

Will harrumphed and scanned the room. His look was intense, his expression full of drama. He turned, met my gaze, and raised the eyebrow again. I wondered if he'd learned that from Perry.

"Why, indeed?" he asked. I shrugged and waited. Finally, he broke eye contact and answered. "Because of the reviews."

Reviews? I frowned. Rod had mentioned that Perry did restaurant reviews on talk radio. He'd said that was why we were doing his profile for the "Bistro Banter" page. At the time I thought it was strange that I had to go to the memorial for a simple obit write-up of someone I'd never even heard of. But if Perry had stirred up controversy with his barbed jibes—that stewed a lot of food people—that was definitely saucy enough for a story.

Ha. Barbed jibes. Stewed food people. Saucy. I amused myself.

Immediately, guilt overcame me. This was not the time or place for levity. I stifled my grin. Okay, if Perry's reviews had been truly controversial, that might be worthy of a story. But was it a motive for murder?

"So did he trash a lot of restaurants?" I bit into a bagel. It was dry.

Will crossed his legs and cocked his head. "You could say that."

I pursed my eyebrows again, knowing they resembled one long, hairy caterpillar when I did. Jenna had told me during one of her marathon labors, I can't remember which one, but the comment had stuck. I relaxed my brow and buttered the bagel bite marks with chived cream cheese. "Was the criticism justified?" I asked.

Will bit his lower lip and crossed his arms. He tucked his hands inside his armpits. He frowned. When he spoke, his words were softer. "Sometimes," he said. "But not always."

Oh.

I nibbled the bagel and gazed out over the dwindling gathering as a flutter started deep inside. It could have been a reaction to too much bacon on an empty stomach, but I didn't think so. Trying hard to play objective reporter, I asked myself the hard questions. Could a nasty radio review ruin a restaurant's business? And, if Lowell had been murdered, how could it have been done so it looked like a heart attack?

I leaned toward Will. "What else have you got?"

"What do you mean?" He tilted his head like a poodle on a dog food commercial.

"Like how his reviews affected people, their businesses? Did Perry ever tell you anything, you know, in private, that supports the murder theory?" The words sputtered out of my mouth.

As I awaited his response, I felt a rush of relief. The intrepid reporter I was afraid had died with nearly four years' of diaper duty reemerged after a long hibernation.

Will hung his head. "People called up the station. They complained about his reviews. Said he'd been unfair. That sort of thing."

"Who called?"

Will didn't look up. "Most of the people here."

Hunh.

I scanned the room again. It was nearly empty now, save for a few speaking with the caterer and the gossiping trio huddled around Callie. The shiver in my spine ended in a stirring in my belly. There might be something to Will's story. It still seemed unbelievable, but then again, murder always seemed unbelievable. I mean, was I the only one afraid of going to hell?

I set my plate on the floor and poised my pen over the paper. "Did anyone ever threaten Perry?"

Will remained mute. I scribbled the date and as many questions as I could remember while I waited for him to speak. He didn't.

"Will?" I prompted.

He took a deep breath. "Yes. They all did."

"What'd they say?" I asked. "Exactly."

Will stared at what remained of the group. "There are lots of ways to threaten people." He turned toward me again. "Not all of it's verbal."

"So how'd they do it?"

Will shifted his attention to his shirt cuffs, unfolded each one, then refolded it in neat, equal dimensions. Afterward, he glanced at me. His mouth worked open and shut a few times like a beached flounder, but no sound came out.

I waited, wiggling my toes inside my shoes. When he didn't speak, I fished a business card out of my bag. "I understand it's hard to talk about. Call me when you feel ready." I held out my card and stood.

Will stared at the white rectangle in my hand but didn't make any movement toward taking it. "They found out."

I sat. "Who found out what?" I didn't know if Will was being evasive, or if there was actually something seamy he had to say but didn't know how. I faced him, prepared to encourage him to spill the beans. "Will?"

Will focused on Callie. She was escorting people to the foyer. As she exited the room, Will's head swung round. "Look, there are things I can't tell you."

I stared at him. His lips pulled tight.

"Why?" I wanted to remind him that there was no sense keeping a dead man's secret. But I stopped myself. He was grieving for his brother and attacking him would only make matters worse.

"Because Perry doesn't deserve to be remembered for something he did wrong." Will grasped my arm again. His eyes threatened more tears.

I softened. I'm a sucker for tears. Especially on guys.

I spoke slowly, enunciating each word. "Will, unless I know what he did, and whom he did it to, I can't research this."

Callie returned. A split second behind her, two men walked in and surveyed the room. The first wore a pair of brown pants and a tweed blazer a lot like mine, but with leather patches at the elbows. The second wore a mismatched blue suit. Both wore black police-issued shoes.

My pulse quickened like that of a romance novel's heroine.

Detectives.

Will grabbed my elbow with his free hand, pinning me in place. I pulled away a bit, instinctively leaning toward the newcomers.

"Please?" Will said. "It's the whole reason you're here."

Vaguely, I registered his words. "What?" Across the room, the cops took in the scene, whispering asides to one another. I'd seen enough detective shows. They were memorizing things, filing details away to be retrieved at will. A moment later, they set their sights on Callie and moved across the carpet.

Callie spotted them when they were five feet away. A puzzled expression gave way to polite acknowledgement, and she strode to meet them halfway.

I stood.

Will tugged at my elbow like a little kid wanting to be picked up. "Please help me. Help us. Both Callie and me."

"I'm trying," I whispered, eyes on the drama unfolding in the middle of the room. "Tell me what's going on."

Will refused to let go of my arm.

I toggled my gaze between Callie and the detectives as they reached one another and shook hands. Hoisting my bag onto my shoulder with my unencumbered hand, I told Will, "I'll call you." I extricated my elbow and pulled away. "But I've gotta go."

I took a step toward Callie, determined to hear what would soon be said. Will jumped up, wrapped one arm around my shoulders and cupped my ear with his free hand. I paused, his spicy aftershave in my nostrils.

He whispered, "I had him autopsied."

I paused. That would explain the detectives.

I faced him. "Really?"

Will lowered his eyes and nodded.

I pivoted, focusing my attention once more on the two cops. They showed their badges to Callie.

"Follow me." I quick-stepped toward the three, dragging a reluctant Will with me.

From across the room I could see Callie's profile take on a half-surprised, half-afraid look. The detectives pocketed their badges. Callie's face rose to meet their eyes.

I inched forward, Will a dead weight on my arm.

The detectives began to speak, their tones too low for me to hear. Each took one of Callie's elbows and led her toward the foyer. Will's grasp tightened. I followed, and of course, so did he.

Callie's stride broke once, and her right knee wobbled. After regaining her footing, the trio continued more slowly. The detectives huddled closer, shouldering her weight.

I broke into a flat-footed sprint. Will nearly lost his balance behind me, but I didn't break stride. When I reached the doorway it was too late to hear the detectives' words, but from Callie's response, I knew what they'd said.

I stopped short and held my breath. Will plowed into my backside but bounced off again. Poised as vertical spoons, we waited.

Callie cradled her head in her hands, a sound of pure misery leaking from her lips.

A moment later, she whispered, "Someone poisoned my Perry?"

Then the room filled with her howls.

Chapter Three

Behind me, Will caught his breath and hung onto my shoulders. His grip grew tighter and heavier each passing second. I placed a hand on each of his and squeezed in a show of support and validation. I had to hand it to him. It looked like he was right. Perry had been murdered.

The sympathy gesture wasn't good enough for him, though. He swung me around and wrapped his arms around my neck, burying his face in my hair. He exhaled once, sending a blast of hot air across my neck, then let loose with a sob straight into my ear. I stared into the flesh of his musky-smelling throat and struggled to breathe with my nose and mouth tight against his cheekbone.

As difficult as it was to get air, it wasn't completely repulsive. If you took away the screaming and tears, it was a little like making out on my parents' couch during my high school years. Then again, it was exactly like making out on my parents' couch during my high school years.

Twisting, I adjusted our necks to swan position and breathed deeply. I patted his back, and whispered, "It's all right" a few times. Every so often I wiped what I sincerely hoped were not boogers from the nape of my neck.

Several sobs later, Will lifted his tear-streaked face.

"Why?" he cried.

If I'd known, I would have told him. But at the moment, all I knew was that someone had killed Perry. And if anyone had the will to figure out who fed Perry the poison, it would be, uh, Will. And me, too.

A moment later Callie returned to the parlor. She walked past us, still stationed at the threshold, her eyes focused on something in the far distance. Will gasped for air and reached out a hand to her. If she saw it, she didn't respond. His hand dropped to his side, and I returned to patting his back as if he were a baby with a reluctant burp.

As Callie continued on her self-defined path, I made like a junior high schooler slow dancing for the first time. Shuffling my feet, I kept Callie in my sights and maneuvered Will, crab-like, across the carpet.

Callie stopped in the center of the room, directly below the brass sun. She turned a slow, complete circle. She stared at the few people there, the leftover food on the buffet table, and the wallpaper and fake foliage surrounding us as though she'd never seen it before. Silently, the group watched. I expected either a meltdown or an explosion, but neither occurred. Instead, when Callie halted her snail-paced twirl, she stood stock-still, facing Perry's picture. Her shoulders sagged and her knees buckled once before straightening again.

The gossipy trio raced forward. They circled her, forming a well-dressed fence, their hands little latches on Callie's shoulders, arms, and back. Each murmured in her own way to an unresponsive Callie.

"Are you okay? Is there anythin' we can do?" asked the Texan, her voice a little louder. She stood in front of Callie, bobbing her head right and left in an effort to meet Callie's gaze, her earrings casting flecks of light onto the sea of curious faces.

Callie whimpered.

The room contracted as we collectively leaned in, focused on the exchange. I stepped closer, tugging Will along. His tears stung hot and wet on my neck, and his breath cooled them, so that I was constantly warmed and then chilled. His face and hands nestled in my hair, causing little pinpricks of pain where my follicles refused to release their hold. If he hadn't been in considerably more distress, I would've howled at the hurt I felt.

I bit my tongue and strained an ear the Texan's way.

"Sorry, darlin'," she said, leaning toward Callie's mouth. Her forehead wrinkled into a Dallas roadmap. "I can't hear you."

Callie's head tilted up slightly. Her eyelids fell closed, but her lips parted. Only a mumble escaped. The three of them leaned in. I inched closer, and Will dominoed behind me.

Finally, Callie spoke again, her tones still too low for me to hear.

I strained forward, Will a quiet, dead weight behind me.

Callie's eyes opened to two tiny slits. "Poisoned," she said. "My Perry was poisoned."

At once, the three released their hold on Callie and reared back, clutching themselves. Miss Texas wrapped her hands over her ears as though not hearing could make it all go away. The handsome woman covered her eyes, refusing to see, and too-thin Trish slapped one hand after the other over her mouth, probably to keep an errant carrot stick from falling in while she was in shock.

With huge effort, I removed myself from Will's stranglehold and eased back. He raced over and joined "See-no, Hear-no, Speak-no" in comforting Callie. I made my way to the group, tentatively at first, trying to see a way to help, but realized in a flash there was no way to improve upon friends and family. I stepped back again.

After several moments of the tearful display, I turned to leave. Will caught my eye. "Help us," he said, his voice raspy.

Without considering the consequences or the implications, I nodded.

Then I turned on my heel, passed the detectives who stood silently watching the group, and walked out the double doors into the drizzle. Instinctively, I picked up my feet and fled across the street. I wasn't sure if I was running toward the Kia or away from the suffocating grief of the memorial. I just knew I didn't belong there.

As the rain thickened, my stride lengthened. I sprinted the remaining two blocks until I'd reached my car, then hopped in and locked all the doors.

I placed both hands and my forehead against the steering wheel, relieved to find the hard plastic surface supporting me. I struggled to catch my breath. My heart pounded a thousand miles a minute and my throat ached like I needed either a glass of water or a good cry. Maybe both.

I stayed that way for several minutes until my breathing and pulse slowed to near normal. Wearily, I lifted my head and twisted the key in the ignition. Instead of shifting into gear, though, I let the Kia rumble in neutral while I watched the rain splatter the window and puddle on the hood.

It wasn't right, I thought, losing someone the way Callie and Will did. I understood Callie and Will's pain. And I got Will's anger, too. To think that they suspected someone who had sat in that same room and grieved with them would have frosted my cupcake. I pondered their misery for a few minutes before the rain eased up and the puddles began to steam away.

What a way to go, I thought, shifting into gear. What a crappy way to go.

I flicked on my signal and waited for three cars to pass. I wondered if the poison would have been discovered without Will's autopsy request. I wondered what kind of poison the killer had used that was that powerful, yet invisible. And then I wondered what kind of person could do that to another human being, not to mention the victim's loved ones.

I shivered, unsure how much was due to my rain-soaked cotton twill pants freezing in the February air and how much to the murder of Perry Lowell.

Without any answers, I checked for a clear road and pulled into traffic. I tried hard to be the objective, logical reporter I knew still lurked inside me somewhere. As I tooled down the city streets, I replayed what I knew.

Perry had been at the Space Needle the night before he'd died. The killer may have been a chef. The motive may have been a bad review. The means may have been chocolate.

I swallowed hard. It seemed too farfetched. And

yet, it was all I had.

Merging onto the main road, I wondered again if I wanted to get involved. Then I remembered the look in Will's eyes. And my promise. And the possibility of a life-changing story.

I changed lanes and headed for the *Sun*'s offices. It was Sunday, but the offices should be quiet and I could work without interruption.

A drip of rainwater coursed from a strand of hair stuck to my cheek down my chin. I wiped it away. What I needed was a plan, a place to start. Motive seemed to be the best bet. I'd start by going back the last couple of months and see what I could dig up on Perry's reviews. Then, armed with a list of names, I'd storm the Needle and find out who on the list had also attended the Chocoholic Ball. A simple process of elimination later, and the murder would be solved. It would be kind of like taking a multiple-choice quiz. I was bound to get at least some of the answers right.

I pulled to a stop at the end of the road, then yielded as a long line of cars zipped past me. Joining them on Lake City Way, I figured I'd start looking for Perry's reviews on the web. I'd look up the radio station Perry worked for and see who he'd most recently panned.

Ha. Panning a chef.

I pondered the possibility of poetic justice for another two miles. At the teriyaki place, I hung a right. I drove around the drive-through lane and into the *Sun*'s parking lot. Jerking to a stop outside the two-story, flat-roofed box the *Sun* shared with the restaurant, I composed myself. I couldn't let on that I had a scoop. It wouldn't be a scoop anymore. Especially if Cherrie were around.

I grabbed my bag and made for the *Sun*'s door. For whatever reason, I'd been given this once-in-a-lifetime opportunity to investigate the underbelly of high society. I would find out which well-heeled, chocolate-eating, red-wine-guzzling Seattle philanthropist had fed Perry Lowell a toxic torte. And I would make a name for myself along the way.

Whistling, I headed toward the *Sun* doors.

Chapter Four

There's a lot of power in knowing something other people don't. Good guys share knowledge with the rest of the world so we can all live better, more informed lives. Bad guys disregard any cost-benefit analysis and keep self-serving info quiet. They enjoy watching the mayhem that ensues when the average Joe's frustration reaches the breaking point. These folks can often be found working as computer technicians and teaching techno-idiots how to run them. A few are politicians.

But I'm a good guy. I'd share the story of Perry Lowell's poisoning with the entire human race when I had it all figured out and there was no danger of the murderer escaping punishment. Then everyone wins. But I wouldn't be sharing anything with Cherrie or Rod until the time was just right, and there was no chance of the story being reassigned to Cherrie.

I shook off the morning mist and swung through the heavy glass doors of the *Sun* building. My grin faded. Seated directly in front of me at the receptionist station was none other than Cherrie Belle. On a Sunday. What were the odds? I braced myself and met her eyes. Since we hadn't had a receptionist for the past six months—one of Rod's cost-cutting schemes—Cherrie had set up shop right there. It was her way of being first in line should a well-meaning citizen drop in to share something newsworthy. It also beat staring at the cement wall opposite our desks. Since the *Sun* building didn't get many rays on the first floor, especially in the six-by-six caves we called offices, I couldn't blame her. I just wish I'd thought of it first.

"Hey, Cherrie." I nodded and hunched forward, fully intending to breeze past her to my own niche in the wall a little farther down the hall. Besides Cherrie, there were only two full-time personal ad takers that worked upstairs on Rod's floor, plus Brad, the *Sun*'s advertising manager who checked in at the office once a day. Brad spent most of his time scraping up sales or chewing peppermint gum in a vain attempt to rid himself of the worst case of chronic bad breath I'd ever encountered, so I had expected a silent, empty space.

Cherrie raised her perfect, brown oval eyes and cocked her head. "Harriet. What's going on?"

She always called me by my last name like we were teammates on a team. "Nothing." I gave a little wave and headed down the hall.

My response was too quick, too forced. I knew that. I'd never been good at lying. Cherrie's chair swiveled with a squeak. Out of my peripheral vision, I saw her stand and walk parallel with me, the counter our median.

I picked up my pace. Just twelve feet and I'd be at my door and out of her reach. At the end of the counter, however, Cherrie intercepted me. She stepped right in front of me, blocking the hallway. I hit the brakes.

"C'mon," Cherrie said, a smile forming on her ripe, frosted plum lips. "I can tell when something's up."

I shifted my gaze toward my office, now a mere six feet away. If I could just get past her, everything would be okay. "Nothing's up, Cherrie," I said, averting my eyes. "I'm just running late."

Cherrie's face froze, but her eyes were on fire. I knew that look. It's a cross between hypnotized cobra and prom queen. Either way, watch out when the music stops.

"It's nothing. Really." Damn my pitchy voice.

Cherrie flicked a clump of long blonde hair off her sapphire sweater that bumped in all the right places. "C'mon, Harriet. You wanna tell me," she said. "What's the scoop? You're never here on a Sunday. There must be something going on."

I frowned, tilting my head to meet her gaze, a full ten inches above my own when she's in heels. And she was always in heels. Cherrie's lips tugged higher. She was young, but she had an uncanny knack for reading people. I'd learned that when I was assigned to train her the first week she worked for the *Sun*. She'd tagged along on an interview I was doing at a local zoo. Instead of observing, though, she zeroed in on a question the monkey handler hadn't wanted to answer. But she'd cajoled it out of him. The resulting headline, "Monkeys Fed Dog Food When Funding Low" became the *Sun*'s fourth highest selling edition in its history. Evidently, we have a lot of animal lovers in Seattle. We actually had to do reprints. So as much as I hated to admit it, a lot of things had risen since she'd gotten there. Our respectability. Our circulation. Our advertising rates. And, of course, our mutual editor's attention.

"Sorry." I sidestepped to the left, then shouldered past her. Sometimes it pays to be the younger sister of three brothers and the older sister of a bathroom-hogging girl. Cherrie may have been the cheerleader, but I could run with the ball.

Her gaze bored holes in my back as I stepped out of arm's reach. But I didn't turn back. I didn't have time to make up a fib, and I couldn't tell her the truth. If I did, she'd march her size four hips right into Rod's office, and before I had a chance to say, "It's my story," he'd be reassigning it to her.

I reached my office, jammed the key in the lock, and pushed the door wide. With one hand I hit the lights. With the other, I fanned the door in an attempt to rid my office of the musty smell that developed every night. The *Sun* building, circa 1962, grew more mold than a penicillin factory. Despite employees' numerous complaints, Rod had done nothing to correct the problem. After a couple tentative sniffs, I closed the door and locked it from the inside.

In one motion, I set my bag on the folding chair in front of my desk and punched the computer on. The hard drive whirred and beeped, warming up. I looked around for a bare slab of desk. Nothing. I piled all my desk papers and books into a stack and swept it into my arms. Where to stash it all? The floor was out. Windowless rooms with an antique air-purifying system ensured that the carpet was almost always moist.

I settled on my handmade two-by-four and concrete block bookshelf. The bottom three shelves were crowded by too many books, CDs, and knick-knacks. The top tier held heaps of supplies, and in-and-out boxes which could be piled one atop the other, but at the cost of obscuring my sole concession to creativity: a poster of a unicorn I'd drawn a goatee on. It gave my whole space a grungy Seattle feel, and I liked it. After several seconds of indecision, I decided the story trumped the beast. "Sorry," I said as I covered all but the unicorn's eyes and three inches of horn. I blew him a kiss, then turned away.

The computer monitor flashed, revealing a password screen. I entered my info and waited for the sluggish Internet connection. I could have used the faster computer with the wireless connection up front, but Cherrie was there.

As the screen came to life, I alternated between drumming my fingers and fiddling with my pen. I skimmed the items I'd already jotted down and added more questions. Did the chefs find out what Will didn't want to tell me? What kind of poison did someone feed Perry? How long had it taken him to die?

The first question I couldn't answer, but if I knew the type of poison and how long it took to kill an adult man, I could count backward to where he'd gotten it and possibly from whom. If it was as I suspected, fed to him at the Chocoholic Ball, a simple guest list would be my next step.

I opened up my email and saw two messages. One from Rod and the other from my sister Jenna. I clicked on Rod's first. He wanted to see me but didn't expect to be in until ten o'clock Monday morning. Fine. I made a note at the top of my questions page and deleted his entry. Jenna's popped up.

Solid blocks of type filled my screen. The first line read "Happy Valentine's Day." I scanned a few paragraphs, then scrolled to the end. Her P.S. said "Do you have any vacation plans this summer?" I shuddered at the thought of traveling to eastern Washington during the hot, sticky summer, knowing when I got there I'd be treated to days and nights of babysitting. I made a mental note to read the entire email and respond later and closed the window. I had a murder to solve.

Since I didn't have Will's phone number, I'd have to call Callie to get it. But I didn't have her number either, so I Googled Seattle radio stations. Up popped KTLK, the station that aired Lowell's reviews. A blinking banner on its home page announced: "KTLK: Seattle's Premiere Talk Radio." Below were several headlines and beginning paragraphs, ellipses indicating more existed a simple click away. I skimmed over the blurbs on the weather, sports, and a prison escape in Walla Walla. To the right was a sidebar with choices from *Contact Us* to *Home Finder*. Near the bottom appeared a snooty-looking cartoon maître d' labeled "Perry's Prattle." I double-clicked on his upturned nose.

An hourglass popped up. For the thousandth time I cursed the *Sun*'s technology budget. I popped a breath mint I found under my keyboard and practiced patience.

The screen spotted, then filled in. A wallet-sized photo of Perry wearing the same sneer I'd seen projected on the wall earlier appeared in the top right-hand corner. In it, he sat at the head of a small table, crystal glassware and bone china in front of him. Where the silverware would have been, though, lay a pencil and pen. Atop the plate a notepad awaited his thoughts. A large silver platter with matching domed lid hovered near his head, held aloft by a white-gloved hand. I wasn't sure what lay under the silver dome, but I was fairly certain Perry wouldn't be eating it with the utensils he had.

Below the picture, a blurb in blue ink appeared and scrolled across the page.

KTLK is pleased to introduce Perry Lowell, host of

"Perry's Prattle," featuring new restaurant reviews Wednesdays and Fridays, with encore presentations every day of the week. Miss a show? Click a link below to look up your favorite restaurant...or just to hear Perry prattle.

I cracked the mint in two with my molars, then read the legend and accompanying icons.

Text Reviews
Bites of Sound
Contact Perry

Under the options, in reverse chronological order, were Perry's reviews with dates, names of restaurants reviewed, and the chefs and proprietors. In the end column was each of the icons: the eyeglasses, the headphones, and the mailbox. It made my job easy. I couldn't help but grin—my luck had finally changed.

First up was Bayou Déjà vu, dated Wednesday, February 11, less than a week ago. More importantly, the last review Perry handed in. A light flashed inside my head. Hadn't the preview page said Wednesdays and Fridays?

If so, where was Friday's review?

I pulled up the calendar function and prayed that viewing two Web pages at once wouldn't make my computer crash. I checked the dating. Sure enough, if Perry had been poisoned on Saturday, February 14, there should have been a review posted the day before: Friday, February 13.

Oh. Friday the thirteenth. Maybe that was a clue. I noted it next to my list of questions, then flipped to a new page in my notepad and wrote down the question. Knowing the lead time required for any written material, and the immediacy of uploading, I figured that

Friday's review should have been posted sometime Thursday and researched a minimum of twenty-four hours before.

If it had been recorded for the drive home, why wasn't it copied to the webpage? It was a lukewarm lead, but I'd follow up on it. Just as soon as I figured out whom to ask. I drew stars around the question, then returned to the screen and re-sized the list of reviews.

I bookmarked the page, then hauled out the phone and wrote down KTLK's number. I placed the call but got put on hold. In the background, an interview with the Walla Walla prisoner played. He'd returned to the prison of his own free will. I held for five minutes of blubbery repentance, then hung up. I'd call again later or maybe Monday. Someone should be answering the phones then.

I returned to the list of review dates and corresponding restaurants and clicked on the review labeled Bayou Déjà vu.

A new box opened. After enlarging it to fill my dinky screen, I read the title.

Bayou Déjà vu—True Grits

I paused. I knew Bayou Déjà vu. It was a barbecue joint that had been a booth at last year's Bite of Seattle. Heavenly smell and great grub. I could still summon the smoky, tangy sauce at will.

Swallowing a mouthful of saliva, I re-read the title of Perry's review. Evidently, he hadn't agreed. I wondered why.

A couple blocks off the waterfront, in one dark corner of Pioneer Park, is a curious little set of doors painted in red, orange, and yellow flames. Reminiscent of the gates of hell, it opens into Bayou Déjà vu,

Seattle's concession to Southern back country dining. Run by the diminutive Chef Jodi Lish, Bayou Déjà vu's menu seems inspired by Satan himself, or as the case may be, herself: all grandeur and promise, but no substance. Cayenne, liberally used, does nothing to cover the gritty corn meal base to every dish. And hot chilies will never substitute for the true gumbo flavor I experienced as a lad in the South.

True, the crawfish, albeit not as fresh as one would find in Louisiana, is palatable, given a good bottle of Chardonnay. Unfortunately, the wine gnomes didn't make a visit to Bayou Déjà vu. Instead, one must choose from a collection of hard-spirited concoctions with hillbilly names like Louisiana Lemonade, Bourbon gone Bayou, and Crocodile Punch. How clever.

Be advised, however: Wear nothing that can't be ruined. Napkins and bibs are standard equipment for this eatery a little north of Hades itself.

I scooted back in my chair and reread the review. Definitely not how I would have described the mouthwatering ribs with the tangy sauce. Perry's Prattle had a vicious bite. But was it enough to murder over?

At the bottom, the physical address and chef/proprietor's name appeared. I backed up a page and clicked on the little headphones. A picture of a miniature tape recorder appeared on the screen. I waited while the green loading bar crept across the page. When it blinked "play," I clicked and settled in to listen to Perry's own words.

He began not with words but with a meaningful clearing of his throat. A pause followed, then a rustle of papers, and finally Perry read from the text I'd just read. I followed along as he read it. It timed in at fifty-nine seconds. I punched it up again and poised my pen over paper. As he repeated his drone, I listened for hesitation before some of the more caustic comments, but there were none. In contrast, he punctuated the phrases "back county dining," "promise but no substance," and "hillbilly names." The rest of the words could have been from a soup label, a box of detergent, or a dictionary for all his inflection and drama. His narration sounded detached, arrogant, and slightly nasal. I set my pen down and listened once more.

As the nasal tone droned on, I pondered him and his words. The review ladled out plenty of nasty about both the restaurant and the chef. Could he do that on the radio?

It wasn't quite slander because he was expected to give an opinion in a review.

But it wasn't like any other review I'd ever heard. And certainly about a popular eatery like Bayou Déjà vu. I shook my head.

The second light bulb of the day flashed on. Wouldn't the unlikelihood of legal recourse make the chefs even angrier? Maybe even angry enough to kill him?

I returned to the review page and focused on the dates. There were two a week in January and February, but the entries decreased to one a week in December. The first one posted was dated November 15. I had no idea if others were archived.

I jotted down more questions: How long had Perry been doing these reviews? How'd he get into this line of work? What were his qualifications? Most importantly, why was I gathering more questions than answers?

I frowned, then highlighted the whole mess of reviews and ordered the computer to print the entire packet. I opted for the old printer down the hall, rather than the newer one up front where Cherrie sat. It would take a lot longer, but hopefully be worth it. When the hourglass disappeared, I left the computer on and punched in the numbers for KTLK on the telephone.

This time I got a busy signal. That was that. When the printer finished, I was out of here.

Chapter Five

I replaced the receiver, grabbed my purse, and headed down the hall, avoiding Cherrie. The old printer was housed at the ass-end of the hall in a closet without a door that smelled of mothballs and, no surprise, mold. Rod decided long ago that buying a new printer when our medium was primarily online would be a waste of resources. To say it was slow was an understatement. So I stood there as the printer hummed, beeped, and clicked, breathing as little as possible of the musty draft. When the first page spewed out, I leaned over the machine and read, my eyes jumping in time with the output.

Friday, February 6.

Bien—French Fries sans Flair

Bien is a smallish, garish hideaway in the upscale section of downtown Seattle. It is easily located by the most obtuse tourist because of its red, white, and blue front side façade. Those are the colors of the French flag, but they also represent most of Chef Laurette Roen's food designs. Red raspberry sauce, white fish, and blue cheese are omnipresent on the menu, yet not a single item stands out as, shall we say, colorful.

There are some decent salads, and certainly Bien makes use of a variety of animal organs that would have otherwise gone to waste in animal food products. But as for me, I'm tired of this saucy chef and her silly sauces. Her famed "Chocolate Torte with Raspberry Sauce" for which she won a James Beard Foundation nod is naught but a warmed-up brownie with red goo reminiscent of Sara Lee.

Boo to Bien.

Holy crap. Bien's write-up made Bayou Déjà vu's review look like high praise. I couldn't imagine the chef—Laurette Roen—being pleased. I couldn't even imagine Perry Lowell's words construed as constructive criticism. The only thing I could imagine was what Chef Roen must have felt after hearing the review. In a word: steamed. I smiled at my own joke and read the next review: Space Needle. Something clicked in my brain. That had also been the site of the Chocoholic Ball. The two things could be connected. My heart jumped a beat as I read.

The Point of Seattle…

Is not at the Space Needle.

Granted, with its gorgeous, near-aerial views and historical significance, the Space Needle does seem like the perfect place to celebrate with out-of-towners. Its menu boasts poultry, beef, and seafood, and would seemingly satisfy the discriminating palate.

This is not the case.

For starters, the poultry is springy, making me wonder if their shipment comes from the Acme rubber chicken factory. Their beef, despite our fabulous Northwest resources, is tough. That goes for the filet, as well as the mastodon flake of bone I discovered while chewing. How the butcher, chef, and server had missed it is beyond me.

And the seafood, spelled "s-e-e-f-o-o-d" by the Needle's misguided marketing department, is named not for the revolving setting, but in my not-so-humble opinion, produced by the same company that makes k-r-a-b.

So if you'd like a dining experience unmarred by disappointment, steer clear of the Needle. But if you'd prefer that those guests never return, by all means, skewer them Space Needle style. As an alternative, may I suggest Union Bay Cabin from last Friday's review? There you'll be treated to a sumptuous meal in a warm and inviting environment.

I exhaled, blowing a clear whistle between my teeth. Lowell's words were scathing, and he had a devastating way with them. But more importantly, why would he bite the proverbial hand that feeds him? If he alienated every restaurant advertiser, how would KTLK stay in business? Honest critique is fair, but these reviews felt like low blows.

Questions hopscotched through my head. I pulled out my notepad and added several to my growing list: Who advertised during Perry's time slot? Who listened to his program?

The only way I was going to find out would be to talk to the advertising manager down at KTLK.

I glanced at the printer's control panel. Twelve pages to go. That meant I had a couple minutes left. I peeked over the partition toward the front desk but didn't see Cherrie anywhere. And no way was I leaving these printouts for her to find. Call me paranoid, but I didn't need to be proven correct to know she'd steal my story.

The next review was none other than Union Bay Cabin. I closed my eyes and tried to remember ever hearing of that restaurant before, but I drew a blank.

That wasn't entirely surprising—I rarely went out, and never to the higher-end eating establishments. I wondered what Lowell found so fabulous about it. I read on.

Union Bay Cabin is Grandma's Cabin in Seattle's Big Bad Woods.

Union Bay Cabin is a bit of a misnomer. It's more like home. Filled with the rich, savory scents of foods prepared with imagination and care by people you love and who love you in return. And, like home, it is a place to which you find yourself wishing to return.

Let me tell you about the appetizers. Steamed clams with clarified butter, oysters on the half-shell, marinated mussels with herbed sourdough points. Does that set your mouth to watering? It does mine.

And then there are the entrees. Roasted chicken with garlic mashed potatoes, prime rib off the grill with ginger carrots and baby peas, puttanesca pizza with California-grown capers. How are your salivary glands now?

Before you leap into your car, or pick up your cell for reservations, let me praise Union Bay Cabin desserts. Seven-layer chocolate cake, pistachio pudding torte, fresh vanilla ice cream with caramel sauce. Mmmmm...

It makes me wish I had more than a minute to talk. See you there: breakfast, lunch, or dinner. They're always open!

I could feel my eyebrows meeting in the middle. Consciously, I released them. After a quick re-read, though, they met again, and I allowed myself the accompanying frown. Not only was the writing less exact, it was nearly all food descriptions. And the foods

48

weren't exotic, not even to me. Mashed potatoes and pizza everywhere, and even I could pronounce all of the foods. How could Union Bay Cabin be that good? Why hadn't I ever heard of it? Most importantly, how could the other restaurants be as bad as Lowell claimed in comparison?

I paused, considering another angle. Would Lowell give good reviews to advertisers? Would he give bad reviews to restaurants that refused to buy advertising? Would a competing restaurant pay to hear another's bad review? I swear a light bulb flickered over my head, bright enough to fill the entire first floor.

Maybe Lowell was ex-torting. Hah! I cracked myself up.

I thought of the picture hanging above the pseudo fireplace at the mortuary. Maybe the guy had a split personality.

I shivered. Even if Lowell had been a hundred percent honest with his criticism, he hadn't been fair in the way he'd told it. But what recourse does a chef have when she, or he, is criticized to that extent, and in such a public way?

Re-course. Funny, but I didn't have time to laugh.

As the asthmatic printer continued, pausing to wheeze after each review, I made a list of places to go. First up was KTLK. I then raced back down the hall and looked up KTLK's address. As I slammed the big yellow book shut, my computer pinged to let me know I'd gotten a new email.

I stepped into the hall. After a quick glance toward the printer closet, I noted that there was no one in sight. That meant Cherrie hadn't gotten curious and tottered down there. I hated to take any more chances by leaving the printout alone, but I wanted to check the email.

I returned to my chair and reentered my time-sensitive password. Another message from Jenna popped up. The time: less than a minute ago. Uh-oh. Two rapid-fire e-mails meant one thing: Jenna had something important to say and wasn't taking a chance of it being ignored. My heart hammered in my chest. I double-clicked, hoping everything was all right with the kids, Mom and Dad, and Jenna herself.

The page opened. In five words, she summed up her world. "I'm pregnant. Please come home."

It didn't take a rocket scientist to know she was due this summer. That's why she asked about my vacation plans.

I stared at the screen. This made baby number three in four years. Jenna would have three babies in diapers by the age of twenty-two. I rubbed my eyes and hit the reply button. I flexed my wrists. I planned to say no, I wasn't going back there. Not this time. But I had to be nice about it. I tapped out several paragraphs, each nicer and more obscure than the previous, but deleted each one, my legs twitching with my need to get back to my printouts. My fingers would not press the right keys, my mouse would not click "send." I closed the e-mail message and vowed to myself to reply as soon as I knew how to answer the question.

I logged off, and as the computer ceased its hum, heard the click of Cherrie's heels in the hallway. Quickly, I grabbed my bag, slammed my door shut, and raced to the printer, passing Cherrie in the hall. Without breaking stride, I gathered the printouts and hugged them close to my chest as I pushed out the side fire door, which wasn't hooked up to the alarm system. I flew past Chang, the teriyaki delivery man who was practicing his Martial Arts moves behind the building, narrowly missed his roundhouse kick, and made for my Kia.

Chapter Six

I barreled over to KTLK just off Northwest 65th and Wallingford in the Green Lake district, stopping only once to purchase a caramel mocha cappuccino with extra whipped cream and nutmeg sprinkles that was too hot to enjoy at the moment. I set it in the cup holder to cool, thinking it would be just right by the time I finished at Lowell's office.

My big plan was to check out Lowell's workspace, then visit the restaurants in the reverse order of when he'd reviewed them. A reasonable plan, in my own humble opinion.

I located the address and noted plenty of pay parking adjacent to KTLK's two-story brick building. I pulled into an empty slot, swiped my debit card at the paybox, then jaywalked across 65th. A gold sign with large red letters spelled out KTLK. In smaller black lettering read Seattle's Premier Talk Radio Station. Directly below it was a set of double glass doors. I gave one brass handle a yank and stepped into the KTLK foyer.

Nice.

The wood floor had been painted red, the walls white. No chairs or couches in this waiting room. Instead, a white, half-circle counter jutted into the middle of the room, and a receptionist sat behind. A shiny red-tiled wall framed her, and a matte brass

KTLK seemingly floated above her head, each letter two feet tall.

As I approached the desk, she met my eyes and spoke. "I'll be with you in just a moment." She returned her attention to the phone receiver in her hand and said, "I don't know. Let me hear it again."

I rested an elbow on the counter and waited for Samantha, according to her name tag, to finish her call. She avoided eye contact as she listened again and ran the long red fingernails of her right hand through her short blonde, pink-and-purple-streaked hair. The tri-colored ends flipped up at ear level, and her ears sported pink hoops that skimmed her shoulders with each bob of her head. She paused for a moment, concentration lines forming between her eyes as she listened to something again.

"Hmmm…" She placed a pen to her lips. "It sounds to me like he's sorry he missed you, and he's hoping to see you again."

Another pause.

"Hell, no." Samantha slammed her pen onto the desk. "Tell me you didn't!" She closed her eyes, waiting for the response, then started in again. "Look, you know any guy who says he loves you on the first date is giving you code for 'Let's sleep together.'"

I cleared my throat.

Her eyes flicked up. She rolled them. I grinned. We've all been stuck on the phone with a remorseful friend.

"Yeah, you made a mistake sleeping with him," she said. "But no, you don't have to wallow in your shame. Just forget about it, and forget about him."

Good advice, I thought, glancing around the space.

Two white half-doors, one at each end of the counter, led in opposite directions. Neither had a handle, so I assumed Samantha had to buzz visitors through. I didn't think it was illegal to wander around an office building uninvited, but who was I? I checked the clock on the wall. Eleven o'clock. They probably had limited hours since it was a Sunday, but I intended to make good use of their time.

"Yeah, yeah, no," Samantha said. "Tiff, I'll call you back. Are you on your cell or at home?" She drew a tiny house complete with chimney and a swirl of smoke in pink ink on her doodle pad, then hung up.

Samantha straightened in her chair. "Sorry about that," she said, shaking her head. "Tiff's my age, twenty-six, but she acts eighteen. She's got some serious man trouble."

"Don't we all?" I replied.

Samantha raised her eyebrows and smiled. "Absolutely. So what can I do ya for?"

I felt no need to lie. We'd already bonded over disappointments in men, and we'd already agreed it sucked. We could be sisters.

"I'm Jess Harriet from the *Sun*," I said. "I'm working on a piece on Mr. Lowell."

Something akin to grief crossed her face. "Didn't you hear?" she whispered. "Mr. Lowell is dead."

I nodded. "Yes. Actually, I was at the memorial this morning." I paused. Surely I would have remembered her hair. "Were you there?"

"Uh-unh. Someone had to man the phones here." She rolled her eyes again before a puzzle knitted her brows together. "Ironic, since I was the only one here who actually got along with the old codger. I'm the one who should have gone. But, I'm the lowly relief receptionist, so here I sit."

"Really?"

"Yeah, really." Her voice cracked. I waited, hoping the silence would draw her out again. Wait for it…"He wasn't exactly everyone's favorite person."

"Why?"

"He could be rather, um, abrasive. But I don't care about that. I can be pretty abrasive myself." She cocked her head. "Wait a minute. How can you do a story on a dead person?"

There it was.

"It's like an obituary, but a little more personal. More like a tribute to him, his work," I said. "That kind of thing."

Samantha's face grew wistful. "Mr. Lowell would have liked that," she said. "So would Mrs. Lowell."

"Is there anyone here who might be able to help me?"

Samantha brought the pen to her mouth and chomped down on the click end. "Well…" she began. "Not really. No one is required to be here on Sundays except for me. All the personalities schedule time in the studio at their convenience. So long as there's a spot open, they can come in at any time."

"It would be so helpful if you could refer me to the manager or to his sound engineers," I said. "I'd only need, like, five minutes." That was a lie, of course, but people have a hard time cutting you off once you start asking questions.

Samantha's expression twisted, revealing an emotional tug-of-war. "That might be difficult."

"Why?"

Her gaze shifted from the two doors back to me. She leaned closer. "Like I said, I was the only one who got along with him. People didn't like him too much." She paused and glanced around again. "He really pissed people off. Like, a lot. I got along with him because I accepted him the way he was. That's something I pride myself on. If I want people to accept me, I need to accept them."

"All I need are a few quotes. Someone to tell me what was meaningful to Perry." I snapped my fingers. "Maybe you could help me."

Her eyes registered a mix of interest and apprehension. "What do you want me to do?"

"Just tell me a little about how he did his shows, how he did the research, how he chose the restaurants he reviewed," I said. "Anything that helps me, and of course, my readers, to understand who he was and how he worked so they can better understand the man behind the voice."

Tiffany nodded and smiled, revealing straight, even teeth. "Mr. Lowell deserves at least that, no matter who he pissed off."

Her statement reminded me of Will's comment earlier that morning. He'd said Lowell shouldn't be remembered for what he'd done wrong. I wondered if they were talking about the same thing.

"What do you mean?"

Samantha pursed her lips and whispered, "Okay, I'm not supposed to leave the front, but if it's only for a minute, it should be okay. Let me just switch my phone over." She punched a button, then stood and walked toward the door to my right. "Come around this way."

She lifted a portion of the counter, and it swung up

drawbridge-style. She held it as I walked through, then replaced it and flipped a latch, sealing us in. One quick glance toward the doors, and Samantha held out her hand. "I'm Sammy, by the way."

We shook. "Good to meet you, Sammy," I said. "I appreciate your help."

We walked through the door, righteous conspirators on a mission, her leading the way. Halfway down the hall, she turned. "I'm going to take you to his office, let you get a feel for who he was. I'll answer what I can, then try to come up with some recent stuff he said."

Somewhere in my cerebral cortex, a thousand slot machines hit jackpot. "Thanks," I said, keeping pace with her quick strides.

She nodded, hoops swaying. As she walked, she wiggled a hot-pink plastic coil from her wrist and fiddled with the keys attached to it. At the end of the hall, she stopped in front of a door. Spelled out in gold script letters on the dark wood were the words "Mr. Lowell." Sammy selected one of the keys and inserted it into the door's lock. She twisted. It clicked in response. Before opening, though, she rapped twice and listened for a reply. Without an answer, she slowly swung open the door.

"This is…was Mr. Lowell's office."

I stepped in and took a good look around. The first thing that struck me was the order and stainless-steel theme. A silver desk organizer and paper clip dispenser sat at his twelve and two o'clock positions, and three mounted pens, all silver and gleaming, stood at attention at eleven o'clock. Directly in front sat a keyboard, trimmed in metal. Mounted to the wall on a retractable arm rested a stainless-steel monitor. Everything was spotless. Even the monitor was smudge-free.

"Immaculate," I said, true appreciation evident in my voice.

"Yeah. Mr. Lowell was…particular."

"Did all the presenters have their own office?"

"No, only the ones that are recorded here. A lot of our programming is syndicated, so there aren't any offices for those presenters. And the advertising salespeople work out of their cars for the most part."

That made sense. Office space was expensive. I turned my attention back to Lowell's office. A black bookcase hung directly over his desk. Wedged between two heavy, trunk-up elephant bookends stood several oversized three-ring binders, each spine clearly labeled in black block lettering on a white background. Arranged chronologically by month, they ran from November through February. My heart zinged. Despite a lack of organization in my own office, I could see how his uber-order would help me immensely if I had the inclination and the time to put it into practice for myself.

I pulled out my pen and notepad, flipped to a new page and wrote, "Perry's office."

I looked to Sammy. I had no idea where to begin. I'd never done an office search. It felt disrespectful, but not so much so that I would forgo it.

Sammy glanced down the hall toward the reception area and then back to me. "So what do you want to know?"

A moment of panic passed. I didn't know where to start but was determined not to let Sammy know. I spit out the first question that came to mind.

"Do you know what his demographic was?" I drew a rectangle with an architect's half-moon and diagonal line to represent the door. At least I'd have a sketch of his office to refer back to.

"You mean who listened?"

I nodded, adding smaller rectangles for his desk, chair, and bookcase on my notepad.

Sammy shrugged. "Regular people."

"People driving home from work?"

Sammy nodded. "And housewife types. You know, pick up the kids from school, go through Mickey D's, then off to soccer or ballet or karate class. Then they sit in their SUVs and call into the radio station on their cells. Mr. Lowell used to brag about how he reached out and touched the common man…and woman."

Jotting that down, I said, "I noticed Friday's review wasn't on the webpage. Do you know why?"

Sammy's gaze searched the ceiling. "It was up there," she said. "I know because I read it. Mr. Lowell sends it to everyone's email. Then right after that, he puts it up online."

"It's not up now," I said, outlining Lowell's window. "Or maybe the process got interrupted. Maybe he sent out the email but didn't upload the review onto the web."

"That's funny," Sammy said. "I could have sworn it was uploaded."

I stopped my drawing and looked her in the eye. "Is there a way that you can check to see if it had been put up in the first place?"

Sammy's face squished into a look of confusion. "I don't know," she said. "Why would we need to find that out?"

The last thing I needed was for Sammy to become suspicious of me and my questions. I shrugged good-naturedly and said, "No reason. I just thought I should read his latest review to get a good feel for what he was working on at the time of his death. It would be kind of an honor to the last reviewed person."

Sammy's frown deepened. "I don't know how much of an honor it would be," she said. "But I can check on it." She shuffled her feet.

"That would be great," I said. "And I promise I won't tell anyone where I got it."

Sammy nodded, then poked her head out the door and peered down the hallway.

"Do you need to get back to your desk?" I asked. "I'll be okay in here alone. I only need five minutes, I promise."

Sammy shifted her weight and played with her earring. "I'm not really supposed to let people in, so I shouldn't leave you alone." She glanced around Perry's spotless office before continuing. "But the man's dead. How on earth could it hurt?"

"Five minutes," I repeated with a wink. "I promise."

Sammy nodded. "Okay, I'm going to lock and prop. Just be sure to pull the door closed shut behind you when you leave. Mrs. Lowell might want some of his stuff. You know, sentimental stuff."

I nodded and held up three fingers in the Boy Scout honor oath. She locked the door, then nudged a white Buddha statue to the door's edge.

"Thanks. I'll be right out." I grinned like a four-year-old at a birthday party.

"Good luck." Sammy winked, swiveled on her heel, and sashayed down the hall.

I liked that girl.

As soon as she was out of sight, I eased the door closed, then pulled down the binder labeled *February* and flipped to the first page.

Perry had done himself proud. Complete with scrapbooking stickers and handwritten notes, he'd even completed a title page for his book of published works. On the table of contents three listings had been printed, each in a different color: Union Bay Cabin, Bien, and Bayou Déjà vu. He had left space at the bottom, presumably for more entries.

I started with the first color-coordinated section— green. It read "February 4th: Union Bay Cabin." It held a menu and business card from the restaurant. On the back, three index cards with hand-scrawled notes appeared glued on. I had a hard time believing someone actually carried index cards to review a restaurant. An astute waitperson would pick him out immediately. And what good's a review if people know they're being reviewed?

I made a note of those questions and moved to the next page. On it, a hard copy of his review had been affixed with more glue. Not wanting to waste precious time reading it since I already had a copy in my bag, I turned the page. More of the same, only a different restaurant—Bien—and accented in blue. I skipped Bien's review and scanned the menu. It was in French, with no English translation. How anyone ordered there was beyond me. The prices were digits without dollar signs. 32. 45. 68.

Finally, I flipped to the last completed section:

Bayou Déjà vu, all in orange. Same format.

The interesting thing, however, was in the next section. Or rather, wasn't in the next section: the missing review for Friday the 13th.

The menu and business card page were empty, but on the next page, three index cards had been glued onto the sheet at angles. I couldn't make out many words—there were lots of accents and apostrophes in a tight, small chicken scratch. No restaurant name there, either. Given time and a menu to compare the foreign words to, I could probably figure it out.

A moral dilemma ensued. Should I sit down and attempt to decipher his hieroglyphics, or should I borrow the index cards? Challenging dilemma. On the one hand, borrowing something that isn't yours is wrong—we all know that. On the other hand, the damage had been done and the owner was dead. What good could they possibly do him? Then again, I could just take a picture with my cell phone. Pragmatism won out. I snapped the pic and checked the resolution.

Not good. I squinted at the script on the actual card but had a hard time making out the words. Occasionally, an "i" or "t" would jump out, mostly by their dots and crosses.

A voice down the hall grabbed my attention. I swung round, my heart racing, and listened carefully. A man's low tone, words undistinguishable. No response from Sammy.

I stared at the page. If I didn't take them now, I'd probably never have another chance.

Shaking the moral angels off my shoulders, I tried to pry the cards off the page. My reward was a tear as the index card ripped over a hard piece of glue.

This wouldn't work.

I'd have to take the whole page if I was going to take it at all.

A click sounded from down the hall. I paused to place the noise. The counter gate. They were coming my way. I released the three-ring mechanism and removed the page.

Just as I wedged the page into my bag, footsteps thundered down the hallway.

I froze. I'd never been caught stealing before. An image of my sheriff's deputy brother, smug smile on his face and a brass ring full of jail keys dangling from his hand, appeared in front of my eyes.

With lightning speed, I replaced the binder on the bookcase. Shoving the elephant bookend tight again, the rings snapped shut.

I stood, pushed Lowell's chair against his desk, and swung my bag over my shoulder. After a nanosecond spent scanning the room for evidence of my presence, I jerked the door open and scooted Buddha back in place.

When I stepped out, the footsteps had materialized into a mountain of a man towering over me. He filled the doorway with a brown suit that had to have been bought at the Big Boy Outlets. He was well over six foot, four inches and at least three hundred pounds. He wore a stony expression below a cap of snow-white hair.

"Who are you?" he asked.

"I'm Jess Harriet," I said, extending my hand. This guy was up to no good. It would be best to play dumb. "It's a pleasure to meet you, Mr. Lowell." I gave myself a pat on the back for thinking up that deception so quickly and stared back at him.

He took my hand and squeezed hard. "What are you doing here?"

I pulled my eyebrows together as if in confusion but stayed with the story. "We had an appointment," I said. "Remember?"

The lines around the man's eyes shortened, but he continued to stare at me hard.

I maintained the goofy grin. "I can come back another time," I said, trying to pull my hand back. "If this isn't convenient."

He held tight and I had no choice but to pretend not to notice that his grip could have ripped my arm off.

As he stared at me, then the contents of Perry's office, I wondered what I had gotten myself into. Here I was, trapped just outside Perry's office, no Sammy in sight, and a killer on the loose. My heart began pounding loud enough to affect my hearing. Could this have been Perry's killer? I swallowed hard and attempted to pull back my hand.

The man's mouth moved, but I couldn't make out what he'd said.

"Excuse me?"

"What were you doing in there?" He loosened his clench long enough to point at Perry's desk. I pulled my arm away, stuck it in my pocket for safekeeping, and stepped back. The look in his eyes told me not to pretend I didn't know where he meant.

"Waiting for you," I said. "When I heard your voice, I came out."

I stepped back to let mountain man see I had nothing to hide. The room was immaculate. Just the way I'd found it.

He scanned the room. His eyes moved across,

diagonally, and up and down. I gulped again and peered around him down the hall. Still no Sammy.

"Who let you in here?"

Rats. I really hadn't wanted to reveal my source. Images of the Watergate reporters sitting in jail cells filled my head. I would not do well on prison food.

I tried evasion and hoped for the best.

"Is there a problem, Mr. Lowell?" I asked. "If this is inconvenient—"

Instead of replying, he took a step into the room, turned, and faced the wall opposite the desk. His gaze skimmed quickly over the blank space. I could have made a break for it, but I would have had to fight off three hundred pounds of flesh when he caught me. And I was certain he'd catch me.

The man's eyes leveled on mine, quite a feat, given our relative sizes. "You didn't take anything from my office, did you, Miss Harriet?"

My heart leapt into my throat and my knees threatened to buckle. It was one thing for me to pretend he was Lowell to get out of trouble. The fact that he played along scared the bejeebers out of me. Pretty ballsy for a security guard. If he was a security guard.

The idea that he could be someone else entirely, maybe even a—gulp—chef, scared me even more.

I fought the urge to pee my pants and made like I lied for a living. "Of course not, Mr. Lowell. I just waited," I said, my voice weak. "I can come back at another time if you'd like."

He evaluated me a moment longer, then swept a last gaze round the office. If anything had been out of place, it would have been immediately obvious. "I'll call you to reschedule," he said. "Don't call me."

I nodded, walked down the hall, and lifted the counter gate on my own. Sammy's chair sat empty. Three red lights flashed on her phone. Where was she?

I would've liked to have called out, maybe searched for her, but with Mr. Mount Everest an uncertain distance behind me, I decided it would be better to pretend everything seemed fine and call her from a distance to make sure she was okay.

I swung through the glass doors and walked to the end of the block. While waiting for the crosswalk to clear, I hazarded a glance back. Mountain man dwarfed the front entry in both height and girth. He stood still as a statue, hands behind his back, staring at me. I gave a little wave, but he didn't respond.

After sprinting across the street, I hopped in the Kia and gunned it. I wanted to put as much distance between me and the human ski resort as possible. If his intention had been to creep me out, it had worked.

Chapter Seven

That creep made me anxious to talk with people who knew I existed and would definitely send a search party if I disappeared.

When I was out of his sight, I lifted the caramel mocha cappuccino from the console and tongue-tested the temperature. Goldilocks herself would have declared it just right. A solid inch-and-a-half of melted whipped cream followed by a thick and dark chocolate caramel coffee coated my throat. Aah. I took several sips and replaced it in the holder. Already my nerves felt better.

At the next stoplight I dug out my cell phone and held the button until its familiar chirp announced it was on and ready for chatting. I set it in the cell holder affixed to my dash and navigated back to the waterfront. Just as I merged into southbound traffic, the cell phone chirped again. Sliding it open, I saw I had two missed calls, both from Rod, and one voice message, also from Rod.

Lovely.

As I toyed with the idea of phoning him back now versus after I returned to the office on Monday, the chorus to "Crimson and Clover" played. That was an actual call. I didn't have to look at the display to know it was Rod. I picked it up and pressed the speakerphone button.

"Jess Harriet."

"Where the hell are you?"

"I'm fine," I said, slowing to allow a speedster in a northbound lane to pass. Suddenly, I was in no hurry to return to the office. "How are you?"

As expected, Rod ignored my niceties. "Where *are* you?"

"I am presently in my Kia, driving northbound toward the office," I replied. "If you give me a moment, I'll triangulate my position and give you the exact coordinates."

"Why didn't you check in with me?" he said. "I've been waiting for you to get here. I even went downstairs looking for you."

"Well, until a few minutes ago, I was there." I checked the digital clock on the dashboard. Almost noon. "Ask Cherrie. She was there, too."

Rod harrumphed. "I already asked Cherrie. She said you hadn't been in this morning."

I considered any number of obscenities. Bitch. Ho. Bitch-Ho.

"Wow," I said. "I could have sworn that was her in the blue sweater. My mistake."

Rod paused only a split-second before plowing forward. "Look, I know it's a Sunday and all, but I want to run this story in tomorrow's uploads. How's the story coming along?"

"Okay." I took another sip of the caramel mocha cappuccino. Oh, yeah. It definitely took the edge off of an angry Rod.

"What'd you get at the memorial?" Rod's persistent voice alerted me that something was up. I frowned. Rod never checked my stories mid-progress.

He must have found out Perry had been poisoned. Maybe he planned to scoop me.

"So what do you make of it?" I ventured, hoping he'd tip his hand.

"Make of what?" Rod's words returned to a slow, measured beat. Whether he hadn't heard the poison news or faked knowledge for some unknown reason was anyone's guess. I'd never figured the guy out.

Major dilemma.

If I told Rod how Perry died, I'd lose the story— probably to long-legged Cherrie. Maybe even to Rod himself. If I didn't tell him, I'd have a little more time to solve the murder and write it up, make my journalism mark on the world, impress the *Seattle Daily Log*, and get offered a fabulous job. I might even have time to breeze into the police station and receive an honorary badge or standing ovation.

"Why are you calling?" I blew noisily into the little sippy hole on the lid of the cappuccino, creating a whistling effect in the earpiece. That kind of thing makes Rod crazy. And provoking Rod had become a way of life for me. It beat dating for hours of amusement and was far cheaper.

Rod cleared his throat. "Why do you want to know?"

He had me there. I fished the straw out, making sure it squeaked on the ridge of the sippy-hole. I pictured Rod cringing from the sound, goose bumps rising below his white Oxford shirt.

"Just curious," I said.

"Maybe I'm just curious, too."

Ah. The stand-off. We arrived here often. Since I was the subordinate, I had to give first. I could prolong the agony, but I couldn't change fate.

"Story's good," I said. "I'll have the dead dude's write-up by tomorrow afternoon as promised." Flip was common for me. Even so, it seemed harsh given the circumstances. I bit my tongue.

A sharp intake of breath passed through the phone line. I thought maybe Rod had had a heart attack or something.

"Rod?" I stopped sipping and set the cup in the center console. "What's the matter?"

Silence.

"Rod?" I stared up at the Kia rooftop, momentarily forgetting that I wasn't in my office cave, one floor below his window-lined office.

"Jess," he answered. "There's something you should know. About this story."

I signaled and moved one lane over to the right. "What?"

The slight creak of the leather swivel chair behind his oversized desk transmitted via cell phone towers. I pictured him sitting, feet propped up on the windowsill, staring at the alders outside. He'd loosened his tie, unbuttoned his shirt at the top, and rolled his cuffs. I flushed at the turn my imagination had taken, then shook my head to clear the image.

"Rod?"

"Perry Lowell was my uncle."

I gasped. "What?"

"You heard right," Rod said. "He was my uncle."

I eased over another lane. My exit was ahead. "Sorry, Rod. I didn't know. Sorry."

"It's all right, Harriet. Actually, Callie's my aunt. On my dad's side."

"Wow."

"Yeah." He cleared his throat, and his tone returned to business mode. "It will mean a lot to Aunt Callie when we get this story completed."

Yeah. So would solving the crime and putting away the murderer. I toyed with my conscience. If he didn't know that Perry had been poisoned, I didn't want to be the one to tell him. But he definitely should know.

"Rod?" I ventured. "Have you talked to Callie this morning?"

"No, I'll be seeing her this afternoon at the family memorial. We're getting together around three." He paused. "Why?"

I leaned over my steering wheel and slowed on the exit ramp. Do I tell him now and get it over with? Or do I tell him in person to soften the blow?

"Why, Jess?" His tone was softer.

I shivered. That always happens to me when his voice gets all nice and he uses my first name. "There's something I've got to tell you," I said. "It's better if I tell you in person. It's about the memorial."

"What is it?"

"Can you give me a few minutes to get there?" I asked. "I'll be there in five."

Rod was hesitant. "Is it that important?"

"Yeah."

"Okay," he said. "But hurry."

He hung up. I tossed the phone onto the passenger seat and merged onto Lake City Way. Once in the right lane, I removed the cup from the console once more. I sipped until I reached the stoplight in front of the teriyaki place.

A minute later, and without knocking first, I

entered Rod's office. Sure enough, he sat in the burgundy leather chair behind his desk, framed by a custom-made bookcase that outlined his window. The bookcase held leather-bound tomes I suspected he bought by the yard online, not by browsing expensive antique stores and collecting one by one. And I doubted he'd read any of them. His face was expressionless, but his small hazel eyes stared straight at me. He was surprised but trying hard to hide it.

My actions surprised me, too. I was always sassy, but I rarely went to his office unbidden. It was the *Sun*'s code of conduct to wait until Rod requested someone's presence before climbing the staircase to the royal second floor.

I settled into the tall, straight-back chair in front of his desk. My feet didn't touch the floor with my butt on the cushion, so sitting there made me feel like a child about to be reprimanded by my stern father.

"There's something you need to know," I said, not sure where to begin.

"There's something you need to know, too." Rod opened his top desk drawer and slid a napkin across his desk toward me. I wiped my chin. A small brownish cappuccino smear appeared on the white surface of the napkin. I rolled my eyes. I really needed to remember to check the mirror before getting out of the car. Especially in front of Rod.

"Okay," Rod said. "What's your news?" He leaned back in his chair and clasped his hands behind his head. When he did that, it made his rapidly receding hairline nearly disappear. At twenty-nine, he was only four years older than me, but he looked an additional five without hair. That was okay. He acted like he was ten years older than me, too, when he shifted into boss mode.

I dabbed above my lip and at the sides of my mouth, then wadded the napkin and dropped it into my bag. I'd throw it away later. "Well," I said, before pausing. I spent a moment in panic wondering if it really was my job to give him the bad news. How do you tell someone their family member had been murdered?

"Today, Harriet." Rod exhaled.

I frowned. It wasn't going to be easy, but it had to be done. "I'm sorry I have to be the one to tell you—it may not even be appropriate—but the cops came when I was at the memorial this morning."

Rod's narrow face cocked to one side, but his gaze never wandered. "Do you know why?"

"Yes. They found something during the autopsy."

"Autopsy? What autopsy?" Rod froze. "What did they find?"

"His brother ordered the autopsy," I said. "And they found poison. Sorry."

I knew I was revealing a side of myself, a softer, more girly side, to Rod, with the inclusion of "sorry," but I couldn't help it. At that moment, I felt bad. Really bad. For Rod. For Callie. For Will. For everyone at the memorial. Even for me.

"Are you sure?" Rod pulled his hands forward, so that his face resembled a Shar-pei's. On him, it wasn't a good look.

I nodded, close-mouthed. When I spoke, my voice became gentle. "I heard the cops myself."

"What kind of poison?"

"Sorry, I don't know," I said. For good measure, I

added another "Sorry."

"Well, I'll be damned." Rod's eyes rolled toward the ceiling. After a moment, he shook his head and one side of his mouth curled up. "The old guy finally got knocked off his throne."

Chapter Eight

I waited as Rod had himself a good little laugh. Sure, Lowell had been high on himself. That was obvious from the smirk he wore in photos and the tone in his voice recordings. But wasn't it a bit rude, given the circumstances, to call your uncle arrogant? I mean, that's exactly what he was doing. Especially when the guy had been dethroned?

I hesitated, unable to join in. Patiently, I shifted in the uncomfortable upright chair. I waited for Rod to speak. He chortled a few times as I stared at the ceiling, the leather-bound books, and the doodle-free doodle pad on Rod's desk. Finally, I gave into the temptation of meeting his eyes.

He'd stopped. Not even a grin remained. "So who ordered the autopsy?" His voice was dry, emotionless, restrained. Vintage Rod.

"The brother."

"Who?"

"Perry's brother."

Rod frowned. "Perry doesn't have a brother. He's an only child."

"I thought he said he was Perry's brother." I frowned, skimming my notes. On top lay the sheet of index cards. I set it in my lap for later. It occurred to me that Rod might be able to read Lowell's writing. I didn't need him to know just yet that I'd already begun investigating Lowell's murder.

Unearthing the notepad, I scrolled down to where I'd made the memorial notes. "Yeah. His name is Will," I said. "Perry's little brother."

Rod rolled his eyes. "That wasn't Perry's brother."

"Who was he?"

Rod rocked in his chair and steepled his fingers in front of his face. Several seconds passed before he answered. "I'm sure this whole murder angle is fascinating to you, Harriet, but we're going to run the story as intended…a profile."

My mouth dropped open. "But…"

"Do you think you can have the profile by tomorrow?"

My jaw worked up and down, but no sound came out. Two things became perfectly clear at this point: One, Rod wasn't going to tell me who Will was, and two, I'd better not push the point about the story angle. It would only result in him asking me to cover for an ad-taker during the vacation months. Definitely not something I wanted to do again. Last time I filled in, a guy doing a personal ad asked me to spell *nipple clamp*.

I stashed the index card sheet back into my bag. "Absolutely." I started to get up.

"And it will be on time?"

I glared. I'd only been late once in the past year. I'd had my wisdom teeth pulled and developed dry socket. Even so, my story was only a day late. Unfortunately, in the news business there's no difference between a day late and a year late. If it doesn't make deadline, it doesn't see print.

"That's what I said." I met his gaze with my own steely expression.

Rod stared at me a moment more, his fingertips tapping the bridge of his nose. He seemed to want to say something, but successfully fought the urge.

I rose. "I'd better get to that story." I'd made it almost to the door when Rod stopped me.

"Let's get together again around lunch time tomorrow, say twelve thirty," he said. "I'd like to check the story before it goes live."

I nodded. That was unusual, but reasonable. "Sure."

I rumbled down the stairs and through the hallway. Once entombed in my office, I set up my desk. I didn't allow myself time to pout about Rod's decision to go with the original story. I would solve this thing on my own time if I had to. I'd made a promise to Will—whoever he was. And myself. Later, when I finished, if Rod didn't want the story, I'd freelance it. Someone, hopefully the *Daily Log*, would want it.

With a buoyant heart, I stacked the printouts to my left, my notes to the right, and smack in the middle the prized index card sheet from Lowell's office. Retrieving a pair of scissors from my top drawer, I cut the index cards apart and discarded what remained of the sheet. I stared at the cards again, but still couldn't make out any words. Either Perry had written them in another language or he had one helluva shorthand. Too bad I couldn't ask Rod to interpret, but it wasn't necessary if I was only writing a glorified obit. And that's what Rod thought I was writing.

I pushed them to the top of the desk and slid the reviews in front of me. I could put the profile together later in plenty of time for my lunch meeting with Rod. My first goal was to create a suspect list for my murder story. I pulled a yellow legal pad out of the bottom drawer of my desk. After drawing a vertical line down the middle, I labeled the left column *suspects*. On the right side I wrote *motive*. Directly under *suspects*, I wrote *Jody Lish—Bayou Déjà vu.* Across from her name, I wrote *bad review*.

Following that entry, I wrote two more: *Laurette Roen—Bien/bad review* and after noting the Space Needle's chef, added: *Doug DuBois—Space Needle/bad review*.

I turned my attention back to the stack of printouts in front of me. Lowell had been writing reviews since November. If all of them had been as nasty as these three, he was lucky he lived as long as he did. I tried to imagine what it would be like to be skewered publicly. It had to be horrible. Especially considering that in the restaurant business it would affect your livelihood.

And I thought getting called at six a.m. was bad.

Maybe Will was right. Maybe a bad review was reason for murder.

Will. Why had he lied about being Perry's brother? It wasn't exactly a perk to be the brother of someone who had an angry mob for a following.

I shook my head again and wrote Will's name at the very bottom of the *suspects* column. A long shot, I realized, but maybe all that talk about chefs who hated Perry was just a way of diverting people's attention from the real murderer—Will himself. In the motive column, I drew a question mark.

After a moment spent glancing over the list, I realized I wasn't getting any answers, only more questions. I needed to get out and talk with real people who knew, and possibly hated, Perry Lowell.

Remembering Sammy, I gave her a quick jingle on my cell, but my call went straight to voice mail. I left a quick message asking her to call me, then slid the phone closed.

What to do next?

I could run with my original plan and head for Bayou Déjà vu, but that wouldn't tell me how someone managed to poison him at the Chocoholic Ball.

I checked the time. Nearly one o'clock. The Space Needle had to be open by now. Stashing the rest of the reviews inside my bag, I logged the computer to standby, then locked up and headed for the front door.

As I passed Cherrie's desk, she said, "Good story, Harriet."

I swung my gaze around. She hadn't even bothered to look up.

"What story?"

Cherrie glanced my way and raised one perfectly-arched eyebrow. "Oh, any story you might be working on." She looked away to a vase on the corner of her desk. In it, a new bouquet of pink tulips blossomed. Delicately, she traced one stem with an index finger, then returned to her paperwork.

I considered asking what she did to earn the flowers but stopped myself. Instead, I mumbled, "Thanks."

As I crossed the threshold to the *Sun* parking lot, I realized Cherrie had been fishing for my story.

But she wasn't going to get it.

It was mine.

Chapter Nine

As challenging as driving in downtown Seattle is, given the one-way streets and vision-blocking buildings, I've learned if I keep Elliot Bay on my right then turn left when I see the Needle, I'll eventually wind my way up the hill and find Seattle Center.

Plan "A" entailed me playing tourist. Not very original, but I couldn't tell anyone I was a reporter. People clam up when they think their words might wind up in print. I didn't have a Plan "B."

I parked and crossed Broad. In front of me, the Needle looked like a mini-fortress. Two stories of thick glass walls allowed those of us on the outside a view in. More glass and steel rose high into the sky, seemingly into the clouds. Holding all of it up were steel girders that yawned open, like crocs in water.

Cupping my hands in front of my mouth, I exhaled and rubbed them together vigorously. The rain had ceased, and the clouds had thinned, but the wind on my damp clothing chilled me to the bone. Living in Seattle in February meant never really getting warm.

I bypassed the valet booth, climbed several shallow cement stairs, then breezed through the glass doorway. The lobby was quiet. A lone Japanese couple strode the aisles. I studied the lay of the lobby. Acrylic cube shelving stocked Needle-themed merchandise. Everything from sweatshirts and salt and pepper shakers to Space Noodle pasta in the shape of the Needle itself were displayed with attention to shape and color. After completing a full circle, I bought a ticket to the top from a skinny kid behind the long counter.

"This is a sight-seeing only ticket," he said, his voice edged with a seriousness only teenagers can get away with. "The restaurant has closed for food service, but the lounge is open until nine p.m."

I nodded, took my ticket, and wound around the center until I found the elevator. Inside, a man in a whimsical guard uniform—white shirt, black pants, black patent leather shoes, and a cartoon-planet patterned vest—awaited.

"Ticket, please," he said.

Something about the voice made me look at the face. Tom Peterson, dating disaster number seven from my freshman year of college, stood at attention.

Groan.

I held the ticket out but turned my attention to the metal outside the glass walls. No way could I forget his face, but there was a distinct possibility he might forget mine.

"Jessie?"

Reluctantly, I met his gaze. He wore the same loopy grin he always had. Clearly, he had better memories of our trysts than I did. I frowned, remembering the roommate he'd dumped me for and the resulting uncomfortable meetings when he came to pick her up for dates.

Wait.

If Tom still thought of me as a friend, I wouldn't have to play tourist.

"Tom!" I squealed, holding out my arms.

He embraced me in a bear hug. "How *are* you?" he asked, clinging tightly.

"Fine." I attempted a pull-away. When he resisted, I asked, "You?"

"Great." He gave me a final squeeze, then pushed me to arms' length. He stared at me like a long-lost treasure, eyes bright, grin a mile wide. "How are *you*?"

I thought we'd covered that, but I played along. "Good, Tom. Really good. Yourself?"

"Never better."

There was an awkward moment of silence as he stared at me. My cheek twitched, warning me I needed to give the grin a break.

"You work here?" I asked.

Tom pointed to his chest. Affixed to the vest, just above a yellow representation of Saturn and all its rings, was his nametag. Tom.

"Yeah," he said. "I work the elevator right now, but that's only till I finish school."

"Oh," I said. He'd been the same year I was, so I had no idea what he'd been doing the past four years. Maybe he'd had a pregnant sister he needed to help, too. "Cool."

He looked at my ticket. "Going up?"

I successfully resisted the urge to ask him where else I'd be going and plastered a smile on my face. "Absolutely."

The doors closed on lobby noises. Tom pressed the top button, and the glass rocket ship launched, a whirring sound muffled by the thick glass. I glanced over my shoulder at the rapidly receding ground.

The whirring grew faint, and the sour taste of pepper bacon worked its way back up my esophagus.

Nausea threatened. I turned away from the wall. Willing my knees to be strong, I shifted my gaze to Tom. He grinned.

"So what brings you here, anyway?" Tom lifted his arms to stretch. Muscular bumps formed under the white cotton. That was new. Tom had been a skinny Midwestern boy when I knew him.

After a quick internal scrimmage with the truth, I took a chance. "I'm doing a story." I cleared my throat. "I'm a writer. For the *Sun*."

His eyes lit up. "Cool. I read that paper sometimes."

Ick. I sincerely hoped he wouldn't ask about the personal ads.

"So what's the story about?" Tom leaned against the wall next to the panel. To his left, girders wound like a ribbon in a breeze as we ascended. They spiraled out of sight, replaced by an occasional door panel and a whole lot of space floating outside. I fought the somersaults inside my stomach and concentrated on his face.

"Chocoholic Ball," I said. "Know anything about it?"

"Yeah. I pulled an extra shift that day," he said. "I worked wine."

"Whine?" I asked. "Is that the complaint room?"

Tom smirked, curling one hand around a make-believe glass and tipping it. "Drinky-drinky."

I couldn't believe he'd just said drinky-drinky. "Ah," I said. "Wine."

Tom nodded, the blue over his chest expanding a full inch as he pulled his shoulders back. "I'm studying to be a sommelier," he said. "I get my certificate in about six months."

"Summer-yeah?"

Tom's grin showed all his teeth. "Sum-ul-yea. It's a wine expert."

"Oh."

"They used to call them wine captains. Now it's sommelier," he explained. "Sometimes all you do is pull the cork, but other times, you get asked about the wine list. If you're really good, you get hired on someplace like Canlis. Then you do the wine buying."

"Hunh. Sounds cool." And it did. I had to admit I was a little impressed.

"So what kind of wine did they serve at the Chocoholic Ball?"

Tom glanced out the window. "We had a red and a white: Pinot Noir and Late Harvest Riesling." Tom pressed a button on the panel. Upward momentum slowed.

"What are you doing?" I reached out, bracing myself on a wall panel.

"Want to see where the Ball was held?"

I placed a hand over my mouth and bobbed my head up and down. "Yes, please." I rooted around in my bag for my notepad and pen.

The elevator slowed, then began to descend. I kept my eyes trained on my no-name black running shoes as my stomach leapt into my chest and held. We stopped somewhere between earth and sky.

Holding my abdomen, I ventured a look out over Seattle Center. The arcade's lights were off, the doors closed, and the skill games hidden behind yellow, blue, and white plastic panels. The roller coaster was parked at the bottom, and the ship ride had docked. All that would change when the sun came out and hordes of tourists and high school students skipping school flooded the gates.

The door slid open. Tom unbuttoned his vest and retrieved a tassel of keys attached to a short brass chain. He sifted through them, settling on a small gold one. With one hand, he swung open a panel on the wall. With the other, he inserted the key. He twisted, then paused. A click. Satisfied, he released his hold, key still cocked to the right.

"That'll keep the elevator here," he said, sweeping a hand out in front of me. "After you."

We stepped into a large room. Balloons, bows, and flowers in every shade of purple filled the room. They formed clusters in the corners and droopy frames for the floor-to-ceiling windows. The twin scents of musky men's cologne and women's floral perfume assaulted my nostrils.

"Must have been a wedding yesterday," Tom said, sniffing. He walked over to a counter and pulled a clipboard from below. After a quick shuffle of the paperwork attached, he said, "It's clear for today. Except for the cleaning staff."

"Nice," I said, fingering a strand of violet crepe paper that draped from one end of the room to the floor. "Must be pricey to get married here."

Tom waggled his hand back and forth. "So-so. You'd be surprised. We're pretty competitive."

Good pitch, but no sale. I wouldn't be walking down any aisle, no matter how high up in the sky, any time soon. I focused on the view out the far window. I moved toward it but stopped a safe distance short of the edge. I looked up, then down. Above, at the top, the restaurant rotated. A hundred feet below lay terra firma.

I stepped back and turned to Tom. "Where are we, anyway?"

"Skyline level," he said. "It's not open to the public. You pretty much gotta have an invite to get in here." Tom pointed toward the window. "Isn't that cool?" A low-hanging cloud crept into view. It cast a pall on the room, like an obese gray ghost. "It feels like you're flying."

What I wanted to say was, No, it wasn't cool, it was terrifying, and I hate planes, too. What I did say was, "So this is where they held the Chocoholic Ball?"

"Yep," Tom said. "All the great events are held here. The Space Needle is the symbol of Seattle. Besides the Ball and weddings, we do banquets, business meetings, seminars. Just about everything— even inaugural events." He held out his hand. "Come on, I'll show you the rest of the space."

I grasped his hand without removing the pen. Less intimate that way.

Tom pulled me toward the window's edge. "This is the Lake Union Room." He pointed at a stretch of blue-green. The water was calm, but a few small sailboats cut across, their sails brightly colored triangles catching the wind.

"Some view, huh?" He rested a forearm on the window and his forehead atop.

"Absolutely." I released Tom's hand and scribbled some notes.

Tom turned, folded his arms, and leaned a shoulder against the window. "So what do you want to know? Anything I can't answer I can refer you to the right person."

"Let's start with the layout," I said. "Did they have a bunch of tables and chairs, or what?"

"We arranged vendors in a rectangle in the center of the room, then lined the windows with bistro tables and straight-back chairs." Tom paced the room, using two fingers of each hand to point out items like a flight attendant on an airplane giving a safety lecture. "This room held the non-chocolate desserts. When people wanted a new dessert, or a glass of wine, they went to the vendors. The restrooms are around the corner to the right so the flow moved that way."

He trotted down the hall. I wrangled my cell phone out of my purse, snapped a couple of shots, and followed.

"This is the area we always designate for the bar." He indicated a long granite counter. "It has hot and cold water, an ice maker, lots of storage."

Three bottles of champagne fastened with a large lilac ribbon stood on the counter. Next to them rested two flutes, pink lipstick smudges on one. Both were empty. A faint sweet scent emanated from the sink.

Focusing on the scene, I tried to think like a murderer. Morning light filled the space unevenly. At night, the moon and stars wouldn't have made up for the blackness of the sky this high above ground. I glanced up. Overhead, four recessed lights fit snugly in their brass sleeves. Spaced evenly down the twelve-foot corridor, their glow would have provided little more than a halo over guests' heads. The bar area and hallway behind would be dim. Empty, it would have been the perfect place to dump poison into Perry's cup. Even occupied, it would have provided cover for the murderer to blend into the crowd. And escaping without

87

notice would have been not only possible, but easy.

A chill shivered down my spine, part excitement, part macabre intrigue. I'd never known a killer, and now I stalked one.

I drew a map on the back of the notepad, outlining the bar, hall, and angle of the Lake Union Room. When I'd finished, I flipped the paper over again and wrote, *What did Lowell drink at the Ball*? and circled it twice.

I returned my attention to Tom. "Who else worked the bar?"

"A buddy of mine named Chaz. Charles is his real name. He's a graduate sommelier." He crooked a finger my way, then continued down the hall.

We entered a medium-size room next, banked by tall sheets of smudged glass on all but the interior wall. "This is the Puget Sound Room," Tom said. "This level doesn't rotate, so people have to move to see the different views. Sometimes people rent only one room or the other, but the Chocoholic Ball always reserves the entire level."

That meant there had been lots of hustling back and forth, guests and waitstaff. Anyone could have slipped something in Lowell's drink. They may even have laced a cake.

Next to the drink question, I wrote, *What did Perry eat at the ball*?

Tom continued. "We served the chocolate desserts in here. We arranged more bistro tables and more high-backed chairs along the windows. People really love the view."

Tom moved toward the windows and gestured for me to follow. "That's Elliot Bay. Puget Sound's beyond that."

From a solid leap away, I gazed out. The teal water was choppier than Lake Union's, but vastly larger. Two ferries crossed at a slow chug, one from Seattle's ferry dock heading north, the other toward us from Vashon Island.

Tom took a deep breath. "Can't you almost smell the salt water?"

I sniffed, smelling only a faint chocolaty residue.

"So what do you think of To-*mas*?" Tom leaned his back against the window.

"Who's Tomas?"

"My sommelier name," Tom said. "You know, after I graduate."

I bit my lip. No one would believe a Spanish handle on a corn-fed Anglo, but who was I to pop his cork? "Sounds good."

He grinned. "Yeah. People like to think sommeliers are European. I think I can pass for British or Australian. If I brush up an accent or something."

I could have pointed out that Australia was like a billion miles away from Europe, but I didn't. "Is there another room?"

"Yep. The Seattle Room." He headed toward the hall again, wrapping an arm around my shoulders along the way. I squirmed, but allowed it to rest there, making sure my hip didn't rub up against his.

Ick.

He led me straight across a similar space to the windowed wall. A pace away, I dropped my pencil. I eased away from Tom and stared outside.

An array of buildings, some taller, some shorter than the Space Needle, stood at attention like a concrete and steel army. Closer in, ornate facades and the occasional gargoyle provided contrast to the glass-paned modern structures. Below, traffic crawled along mist-slicked streets. I picked out the Kia in the parking lot—a faint tan dot. When I forgot about how easily I could plummet to my death, it was pretty amazing.

"It must be dark at night." I angled my stare up into the gray sky.

"Dark and romantic." Tom's eyes grew sleepy.

Double ick.

I stuck to business. "Was it dark the night of the Chocoholic Ball, too?"

"Definitely."

"How'd people see to make their way to the desserts, the wine, the bathroom?" Talking about bodily emissions usually throws buckets of cold water over horny men.

Tom straightened. "Oh, there's recessed lighting in the hall, and we have torchiere lamps we bring in. They have heavy shades, so the light's muted. It's gotta be that way so the windows don't glare." Tom rapped a knuckle on the glass. A dull thump, rather than a ping, echoed through the room. "It was Valentine's Day, you know."

I bowed my head to stare at the words on my notepad.

"So what'd you do on Valentine's Day, Jessie?"

Triple Ick. I knew where this line of questioning was headed. I begged my brain to create a good lie, just once. As usual, it came up clean by the time I opened my mouth.

"Oh, I had an early night." The truth was, I'd ordered my regular from the teriyaki place, then settled in for a horror flick. I got through half it by eight o'clock, then switched to cracking open the bag of books I'd bought at the used bookstore.

Tom's lips curled into a smile. "So, Jessie…"

I gulped. Please God, don't let him ask it.

"Are you seeing anyone special?"

Finishing a scrawl across the paper, I looked up. I considered saying I was, but then he'd barrage me with questions about what his name was, where he worked, how long I'd known him, et cetera, ad infinitum, ad nauseum. I'd have gotten caught up in a lie, he'd have realized it, and that would be the end to my "in" at the Space Needle.

"Uhm…"

"Uhm…" he echoed, his lips pulling into a smug smile.

In the end, when no lightning bolt issued from the sky, I answered truthfully. "No."

Tom's grin widened.

There was no level of ick left. I needed a shower. And quick.

"So who all attended the Chocoholic Ball?" A lame attempt to change the subject, but worth a try.

Tom shifted back on his heels. "Tons of people. Lots of big Seattle names."

I pursed my eyebrows. "Like who?"

Tom shrugged.

"What? Is it a secret, or something?"

"Well," Tom faltered, tracing a seam in the windows with one finger. "Kind of."

"Why?"

Tom shook his head, looked around, then dropped his voice. "I don't really know. Honest. What I do know is that we aren't supposed to talk about who was here. Chef's orders."

"I don't get it."

Tom shrugged again. "Neither do I. He said it was because it was the one opportunity each year where the charity, not the publicity, is the focus."

"But you don't believe it?"

Tom shook his head. "No. It doesn't make any sense."

"Why not?"

"Because. If the point is to increase awareness and raise money, why not use the press coverage?" He scratched his chin.

"I agree." He had a point. So why the secrecy? Could the killer have known about the privacy pact? If so, it would have provided a sense of anonymity, enough to tempt someone intent on doing harm to another. I jotted that on my pad.

"I mean, they could have televised it," Tom said. "The chefs could have created unique desserts, sold them online, maybe even auctioned them off. Local celebrities could have made 'yum-yum' noises in the background." Tom scooped imaginary foods into his mouth. "I mean, if the point is to raise money, why not raise as much as you can? It's a worthy cause."

He was right. It didn't make sense from a business standpoint. It was, however, making some sense to me. A killer wouldn't want any proof he—or she—had been there.

"Whose idea was it to make the guest list secret?" I asked.

Tom shrugged. "I have no idea. It came down from above."

"But there's gotta be a list somewhere," I said. "I

mean, how else could they have invited people? That would have to be some phone tree. And how could they have gotten past the elevator guard?"

Tom shifted his gaze. He was hiding something.

"Tom?"

He didn't respond.

I steeled myself and put my hand on his upper arm. "Tom, do you know where there's a list?"

The muscle I'd noticed before flexed and Tom's chin bobbed.

"If I promise not to use any names in my article, will you let me see it?"

Tom pondered that a moment then turned to face me, his eyelids droopy again. I dropped my hand.

Uh-oh.

"I tell you what," he said. "I'll get a list and give it to you over dinner."

It had happened. The sum of all personal fears. He'd asked me out on a date I couldn't refuse.

I considered my options at warp speed. If it were simply a list from his memory of working that night, it wouldn't help. Chances were the killer had been ultra-discrete, non-descript, maybe even used a fake name. Tom probably never even noticed him. Or her. On the other hand, an official list would enable me to narrow my suspect list significantly. It might be the key to my whole story. Rod's face appeared in my mind. Then Cherrie's. No way was I going to blow this lead.

"Would this be an official list, or what?"

"Official attendee list."

"How would you get it?"

Tom whispered, "Computer database downstairs. Everyone who comes to the Chocoholic Ball has to be accounted for. Ever since 9/11, the Needle's been a target."

"So you're getting the official list from security?" I sounded like a skipping record, but I didn't care. If I had to spend an evening gazing at Tom over a dinner table, I wanted something more than a free dinner.

"Yep."

"Okay."

Tom smiled like the Cheshire cat. "Mouse Hole. Pier fifty-two. Seven tomorrow evening?"

Mouse Hole was a bar he and I had always talked about going to when we turned twenty-one. Of course, we broke up a full year before either of us could have stepped across its threshold. I couldn't help but smile at the memory. It was semi-flattering that he remembered. "Sounds great," I said.

Tom gave me the thumbs-up. He took my hand and led me back to the elevator like I couldn't find my way back.

"By the way, who's the chef here?" I asked as he wrangled the key from the locked open position.

"The executive chef is Doug DuBois."

"Do you think you could set up a meeting with him?" I asked. "Maybe I could ask him a few questions, too."

Tom stuck the key back into his pocket. "I wouldn't do that."

"Why?"

Tom paused, buttoned the top of his vest again. "Because Douggie wasn't invited to the Chocoholic Ball. And he's not too happy about it."

Chapter Ten

Word Slut.

It was all I could think. For a lead, not even the name of the murderer, I'd agreed to go to dinner with a man I'd despised for the past four years. How could I sink any lower?

Disgusted, I pumped the accelerator and twisted the key in the ignition, consoling myself with the thought that I wouldn't have to deal with any of his friskiness. We were, after all, meeting at Mouse Hole. I would drive myself, so there'd be no awkward drive home, no frantic attempt to unlock the door before he leaned in for the goodnight kiss.

Taking a deep breath, I checked the clock. Nearly three o'clock. I had the entire evening to gather my notes and come up with new ways to investigate before my mandatory lunch meeting with Rod the next day. More importantly, I hadn't spilled my guts to Tom about the real story. And I hadn't had to lie. I felt just like a real reporter.

After a quick mental pat on the back for that sliver of integrity, I headed for home. Once there, I climbed into my pajamas, logged onto my computer, and printed out the rest of the reviews on my infinitely superior home printer. Pawing through the printouts, I set Bayou Déjà vu's atop. Perry had reviewed Bayou Déjà vu most recently before the missing review, so it made sense to put its chef, Jody Lish, first on my list to visit tomorrow.

But then I had another thought. Everyone had had bad reviews, but Will had admitted that the bad reviews weren't justified. Bayou Déjà vu's and Bien's were most recent, but probably the tip of the iceberg. Union Bay Cabin's critique, on the other hand, had been good. Too good. It made more sense to see what Perry raved over.

I pulled up Union Bay Cabin's address and used the satellite view. Along Union Bay, the steely city gave way to old growth Madrona. I had never driven that road in all the time I lived here, despite its lush, green park-like setting. Homes were, of course, pricey there, and no one I had ever known lived in a mansion like that.

Sure enough, just across the street from the water's edge, Union Bay Cabin stood. I panned the view right and left, then used the street view, searching for a restaurant or marquee. I saw nothing. I had just about given up when I spotted it. A squatty shack with darkened windows nearly obscured by untended foliage, gravel parking lot adjacent.

I frowned. To say it was out of place in that neighborhood was an understatement. Something about this felt off. Very off. So I hopped into my black duds, pulled a comb through my bushy hair, grabbed my beach bag, and headed for Union Bay Cabin. If I were lucky, I'd get there before the dinner rush. Maybe even speak with the owner.

I followed the GPS directions and drove to the eatery. Its log exterior screamed for sealant, and its roof looked as though patched with moss. It could have been for rustic effect, but I doubted it.

After a quick left against traffic, I rolled into the parking lot. Eight makeshift parking spaces, and three had Chevrolets or Cadillacs from the mid-nineties stationed in them. I checked my watch. Nearly five o'clock on a Sunday. Not too busy. I decided to trust my luck. I slipped the Kia into the back of the lot and got out.

A dirt trail led from the parking lot to the front door. Along the way, smelly junipers grabbed at my clothing. Not very appetizing. In fact, nothing about Union Bay Cabin was appetizing, not even to me. And I'm not a picky eater.

At the door, I noticed that the hours of operation had been posted in a handwritten scrawl directly onto the scarred wood surface. M-F 7 to 11, S-S 8 to 8. I pulled on the leather strap that served as a handle, yanked, and hoped for the best.

The door swung wide with a creak straight out of an old-time horror movie. I hesitated a moment in the dark, smoky room, my nose wrinkling in response to the heavy scent of old, charbroiled meats and rancid grease. Within seconds, my eyes adjusted. Heavy, open-beamed ceilings and rough-hewn log walls with an open fire pit in the middle appeared. Surrounding the pit was a bent metal screen, and directly above it, a circular vent that led up and out. To the right of the pit, a man squatted, poking at the fire with a long metal implement. The fire sputtered and crackled in response.

Two shallow tiers held a scattering of tables. A few tables huddled close to the fire. A step up provided a platform for more tables. It looked like priority seating, greasy spoon style.

I took a good look at the people there, getting a feel for who may have paid heed to Perry's advice. At two of the tables sat men in shirts and pants, no ties. I made them out for salespeople or managers of local businesses. We were too far out of the way for the downtown or university crowd.

An older man and a younger woman sat at the third table. The way they held hands suggested they probably weren't father and daughter. A solitary man sat at the last table. He wore a tangerine scarf at his open collar that reminded me of an old war movie—something with Fred Astaire or Humphrey Bogart. As I watched, he leaned forward and spoke to the fire-stoker. The other man coaxed a few more sparks, then turned my way.

In the murky light, I made out dark hair and a slight build. As he rose, however, I recognized the shirt: a black and white polka-dotted number with full sleeves.

Will Doninger, Perry's un-brother.

Huh. I had a hunch why Perry had given this place a rave review.

Will hung the poker on a hook attached to the pit vent, then walked toward me. As he drew nearer, he smiled.

"Hey, Jess."

I nodded, concealing my surprise. "Hey, Will."

Will cocked his head. "What brings you here?" His eyes brightened. "Do you have a lead?"

I shook my head. "Not yet. I just came in for a snack," I lied. "I've been reading Perry's reviews. Trying to gather some clues. He made Union Bay Cabin sound really good." I paused a moment and looked around. "I didn't realize you worked here."

"Yeah," Will said. "I've been here for-*ever*."

"Cool."

Will raised an eyebrow. "Maybe. Maybe not." He poised a wax pen over a plastic-coated diagram of the restaurant. Tell-tale smudges within little squares revealed that the front tier and the very back tables were the most popular. He glanced over his shoulder once at the empty tables, then drew a perfect number one inside a square, and circled it, careful to stay within the lines.

"Follow me," he said, pulling a piece of wood from under the reception podium.

Like I could get lost.

But follow I did. Will stopped at a table in front of the fire. It sandwiched me between the May-December couple and the scarf-wearing former spy. When I sat, Will handed me the piece of wood. It turned out to be a menu bound together with leather strips woven through holes at the top. On the front cover, Union Bay Café had been burned into the wood in recessed black lines, the letters uneven.

"Thanks."

Will smiled, a genuine pleased-to-be-of-service grin. "Enjoy your meal." He turned to scamper off, then pivoted and leaned in. I could smell his cologne and his breath. Both fifty-proof.

I stayed perfectly still and perked my ears. Maybe he was going to confess to the murder. Or at least tell me why he lied about his relationship with Perry "the Prattler" Lowell.

"Stay away from anything from the pit," he said. "I found a dead bat at the bottom of it today."

I nodded.

Will grimaced and shook his head. "Nasty." He

headed for the front again.

After waiting a beat, I opened the menu, trying to avoid slivers. It was, after all, dinner time, and I had missed lunch.

All the lettering had been burned in. It reminded me of my middle brother Brian's wood-burning kit when we were kids. One summer he'd labeled just about everything in the house, including the wood grain on the television set. I ratted him out, and he chased me with the little red tip into a spider-filled cellar. I stayed there until dinner time when my dad came and got me.

Ah, good times. Now, Brian's a firefighter and I'm still trying to tell secrets.

I focused on the top half of the menu first. Salads, sandwiches, soups, and Lite Bites rounded out the simple choices. Three misspellings jumped out at me: "mayonaise" "tarter" and "catshup."

A full list of rotisserie items covered the bottom half. Choices there were more interesting. Chicken, beef, fish, and shrimp held the center position, but down below, alligator**, Copper River Salmon*, elk*, hippo**, and rattlesnake** were added. I scanned the bottom for the asterisk legend. One star: seasonal, ask your waitperson. Two stars: limited availability, ask your waitperson.

The back page listed a bizarre mix of items under the heading Family Favorites. It included Fried Pickles with Dill dipping sauce, Cajun Popcorn Shrimp, Grilled Clams with Spitfire Glaze, and Crab and Squid Pizza, Mussel Pizza, Pesto Pizza.

I frowned. The menu appeared inspired, but by what I didn't know. Together with the building and interior, Union Bay Cabin embodied a failed theme park. Nice try, but instead of fanciful, it struck me as just plain creepy.

I surveyed the plates on the other tables. All but one diner had chosen standard fare: sandwiches with mini bags of chips. The exception was a businessman across the pit who had a platter of ribs and fries in front of him. As I watched, he tore off a chunk of fatty red meat and stuck it in his mouth. Evidently, he hadn't heeded Will's bat warning.

I closed the menu when Will appeared.

"So what'd you decide?"

The only thing I was hungry for was the truth. But that wasn't on the menu. "Whole grain muffin and iced tea."

Will scribbled my order on his palm-sized pad. "Would you like that muffin grilled?" He shook his head no.

"No thanks." I didn't bother to ask him why anyone would grill a muffin.

"Didn't think so," Will said, "But I've gotta ask. Rules, you know. Be right up." Will headed for the kitchen with his little pad. He swayed only once. My best guess is it was bourbon-inspired.

I wasted only a split-second judging him for working while drunk. Death does strange things to people, and everyone has their own way of coping. My brother Brian coped with our Nana's death by burning RIP into her casket.

A moment later Will returned and began poking at the fire again. Heat waves drifted through the room. I slipped off my jacket.

As I watched Will toy with the fire, the door creaked open. Two women in fur coats stepped into the restaurant, the door clanking shut behind them. They paused at the podium, their faces slowly taking on expressions of horror as their eyes adjusted and they took a quick look around.

When their eyes met mine, I recognized one. The tall Texan from Lowell's early morning memorial. Callie's friend. If she recognized me, she didn't show it. Her companion was someone I'd never seen before. They held a quick whispered conference, then high-tailed it out of Union Bay Cabin as quickly as their salon shoes could carry them. How they'd navigated the dirt trail was beyond me.

"Come again," Will called out. He veered my direction, two saucers in hand. One held a muffin, sliced in half and pre-buttered. A tall glass of tea perched atop the other. Will set both in front of me.

"Thanks."

"Anything else?"

"Actually, yes." I unfurled the straw wrapper and sipped the iced tea. Lukewarm and full of lemon seeds. I pushed it away. "Do you have a minute?"

After a quick glance toward the kitchen, Will said, "Sure." He slid into the chair across from mine and crossed his legs.

I pushed the muffin away and set my tote bag in my lap. I wanted to take notes but didn't want Will to know I was tracking his words. I stuck both hands into my bag and groped for my pen and pad.

Will stared at the uneaten muffin. "I guess you're not very hungry, either. After this morning, I have no appetite." He paused in reflection a moment. "Grief filled me up."

I nodded. Inside the tote bag I flipped open the

notepad and clicked the pen. "I'm sorry for your loss."

Will sighed. "Thanks. It's been tough." He shook his head and stared at a dingy space on one wall. "The only thing I want to do is make up another big batch of appletinis. Perry loved appletinis."

Something about the lilt in his voice started my neurons firing. Who was he, anyway? He wasn't Lowell's little brother as he'd claimed. Rod wouldn't lie about that. And he couldn't be Lowell's boyfriend, because Lowell was married.

I couldn't just ask him.

Or could I?

Of course I could.

"I'm impressed you're able to work," I said. "It's tough losing your big brother."

There was no register of surprise, no silent regrouping about the lie. Instead, there seemed to be a flash of anger.

Will's eyes narrowed and he stared at the door that led to the kitchen. "Asshole I work for said, 'Just cover the lunch crowd and you can take a couple days off.' Of course, lunch bled into dinner." Will shook his head, but the anger couldn't be dismissed that easily.

I had no choice but to play along. "Wow, and after the great review Mr. Lowell gave him."

"Yeah, well, that's part of the problem."

"What do you mean?"

Will rolled his eyes. "There was a falling out."

"How could there be a falling out with such a great review?"

"Well, Bruce wanted one thing and Perry gave another."

"Bruce is your boss?"

"Boss, chef, owner. You name it, he's it." Will's gaze shifted toward the back again.

"Huh." I paused a beat.

"What did Bruce want?"

Will rolled his eyes. "A five-star rating. Totally ridiculous. Bruce doesn't know what the star system's all about. He just wanted the best. Thought people would believe it, coming from Perry."

I didn't know what the star system was all about, either, but I didn't let on. Instead, I said, "So you were right."

Will cocked his head. "About what?"

"About the poisoning."

Will slumped. "Yes. I was right."

"So who do you figure for it?"

Will shrugged. "One of them. What's the difference?"

He had a point. Dead was dead, no matter who did it.

Will propped both elbows on the table. He formed a cradle of his hands and set his chin in it. A moment later, slow, salty drips splattered the table, settling into the varnished grooves.

"I'm really sorry," I said, putting a hand on Will's arm.

Will sniffed but didn't wipe away the tears. "Thanks." His face contorted, then he hid it in his hands. He sobbed once, then without raising his head, removed my muffin, drew out the napkin below, and replaced the muffin on the saucer. After fanning the napkin, he blew his nose and wiped his cheeks with it.

Finally composed, he lifted his head. "Thanks for your concern." He formed a small smile. "Not everyone understands what it meant to have a man like Perry in their lives."

"You mean brother."

Will began to roll his eyes but stopped and focused on me. "Whatever."

A-ha. Will and Lowell weren't brothers in the family sense.

So what were they? Brothers in a fraternity? Brothers in a religious community? I found it hard to picture Lowell in the Big Brother program, but maybe that was it. Before I could think of a way to ask, Will spoke.

"Help me find the killer," he said, his voice tiny against the roar of the fire behind him.

"I will," I said. "But first I've gotta know the answer to my question from the memorial."

Will didn't answer. He just nodded, head hung low.

I leaned closer, my voice a whisper. "What did the chefs find out?"

Will's cheeks worked right and left. He gulped. He shook his head.

I waited.

One muffled sob escaped before Will spoke. "I can't," he said. "I really can't."

"And you know it may make the difference of whether Perry's killer is caught, right?"

Will closed his eyes and nodded with supreme effort. "Yes," he said. "But if we find the killer using the information, it won't be any good."

I frowned. I had no clue what he was talking about. The front door squeaked open, and four men in Quickie-Lube uniforms walked in.

Will glanced over, raised his index finger, then

turned to me. "I've gotta run. Dinner crowd's arrived." He nodded toward the men. "And I'm sorry. We'll just have to find another way to find Perry's killer."

He strolled off, tucking the ballooning shirt back inside his black jeans.

"When can we talk again?" I called out.

Will glanced at his watch. "Tomorrow, maybe."

I pulled the muffin toward me, remembered Will's hands on it, and pushed it away. No big loss. It looked like spongy cardboard with raisins. I took another quick slurp of the tea, frowned, and made my way up to the podium to pay.

Within two minutes, Will joined me.

"Six dollars," he said.

I grimaced, but handed him a five and three ones. "Keep the rest."

Will smiled and pocketed the change. "Keep me posted?" It came out as a question.

"Sure," I said. "But I doubt this investigation's going anywhere without a motive."

"I know." He hung his head. "But just try. Please?"

I agreed. I'm such a softy.

I took three steps toward the door, then whirled. Will stood at the podium and raised a green, liquid-filled tumbler to his lips. Appletini?

"One more question," I said.

Will swallowed and focused an uneven gaze at me. "Shoot."

"Do you happen to know who Perry reviewed for Friday the 13th?"

Will shrugged and replaced the glass below the podium top. "Whoever was next on the list." The words slurred out.

I cocked my head. "What list?"

Will slung his hips to one side. "Perry's list."

I took a step closer. "What was Perry's list for?"

Will's expression remained unchanged a moment, as though he hadn't heard me. Then his eyes widened and his hand flew to his mouth. "Oh no," he said. "You aren't supposed to know about the list."

Chapter Eleven

Will scurried away, polka dots parachuting from the sheer force of his stride. I could have called out, stopped him, demanded to know what he knew. But it was no use. He was determined to keep Perry's actions in the past. As much as I hated to admit it, I knew I'd do the same for a loved one.

Outside, the sun had begun to set, still shrouded in cloud. Although the wind blew chilly, the junipers had remained wet, and beads of water from their sticky yellow tips leaped onto me as I walked by. By the time I reached the Kia, my pants had horizontal streaks across the thighs, always an attractive look.

I sighed, brushed my legs with my palms, then hopped in the Kia and revved the engine. After setting a course for home, I did a mental timeline. I'd have just enough time to meet up with some additional chefs tomorrow morning before meeting with Rod at noon.

****

The next morning, after compiling my notes and feeling even more determined, I merged onto Interstate 5 a newer, ballsier Jess Harriet. I exited onto James, hooked a left onto First, and followed it all the way to Yesler. After circling Pioneer Square for at least ten minutes, gnashing my teeth in frustration, I considered bucking up for a spot in an overpriced garage. Before I could say, "Looks like it's going to rain again," I

108

spotted an ice-blue BMW Roadster zipping out of an angled spot. I pulled in, narrowly avoiding the silver Lexus in the next space over, and flung off my seatbelt.

A quick check at the meter revealed fifteen minutes left before the meter needed feeding. I calculated the chances of a meter maid puttering down the road at exactly the wrong time. I'd chance it.

I jogged past the Tlingit totem pole and entered Pioneer Square. A few blocks removed from the glitz of the Seattle skyline, the Square was a one-third acre brick-laid courtyard commemorating Old Seattle. Known for its funky bistros and boutiques, the former Lusty Lady peep show, and the Below Seattle tour, Pioneer Square was Seattle Bohemian. Trendy and cool. But I still didn't want to be there alone at night.

From the middle of the Square, I saw a crowd forming in the far-right corner. Another five yards and I caught the scents of burning wood and hot, spicy meat. At just past ten o'clock in the morning, it was early for lunch, but the people in the line didn't seem to care. My stomach didn't, either. It quaked in recognition. All this sleuthing had given me an appetite.

Ten paces later, the bright red, orange, and yellow doors of Bayou Déjà vu came into view. Two lines of at least ten patrons each snaked out of the doors and onto the brick surface.

The processions moved forward, single file, with the diligence of ants at work. The lucky heads of each line approached a red counter and placed purses atop, umbrellas below. While I waited, I read two white signs with red lettering. "Eat In" and "Eat Out." I debated. They were equal in terms of length, but the "Eat Out" line promised quicker sale-through. I glanced in the window at the dining room. Several people race-walked across the highly polished orange floor toward round, red-lacquered tables. Once there, they grabbed matching stools, holding their places with packages and sweaters and motioning to friends still in line.

I got in the "Eat In" line. Maybe I'd get lucky and wrangle an interview with the chef as well as a decent brunch. I would need stamina to get through the meeting with Rod.

Almost immediately, the jeans and flannel-clad man ahead of me shuffled forward. I stepped up, studying the gray, curly ponytail at the base of his neck.

I grinned.

This place felt like the county fair back home.

He stepped forward. I followed. The powerful twin aromas of mesquite and hickory woke my senses better than a bone-dry, quad cappuccino ever had or ever would. My stomach rumbled in response, and my mouth drooled just a little. I took a good look at the tables. They were filling quickly, but the counter held plenty of empty stools.

The man trudged forward. "Seein' Double Twin Pack," he said, pulling a black leather wallet attached to a chain from his back pocket.

I glanced at the menu board overhead. Created from little pre-formed black letters and numbers, I noted thirteen meals and a side board of everything from corn on the cob to deep-fried okra. Yum.

The man slapped a twenty onto the counter. "Keep it."

"Thanth," the cashier said, placing a red plastic teepee with the number sixteen etched in white in the guy's hand.

He grabbed a wad of napkins in one hand, the teepee in the other, then lumbered in the general direction of a corner.

My turn.

"Whatcha eatin'?"

I paused. The grumbly, lisping cashier wore a black button-up shirt and low-riding black jeans, a pudge of belly exposed somewhere below the navel and above a spiked black belt. The hair was cut short and tipped in yellow. It stuck out in all directions like a sundial. The face was scrubbed clean in an attempt, I assumed, to decrease the chance of infection in one of its many piercings. I couldn't help but count. One at the tail end of each eyebrow, one through the cheek, one through the right nostril and a bull ring, plus one at the lip. That was six. Including the wink of rhinestone at the belly button through the gape of the shirt, seven.

It spoke again. "I said, 'Watcha eatin'?'" Metal flashed atop its tongue. Eight.

"Excuse me?"

The cashier rolled their eyes.

The pink-haired cashier to their right opened her mouth wide. "*Ninety-One!*"

A young female office gopher in khakis and a polo shirt raced up. She traded her teepee for two white bags.

"Watcha eatin' what we thay here."

Suddenly, I understood the reason for the lisp— piercings. And the grumble? Probably earning minimum wage without a break in sight.

I studied the menu overhead. Same overwhelming choices. A guy in green plaid flannel couldn't be wrong. "Seeing Double Ribs, please," I said.

After adding an iced tea, the total was rung. I

shelled out twenty-two bucks, the most expensive lunch I'd ever paid for myself. I reasoned that if I actually spoke with Chef Jody Lish, I could write it off on my tax return. If I solved this murder, I might actually make enough to need a deduction this year.

A few coins and a teepee were slapped into my hand. "Up in ten."

Again, the pink-haired girl opened her mouth. "*Thirty-Seven!*"

A young kid in baggy jeans scooted up. Shifting the skateboard he carried under one arm, he dragged a large bag across the counter.

"Great," I said to the lisper. I leaned in close and caught a whiff of something sweet and powdery. Not a man's scent. Not a woman's, either. "By the way, is Chef Lish available?"

She turned and yelled, "Jody?" With their back momentarily facing me, I noticed the unmistakable outline of a wallet in one pants pocket and a rolled-up rubber in the other.

After waiting a scant few seconds, they hollered again, louder this time, "*Jody!*"

A small head appeared over the half-wall. "Quit yer hollering, Zit," she said. "For cryin' out loud."

Zit?

"This one wants to talk to you," Zit hollered, their voice not a bit lower.

Jody made eye contact. Fair, blondish tufts of hair stuck out from below a baseball cap, the visor spattered in red. Small blue eyes peered at me. "Can I help you?"

Before I could respond, Zit motioned for me to get out of the way. I side-stepped twelve inches. "Whatcha eatin'?" Zit asked the person behind me and placed both hands on the counter revealing three chunky bracelets and nails painted alternately red and black.

"Hi, Jody. I'm Jess Harriet. I'm a reporter for the *Sun*," I said. "Do you have a minute?"

Jody's focus shifted to the two lines at the counter. "Reckon I will in about ten. Slows down a little after the first wave comes through."

"Thanks." I pointed toward the counter where the skateboarder had been waiting. "I'll be over there."

I hot-footed it to the counter and laid claim to the stool with my bag and teepee. The stool, shiny red faux leather, had been wiped clean so often the texture had worn off, making it smoother than a baby's butt. People continued to come and go quickly, and I was glad I snagged the stool when I did. Within ten minutes, and as if by miracle, "Eat Out" cashier's voice carried across the room at that moment.

"*Eighteen!*"

I grabbed my order, settled at the counter again, and brought out the notes from my bag. I'd read Perry's reviews through January 30th, and still needed to drop by Bien and talk to Laurette Roen. Before Bien's review was Ulrich Alford's, executive chef of the swanky Emerald Room, and Dave and Debby Junette, owners/chefs of Green, a vegetarian restaurant. After checking the addresses, I decided on a convenient travel loop. I stacked Emerald Dining Room's on top, Bien's below, and Green's at the bottom. If I was lucky, I'd be able to go to all three that afternoon after meeting with Rod.

I dug out my notepad and went over my list of questions. First, who had Perry reviewed last Friday? Second, what was on the index cards? Third, what, or more importantly, who, was on the "list"? Fourth, what was the "list" about?

Squeezing lemon into my iced tea, I focused on what I knew about Perry Lowell, his murder, and the possible motives and methods.

Perry had been poisoned. He'd most likely gotten the poison at the Chocoholic Ball. He'd pissed off a lot of chefs, and most of them had been at the Ball. Except Douggie DuBois, the executive chef of the Space Needle where the event was held. Ironic, but a lead worth pursuing. Perhaps he left something to be served? Maybe he conspired with someone?

Despite the toasty heat in Bayou Déjà vu, I shuddered. I'd have to weasel that info out of Tom later tonight. I didn't want to think how.

Zit continued asking "Watcha eatin'?" and the pink-haired waitress kept calling out numbers. I checked my watch. It had been twenty minutes already. I set my pen to one side and focused on eating the steaming red slab of ribs sided by thick-cut, skin-on, sizzling fries. Heady wisps of smoky spices filled my nostrils. My mouth watered in response. The meat cleaved off in thick hunks with light pressure, and there was only a slight resistance as the tines pierced the seared surface. I could wait another ten minutes for Jodi before I'd be compromising my commute back to the office and Rodman, I reasoned.

Each bite beat the last. Sauce exploded in sweets and spices. Sweet and hot peppers, tomato, molasses, black pepper, paprika, and what was it? A hint of cinnamon, maybe clove. Then the satisfying firm crunch of food from a grill and the tenderness of a slow-cooked rib.

I closed my eyes. Food this good was a religious experience. What could Perry have eaten here that made him write that hateful review?

I considered his motives as I chowed down. Chef's day off? Bad batch of ribs? Somehow, I doubted it. Probably personal. With half the slab and a handful of fries left, Jody appeared.

"Pretty damn fair, huh?" She heaved a stool from a table three feet away, swung it overhead, then set it down across from me. She sat, hooking one ankle over the other knee, and slouched, hands behind her head.

I nodded, certain that sauce covered my lips, possibly my chin and nose, and strands of meat clung to my teeth. I didn't care. "I'd shake your hand, but—" I held up my sauce-covered paws without shame.

Jody guffawed, her mouth wide. "Best barbecue you ever had?"

I nodded again, wringing my hands on my dissolving napkin. "Absolutely."

"Damn straight." Jody flicked her baseball cap with her middle finger, then pulled a cigarette from behind her ear. "That's what everyone says. Well, almost everyone."

She stuck the unlit cigarette in her mouth and stared at me as I drained my iced tea. She rolled the white stick back and forth a few times before locking it between top and bottom teeth to speak. "So what can I do ya for?"

The barbecue sauce was like truth serum. "I'm doing a story. On Perry Lowell."

Jody grimaced, the cigarette sticking out of the right side of her mouth. "About fucking time." She turned toward the kitchen. "Zit! Bring me some of that lemonade."

"In a minute," Zit hollered back. Jody faced me again.

"That one." Jody jerked a thumb Zit's direction. "I don't know what name Zit's parents had in mind, but that's what Zit wants to be called." She lowered her voice. "I guess it don't matter. All I know is that they wrote they/them on their employment application. That's enough for me."

I took a sip of tea. "So what's the secret ingredient?"

"Ain't none. It's the basics—ketchup, molasses, paprika, some spices, brown sugar." She removed her cigarette. "But you gotta render the fat off before you cook 'em. And when you cook 'em, do it real slow like."

Zit arrived, bearing a glass of lemonade and a pitcher of iced tea. Zit set Jody's lemonade on the table and swirled the pitcher. Thick juicy slices of lemon bobbed at the top. Zit turned toward me. "Top ya off?"

I scooted my glass forward. "Yes, please." See. I do have manners.

Zit poured the amber fluid, small chunks of ice clinking against the sides, then moved off to another table and offered iced tea all around.

"Criminy. You do a damn good business here."

"Sure do," she said. "It fell off a little this weekend. I only saw my regulars. But that's on account of that damn Lowell. All the tourist folk listen to him." She snorted. "You are gonna tell the truth about that sonofabitch, ain't ya? I mean, that's why you're here, right?" Jody asked, eyeing me. "You're gonna tell Seattle that Perry's a damn prick?"

I nearly choked.

Jody's face contorted. "Hey, wait. I remember you. You were at the memorial yesterday."

"Yep."

"I was there, too, but I betcha don't remember me."

"Sorry," I said, wiping my mouth. "I don't."

"No matter." She rolled the cigarette back and forth a few times. "People don't always notice me. I'm what you call short of stature."

She was right. Behind her, a man swiped a stool. He couldn't have been more than five-ten, but her head barely topped his belt buckle when she was seated. That put her at five feet, tops.

I decided to come clean. "Okay, look. Since you know who I am, and you've probably figured out why I'm here, why don't you tell me why you went to his memorial if you hated him so much?"

"Oh." Jody shrugged. "I wouldn't have. He's a two-bit nothing who's cost a lotta good decent folk a lotta money."

"But?"

"But Tracy asked me to help out."

"Who's Tracy?"

"Black fella they hired to do the catering. Tracy owns Eirambique over in Belltown." Jody frowned. "He couldn't get anyone else to help him. Everyone's pissed at him, but he won't tell me why."

I made a note. "You know, Jody, everyone knew Perry was a...caustic critic." She nodded. "Why don't you tell me how people really felt about him?"

"They hated him. Especially the folks with GAAS."

I frowned. Not everyone hated him. "What does

having gas have to do with Perry's reviews?"

Jody pursed her eyebrows together a moment before bursting out with a belly laugh. Under control again, she said, "No, not having gas as in farting. G-A-A-S. GAAS as in Gourmands And Artisans of Seattle."

"Who are they?" I made a note of the acronym on my notepad.

"Private group," Jody said. "You've gotta be invited to join. Like a sponsor."

"Huh." I wrote down the name of the organization, then the acronym. "They call themselves GAAS?"

Jody tipped her baseball cap up. "Sure do. They think everything they do is artwork and they're serious as hell. That's the difference between me and them. They think they're in charge. Me, I think the customer's in charge." The cigarette bobbed up and down between her lips. "That's also why I left the group."

I filed that tidbit away. "So the GAAS members didn't like Perry much?"

"Hell, no," she said. "In fact, they're probably glad he had the heart attack."

A chill traipsed up my spine and settled in my shoulders. Jody didn't know Perry had been poisoned. "Sounds like you're happy about it, too."

"I ain't sad, if that's what you're asking." She laughed. "Heart attack. Hard to believe since he didn't have no heart."

I let her have her moment. "You know," I said, leaning in, "It wasn't really a heart attack." I gave her the details.

Jody frowned again. "What do ya mean? I was there at the memorial. Everyone was talkin' about it."

I let her question sit in the air a moment before

answering. "He was murdered. Poisoned, actually."

The cigarette dropped from Jody's lips and fell to the floor. It bounced twice, then rolled into a crevice where the wall and floor met. "Get out," she said.

I stared, not quite believing she had ordered me to leave. She didn't move, though, so neither did I. I still had ribs on my plate.

"No shit?"

I realized then she was using colloquialisms, not demanding I vacate the premises. I shook my head. "No shit," I confirmed.

Jody was silent, staring into the space just above my head. After a moment, her eyes shifted, and she searched the floor. When she spotted the cigarette, she scrambled over, picked it up, and stuck it back into her mouth. Settling again in her chair, she shoved two fingers between her baseball cap and head and pulled out a pack of matches. She broke off one red-tipped stick, then wedged the matchbook back up inside the hat. Bringing her right ankle to her left knee, she scraped the match against the bottom of her cowboy boot. A spark ignited, and Jody bent over and lit her cigarette.

She straightened, inhaled deeply, then said, "I'll be damned if they think they can tell me I can't smoke in my own goddamn restaurant."

Smoke billowed around her face. A few patrons turned and glared, but Jody either didn't notice or didn't care. She took another long drag, the red tip glowing fiercely, then rounded her lips and blew circles. By the time she finished, she'd blown five that ran the gamut from fuzzy doughnut to crisp halo.

"That's why you're here, ain't it?" she said,

inhaling again and staring at me hard through the smoke. "This ain't an article about Perry at all. You're trying to find out who killed him."

I shrugged.

Her eyes narrowed. "And you think since I hated him and got a bad review I killed him." She shook her head and raised her voice. "You do. You think I killed the old ballsack."

I held her gaze, but dodged the smoky emissions. "Did you?"

"Hell, no." Jody dragged again. "I hated him, but I didn't kill him."

"Who did?"

"I couldn't tell ya. But I know a lot of folks who'll be glad it was done."

I cocked my head and stared. "Level with me."

Jody looked over to the counter. Zit punched buttons on the register, and the lines had trickled down to one customer per cashier. The dining room crowd had thinned, and a busboy appeared out of nowhere and began swabbing down the tables and pushing stools around.

"Jody?"

She returned her gaze to me, indecision written all over her face.

"You know the cops will be sniffing around here," I said. "All they have to do is look up the reviews like I did. Your name is right there in black and white."

"Ah, hell." She took the last drag, burning into the filter.

"Just tell me what you know," I said. "I'll help you clear your name."

Jody shook her head and pushed a strand of hair

behind her ear. She twisted her neck and gazed out the double doors. The cigarette extinguished itself but remained firmly clenched between Jody's teeth.

I waited a moment, letting the idea digest. "Come on, Jody. Who hated Perry Lowell enough to kill him?"

Jody made no movement, just kept her eyes on the double doors.

"Jody?"

"He was a real dickhead." She didn't meet my eyes. I waited. Slowly, Jody's gaze focused on the front counter.

"Who hated him the most?"

She didn't answer, but she did turn full around. Without meeting my gaze, she took what was left of the cigarette and tamped it out on the table. After working her pant leg up to the top of her boot, she stuck the butt in, then eased the jean back over the leather. She set both feet on the floor and crossed her arms.

I shot her a curious look.

"If the health inspector comes in and sees a butt, I'm screwed," she said. "I figure he won't ask to see the inside of my boot."

"I bet you're right."

Jody eyed me in silence a moment. "Okay, I'll help you," she said. "But just so's you know, I'm not with GAAS anymore."

I nodded.

"Write that down on your little pad," Jody ordered, pointing to my notebook.

I did. Finished, I returned my gaze to her.

She tilted her head at the writing I'd made, her mouth forming words as she read. She met my eyes. "Truth is, I don't know who did it. It could be a lot of people. He gave a lot of shitty reviews. Made personal attacks. It just weren't right."

Jody scratched the back of her head. "He also overcharged for ads. He called 'em 'invitations to sponsor'—at ten times the going rate."

"You mean he was extorting?" I smirked. "Get it? Ex-torting?"

Jody stared at me without expression. I wiped the smile off my face.

"That's funny," she said, no trace of a grin. "You're all right." She leveled her gaze and stared at me. "You know, most people don't know it, but Lowell didn't get paid for Perry's Prattle."

"Really?"

Jody waggled her eyebrows. "What kind of a scumbag tears people apart for nothing? What kind of a guy destroys businesses for free?"

Good question. "I don't know," I said. "So who lost the most by his reviews? Rather, who had the most to gain by his death?"

Jody harrumphed. "I don't think there was anything to gain. And a lot of us lost a lot. I didn't fare so bad, on account of being well-established, and being the kind of place I am. But some of them with GAAS had it pretty rough."

"Like who?"

She paused, her face taut. "I don't know."

I knew she knew. "Tell me again why you left GAAS."

"I'm still a member of sorts. My membership don't run out until next December. But I ain't on the board of directors. And I don't go to meetings no more. Write that down, too."

She paused. I wrote it down.

"What position did you hold when you were on the board?"

"Secretary." She laughed. "Ain't that a hoot? A secretary with piss-poor spelling."

"Why'd you resign?"

"Well, I didn't like the way some folk treated other folk," she said. "And they got so worked up over nothing."

"Like what?"

"Just nothing." Jody shrugged.

"Give me an example."

Jody thought a moment. "Take Laurette. She's a French chick. She was always saying they need to 'discuss their options.' Ulrich was always agreeing with her. I think he had his head up her apron most of the time, anyway."

"Uh-huh." I flipped back to my suspect list and drew a line between Laurette and Ulrich.

"Who else was pissed?"

Jody furrowed her eyebrows. "Ya know, the Junettes were always so honky-dory with everything. But you know they had to be faking it. No one's that happy, right?"

I shrugged. Maybe. Maybe not.

Jody continued. "And Tracy. I love him to death. He's good people. But he gets on this tirade about how he's a slave to his art and shit like that." Jody shook her head.

I waited just long enough to be polite before hammering her again. "They were all on the board?"

"Yes, ma'am."

"So what position did Laurette hold?"

"President."

"Who was vice-president?"

"Ulrich Alford." Jody paused, and I wrote it down. "Junettes are co-membership chairs. Good job for them. California types, laid-back, you know. Vegetarians." Disbelief spread across Jody's face. "Why would anybody give up meat?"

I shook my head. "Dunno. They must never have been to your restaurant."

Jody smiled, showing lots of teeth. "Damn straight. I like you."

I scribbled furiously, and caught up. "And what about Tracy?"

"Treasurer."

"Who's the new secretary?"

"Doug DuBois. Space Needle."

A tangy bit of cayenne worked its way out of a tooth. I held it between two teeth and squeezed. Its spice filled my mouth.

"Look, I gotta get back to the kitchen." Jody stood. "There's a second lunch rush coming just after noon."

"Thanks for your time," I said. "Just two more quick questions."

Jody paused and held up two fingers. "Okay, but only two."

"Do you know who Perry reviewed last Friday?"

She shook her head. "Nah. I don't listen to that asshole."

"Do you know anything about a list?"

Jody looked surprised. "Everyone knows about 'The List.' It's a list Lowell made. The most profitable restaurants in Seattle are on it."

Jody turned, adjusted her cap, and headed for the

kitchen. Tossing everything into my bag, I ran after her, hollering, "Hey, Jody."

She swiveled on one boot heel.

"Do you want to make a guess who did it?"

Jody shook her head. "That's three," she said. "And no, ma'am, I do not."

Chapter Twelve

After wrapping up the rest of my ribs and taking a last swig of iced tea, I made a dash for the Kia. Fortunately, the traffic gods had spared me a parking ticket, and I was free to race back to the *Sun* office for my meeting with Rod.

When I breezed through the doors, the clock that hung above the receptionist's desk read 12:03. A clog in the flow of traffic outside the U District forced me to take University Way to Lake City Way, and I'd been afraid I'd be late. I breathed a sigh of relief, then smiled as I passed Cherrie's empty chair. She was probably out tracking a lead...or a rich boyfriend. Maybe the same thing in Cherrie's world.

I headed directly for my cave. Inside, I bent over, fluffed my hair as best I could, then bared my teeth at the mirror that hung on the back of the door and checked for remains. Surprisingly, all clear. Next, I dug the tube of lip gloss from my bag and applied a little sheen. Satisfied with my appearance, I reminded myself that I didn't care what I looked like. And I definitely didn't care what Rod thought about the way I looked.

I reassembled all my notes in the order of when I took them. Supporting documentation went on the bottom of the stack. The whole caboodle got stashed into my bag and the bag slung over my shoulder.

One quick tuck of shirt into Dockers later, and I ran

up the stairs. I paused at Rod's door, took a deep breath, then rapped twice. I arrived just ten minutes late.

"Come." Rod's idea of a welcome.

I swung the door wide, determined to get back onto the right foot with my boss. I'd be polite and professional, maybe even pleasant. My half-grin drooped, however, when I saw whose butt occupied the chair in front of Rod's desk.

Cherrie. She wore her smart glasses, the ones I suspected held glass in the frames and not true prescriptions. Her hair was swept up in a bun and secured by a pencil, a style that defined her as both sophisticated and hard-working. Worst of all, though, she had her legs crossed so Rod had a view of six inches of lean, muscular cheerleader thigh.

Stifling a groan, I closed the door, retrieved the folding chair from behind it and set it at third-wheel position. Cherrie didn't budge, so I sat adjacent to the two of them. Worsening the power dynamic, my chair was at least three inches shorter than the others. I felt like a kid at the Thanksgiving table without a booster seat.

I was doomed.

"Hey, Rod," I said. "Cherrie."

"Harriet." Cherrie's smile exemplified perfect grace under pressure. Her lipstick, some shade between pink and red, brought attention to her expensive orthodontia and cosmetic dentistry. The strand of pearls at her neck mirrored her teeth. Combined with the hair and heels, her appearance put me to shame. I felt like a drag queen next to Miss America, superior in some ways, but not welcome everywhere.

I clamped my pen between my teeth and balanced

my stack of papers on my lap.

"So you both know, I've given this a lot of thought," Rod said. "I've decided to address the cause of death in the article. That's why I pulled Cherrie into the meeting."

Ah, rats. I knew what was coming.

Rod dipped his head toward Cherrie. Cherrie gave up a shy smile. I wondered if they taught that at cheerleading school.

"Tell me what you've got," Rod said.

I knew this game. Whoever went first gives up the good info and the second person has automatic trumping potential. Unh-uh. I avoided both sets of eyes and rummaged through my papers.

After a moment's silence, Rod exhaled gustily. "Harriet. Go."

Dammit.

I bit my pen and flipped through the reviews, collecting my thoughts. When I spoke, I would stick to the facts. "What I know," I said, "is that Perry was murdered. It was no accident. Unfortunately, there seem to be more suspects than not."

I hazarded a glance up. Rod stared at me intently. I took it as a good sign.

I cut a look Cherrie's way. She was glaring. An even better sign. It meant I had something. Or she thought I did. Either way, good for me.

"So what I looked at next was motive." I paused, enjoying my moment in the *Sun*'s, um, sun. "Who would kill a talk radio restaurant critic?"

"Great question, Harriet." It was Cherrie. Her comment, as always, served two purposes. First, it made her look like a team player in front of Rod.

Second, it made me aware that I had entered "duh" territory. I hurried along.

"He was pretty nasty in his reviews, and he made a lot of enemies." I chose my words carefully. "The way I figure it, someone, or someones, slipped something into Perry's food or drink at the Chocoholic Ball."

"How?" Rod asked.

I handed Rod the drawing I'd made of the Skyline level. He set it on his desk, righted it, then held it in place with his fingertips at the top edges.

I leaned in. So did Cherrie, obstructing my view as well as my ability to point out relevant spots.

"Excuse me," I said. Cherrie had no choice but to nudge over a bit.

"This is the Skyline level of the Space Needle. It's for private functions only. Weddings, banquets, that sort of thing. The entire level is designed for mood lighting, and given the weather conditions the evening of the Ball, I imagine it was pretty dark." I pointed to the sketched-in corridors and made an arrow. "Traffic flowed this direction through the halls, and the hallways are fairly narrow. Anyone could have done anything in there. It would have been easy."

Rod studied the map, bracing his chin with his fist. I'd never seen that expression on him. It was half-surprise, half-respect. Like when a teacher calls on a student who's goofing off, but the student answers the question correctly anyway.

"Do you have a list of the vendors?" Rod asked.

I shook my head. "Not yet. The guest list is top secret. My 'in' at the Needle said he thought it was a publicity ploy to get people more interested in the charity than the people involved in it."

Rod harrumphed.

"Yeah," I said. "Seems farfetched to me, too."

Cherrie wedged in and exhaled, her breath hot on my arm.

I dropped my hands into my lap. "However, I'll have a list in a few hours."

Rod's head tilted my way, and he eyed me. "How are you going to get it?"

I fidgeted. I didn't really want to explain Tom, or how I knew him. I especially didn't want to let either one of them know that I'd agreed to have dinner with him to obtain said list.

Rod's attention never shifted from my face. Cherrie cocked her head and stared. Both waited for my reply.

"I've got a friend in high places." I laughed, but neither Rod nor Cherrie showed amusement. Rod stared a moment, then returned his gaze to the drawing. Cherrie's lips pulled back in a way I'd only seen on feral children facing a predator on the National Geographic channel.

I eased back into my chair. "I've also spoken with the wife and brother—" Rod glanced up and I corrected myself. "I mean best friend—and gathered Lowell's photo and hard copies of all of his reviews." I considered revealing the missing critique, but reserved it for last.

Rod's expression went blank. "And?"

I frowned. "He made a lot of enemies, according to the, uh, best friend."

Rod's eyebrows knit together. "Is that all?"

Cherrie took this turn in the conversation as an invitation to pounce. "I've got a little more I can add to our info pot, Chief."

Chief?

A bit of ribs threatened to escape.

Cherrie set both elbows on his table, effectively pushing me to the far side. "I have an angle Jess missed."

"Okay, Cher," Rod said, faintly smiling. "Let's hear it."

Cher? What, had there been a nickname-giving party I wasn't invited to?

My teeth gnashed.

"I've done quite a bit of research and talked with some people who knew Perry well. Then I took a look at the statistics on murders, particularly poisonings. The significant others in this case are the wife, Calendra Lowell, and the boyfriend—or as Jess called him, best friend—William Doninger."

My mouth dropped open. I wanted to slap my head. Of course. It all fit. Will was gay, and it explained why he referred to himself as Perry's best friend. It also explained Rod's comment about Perry being knocked off his throne. But why was a gay guy married? Did Callie know?

More importantly, did Cherrie know that Rod was Perry's nephew?

I chanced a peek at Rod. His hand covered his mouth, but his eyes were as cold and hard as cement. Even if it were all true, it couldn't have been pleasant to hear his family's private information dug up for public inspection.

I tried to think of a way to stop Cherrie from going any further. I coughed once and scooted my chair around. Nothing worked. Rod's expression and attention were fixed on Cherrie. And Cherrie kept yammering.

"Calendra Lowell is a former hippie. She attended the University of Washington, way back when, and met Perry Lowell there. She is also much older than Perry—fifty-eight to his forty-five.

"William Doninger, who goes by Will or Willy, depending on the circumstances…" Cherrie laughed. Rod's mouth had set in a straight line, and his jaw worked just below the skin. Her joke at his uncle's expense didn't go over very well. I decided to settle in and wait it all out.

Cherrie's smile faded and she cleared her throat before continuing. "Will is something else. He's twenty-eight, single, and commonly on Perry's arm when the trio goes out in public. He works as a waiter at a restaurant called the Union Bay Cafe, and lives in the University District."

She'd gotten a lot of the facts straight, but at least one wrong: she'd called the Union Bay Cabin the Union Bay Cafe. I suppressed a grin. The problem with getting something wrong is it puts a stain on the fabric of the argument. It makes the listener evaluate if the whole garment's ruined.

I relaxed and listened for more gaffs in her story, determined to keep a tally.

"And despite Jess's assumption that he was killed by a chef because of his reviews, there just isn't any support for that." Cherrie tossed a self-satisfied smile my way. "In cases such as these, it's almost always the wife or…significant other."

Cherrie uncrossed, then recrossed her legs, her skirt riding higher. "I really think we need to look at

Calendra Lowell and William Doninger."

Rod's face tightened all the way to his ears. It was clear he was embarrassed, as well as angry at the implication that his aunt had killed his uncle, not to mention all the talk about Will and the well-known dalliance between his aunt's husband and a younger man. And Cherrie was treading on dangerous, libelous thin ice. She was the only one who didn't realize it.

"What support have you got?" Rod's voice was strained, but under control.

Cherrie noticed something in the tenor of his voice and her eyebrows furrowed. "Common sense and statistics," she replied, but her voice sounded weaker.

Oops. Wrong answer. Journalists may follow leads based on common sense and stats, but they don't write anything without facts. Usually facts and more facts to back them up. Rookie mistake.

The problem, however, lay in her theory. It held merit. We all knew it. Most murder victims not only know their killer but have a relationship with them. Murder is a crime of passion. Who has more passion than the person who loves him or her? I saw the same concern on Rod's face.

Rod turned toward me. "What do you think, Harriet?"

I scratched my head. "I agree with Cherrie's take on the statistical side of things," I said, my words careful. "But I just don't see it. I don't see Callie or Will as killers, and I think there are a lot of leads in other directions that have to be followed up on."

I straightened in my chair and crossed my ankles. "Like I said before, I think it's a chef from the Chocoholic Ball. Everyone there had motive, and a perfect opportunity."

Rod nodded and leaned forward in his chair. He braced his elbows atop my sketch of the Space Needle's Skyline level and stared at a spot equidistant between Cherrie and me. The time had come to make a decision. He tapped his forefingers on the bridge of his nose.

Every muscle in my body tensed. Beside me, Cherrie perched on the edge of her chair and leaned forward.

This was a big decision, and we both knew it. It was more than just a story for me, though. It was my future. My dream. My cheek twitched and I held my breath.

Finally, he spoke. "I'm going with Jess on this one."

Chapter Thirteen

Rod chose me to cover the story.

Over Cherrie.

That had never happened since the monkey story.

Silence expanded. The first to move was Cherrie. She nodded, then rose and strode out the door without another word. After the closing click of the catch, we listened to the steady clack-clack-clack of Cherrie's heels down the hallway.

I had to admit, she was a good loser. Or appeared to be. My opinion of her grew.

Rod stared at the drawing again. When he spoke, his voice was softer than usual. "Her hunch is solid, Harriet. You know that. I know that. She knows that. It all makes perfect sense. Except for one thing."

He rubbed his chin, then shook his head. "I know my aunt. She didn't do it. I know it in my gut. She was a flower child...acid dropper...groupie...way back when."

Rod met my eyes. I nodded.

"I can still remember her saying, 'Make love, not war.'" Rod sighed. "She was a nude model, for Christ's sake."

Okay, way too much info. I flashed on an image of Callie's plump, diamond-studded hand resting atop one ample, bare hip, a gentle smile on her face. I shook my head to dispel the image.

Rod picked up a pen, twirled it on end, then slammed it onto his desk again. "She's as gentle as a gnat," he said. "But more importantly, and what Cherrie doesn't know, is that Aunt Callie had all the money. Perry didn't have squat. She paid for everything—the house, the travel, the clothing."

He set his gaze squarely on me and his voice became all business again. "Regarding the Will situation, Aunt Callie's known about that for a long time. She accepted it. It was weird to the rest of the family, but we love Callie, and we don't question it. Even when Will joins them for family gatherings."

I remained impassive. Inside I agreed with Rod. The whole situation felt weird. On the outside, though, I played objective reporter, non-judgmental and open to facts.

Rod's eyes narrowed. "The one thing I know for sure about Aunt Callie is that she loved him. And as much as I disliked Will, he loved Perry, too."

I cleared my throat, unsure what to say. Rod was uncharacteristically human at that moment, something I'd never seen before. Kind of like the two-headed calf my neighbors' cow birthed when I was ten. It seemed impossible. I couldn't help but stare.

After a moment, I spoke. "Wanna play devil's advocate?"

Rod leaned back and clasped his hands behind his head. "Go for it."

"Well," I began, tiptoeing around the words. "You know what people are going to say. They'll say she just got fed up with the whole situation."

"Nah," Rod replied. "No support. If anything, the three of them just got closer over time. There was talk at one point that Will would move in with them."

Bizarre. I strained to remain objective, but felt my eyebrows rise.

Rod stared at me, reading my face. "Yeah," he said. "I know." He shifted in his seat. "What else have you got?"

I thought a moment. "Did Perry have a will?"

Rod smirked. "He had at least one," he said. "But that was the kind he exercised before his death, not after."

A moment passed before I caught on. Exercising a will—as in Will Doninger. I laughed, averted my eyes, then frowned at the images he conjured up. "You know what I mean."

Rod moved forward and brought his hands to the top of his desk. "Perry and Callie probably did, but it wouldn't matter. The trust was in Aunt Callie's name, and Perry wasn't worth anything without Callie."

"Are you sure?"

"I'm sure," Rod said. "The guy had a negative effect on their household income."

I grimaced. "Yikes. Remind me never to get married."

"No kidding." Rod scowled. "The worst part about this, though, is that my aunt's reputation will be tainted if this came out. So would my family's. That's still the way it is with old money. One mention of scandal, and it won't matter that Aunt Callie's innocent. She'll be crucified in the media. So will my entire family. They'll start looking into tax returns, dig up dirt that isn't there…and other dirt that probably is there."

Rod shook his head. "It won't matter how many non-profit boards my mother's chaired, how many charities my family's given to. It will ruin us for a long time."

Stunned, I reflected on his words. I'd never really thought about the disadvantages of having money. I'd always been too focused on how to get more.

"I agree," I said. He had a point. There was no reason to drag someone's name through the mud if they were innocent. That's bad journalism.

"Thanks, Jess." For a moment he held my eyes. They were like chocolate chips in a cookie straight from the oven. They held their shape but were all soft and smooth on the inside.

Just as quickly, Rod cooled. "Let's do what we can, and carefully choose what we report."

"Got it."

Rod straightened the papers on his desk. "So what were you holding back during the meeting?"

"What do you mean?"

Rod cocked an eyebrow at me but didn't say a word.

He knew me better than I thought. It sent a wave of satisfaction through me. Gingerly, I spread the printouts on his desk and moved to the big chair. It still held Cherrie's warmth.

"Listen to this," I said, picking up the stack of reviews. I read a couple to Rod.

At the end, Rod shrugged his shoulders. "That's vintage Perry. He talked like that all the time."

I waited a beat, then asked, "What were Perry's qualifications?"

Rod picked up his pen and turned it end over end, letting the shaft slide through his fingers. "He didn't have any, not really. Except for marrying into a family that owns the radio station."

An entire stadium of lights flickered in my head. "Your family owns a radio station?"

Rod nodded. "And four more—three in Washington, one in Idaho."

"Wow," I said. "I knew your family owned the *Sun*, but I didn't realize you had a media empire."

A belly laugh rumbled out of Rod. He grinned. "Media empire. That's funny, Jess."

"So what else do you own?"

"Another paper here in Washington, and two small papers in Oregon. They're a lot like the *Sun*."

"My family owns six dairy cows and a flock of chickens," I said, thinking of home. "And we had to save for that."

Rod smiled, but he didn't laugh. "So what else have you got?"

I wanted to get back to how rich his family was. I'd never known rich people before. I also wanted to ask why he worked at the *Sun* when they had so much money.

None of that would be polite, though. I answered his question. "Two things." I set the papers on the desk and fished out the index cards. "Have you ever been to Perry's office?"

Rod shook his head. "Have you?"

"Yep."

"Really?" Rod's mouth turned up. "What'd you find?"

I held up the cards. "These."

Rod took the cards and examined each one. "What are they?"

"I don't know," I said. "I can't read the writing.

But I think they're notes for the missing review."

"What missing review?"

"Last Friday. The thirteenth. According to Sammy, it got pulled."

"Who's Sammy?" Rod asked.

"Receptionist," I replied. "Haven't you met her?"

"Sammy?" He cast his gaze toward a corner of the room. "Weird hair, right?"

I nodded. I didn't find her hair weird. In fact, I kind of liked it. But Rod's a different beast.

"Yeah, I know her."

I waited for anything that said he'd noticed her the way he'd always noticed Cherrie. Nothing. I said, "Sammy said she got along with Perry better than anyone else at the station."

"That's probably true." Rod set the cards down and looked up. "Why was it pulled?"

"She didn't know. It hadn't been uploaded on his website, and the hard copy wasn't in his scrapbook."

"What scrapbook?"

"The scrapbook in his office."

"What do you mean 'scrapbook'?"

"More than a scrapbook."

Rod ran a hand over his face and breathed deeply. I knew what he was thinking. It's acceptable, even expected, for a journalist to keep clips of their published work, especially the well-written, well-edited pieces. They come in handy for resume-building or interviews. But no one I knew kept a scrapbook. It was too vanity press. Too star-reporter-of-the-school-newspaper.

Except Perry Lowell, of course.

Disgust shifted to acceptance, then interest. "So

what's in the scrapbook?"

"The usual," I said. "Matchbooks, menus, index cards for notetaking, hard copies, stickers of pens, pencils…"

"Okay. Get back to the missing review," Rod said. "When was it due to his editor?"

"It was supposed to be read on Friday, but I have no clue when it was due for editing."

"Was there a file in his computer?"

"I didn't have time to look." I grimaced. "I got interrupted."

"By what?"

"Not by what," I said. "By whom."

"By whom, then?"

I thought back to mountain man. He hadn't given me his name. "Some Neanderthal. About six-six, three hundred pounds on a good day. He might have been station security, but I doubt it."

His eyebrows furrowed, meeting in the middle. "KTLK doesn't have a security guard."

Fear trickled down my spine. At the back of my mind, I'd been hoping that was all he was.

"Actually, when he caught me, I pretended he was Perry," I said. "He played along."

"Really? He pretended to be Perry?"

I nodded. "So who do you think he was?"

"I have no idea." He shook his head and stared at the index cards again. "I'll give Sammy a call later."

"Oh, one more thing," I said. "Sammy wasn't at her desk when I left the not-a-security-guard guy. I called her once to check up on her but got her voice mail."

Rod wrinkled his nose. "I wouldn't worry about

it," he said. "Sammy's rarely at her desk."

"Oh." His response didn't set my mind at ease. But if he wasn't concerned, I wouldn't be either. Still, I'd try calling her again before the end of the day.

Rod held one card up to the ceiling light and squinted.

"Can you make out anything?" I asked.

He shook his head. "Not at all. I think some of the words might be in French, though."

"French?"

"Maybe not. Maybe English, but British English or something." Rod slid the cards back to me. "Are you sure these are notes for the missing review?"

"I can't be sure. All I know is that they were on the next page in the scrapbook, laid out the way the other restaurant reviews had been laid out." I thought back to the title page of Lowell's scrapbook. "But there wasn't a name listed on the first page, either, so I can't be one hundred percent certain."

Rod thought a moment. "I think they're review notes. You think they're review notes. They're probably review notes."

"Do you think Callie would be able to read his writing?"

Rod thought about it a moment. "Worth checking out." He lifted the receiver on his phone and began punching numbers. Abruptly, he stopped and replaced the receiver. "I'll talk to her later," Rod said. "The family is gathering for the burial this afternoon. I don't want to bother her now. She might be resting or something."

"Do you want to take them to her when you go?" I held the cards out to him again.

Rod nodded. "Good idea." He slid a paper clip from the edge of his doodle pad and fastened the cards together, then set the group in his top desk drawer. "I'm also going to ask what kind of poison killed him."

"Yeah," I said. "It would help to know that."

"So what's the other thing?" Rod asked.

"What other thing?"

"You said you had two things."

"Oh!" I leaned on the desk. "Do you know anything about a list?"

"List?" he asked. "List of what?"

In the old days, or even half an hour ago, I would have reminded him that if I knew what was on the list I wouldn't have had to ask him. But the delicacy of the subject had made me cautious. Instead, I said, "I don't know. But Will told me yesterday that they'd found out about a list. He wouldn't tell me any more than that. Wouldn't tell me who 'they' were or what was on the list. I assume he meant the chefs, but I don't know."

I paused a moment, retracing my steps of the day. "When I went to the Union Bay Cabin—"

"You went to Union Bay Cabin?"

"Yes," I said. "Why?"

Rod grinned. "You've been busy, haven't you?" He regarded me a moment, his eyes starting to go all soft again. "Continue."

I shook off the unwanted tingles I felt when he smiled. "So anyway, I went to Union Bay Cabin and I was trying to get Will to tell me about the list. But he wouldn't. When I went to leave, though, I asked him who Perry had reviewed last Friday. He didn't know, but then he said 'Whoever was next on the list.' "

Rod's grin fell. "Just like that? Those were his

exact words?"

I nodded. "His exact words. I should mention he'd been drinking."

"Drinking?" Rod asked. "As in alcohol?"

"Yep," I said. "I smelled it on him when he spoke. Then, as I left, I saw him take a drink of what looked like a martini in a highball glass. He said something about appletinis."

"I've heard enough." Rod grimaced and straightened in his chair. "Okay. We've got a plan. I'll talk to Callie at the family memorial and get her input on the cards. We'll meet again tonight at—" Rod twisted his wrist and glanced at his watch. "It's one fifteen now. Let's meet again at six thirty."

I wrote six thirty on my left palm. It would be impossible to meet Tom at seven. "Can we make it a little earlier? I need to be downtown by seven."

He stared at me a moment, his mouth working open and shut, and finally said, "Okay. Six."

"Thanks. Do you want me to wait until you talk to Callie? Or can I go talk to some more chefs?"

Rod reflected on that a moment. "We don't want to arouse any suspicion. Whoever did this obviously knows my aunt, and maybe the rest of the family. Then again, we want to investigate before they have a chance to get together and coordinate their stories."

He stood, turned, and stared out his window. "Which chefs were you thinking about interviewing?"

"The restaurants he reviewed. In the reverse order of when they were reviewed." I hoped my reasoning didn't sound stupid. I took a breath before continuing. "I figure the more recent reviews have the most pissed off chefs."

"Sounds about right," Rod said. "So who was the last reviewed?"

"Bayou Déjà vu. But I already spoke to her."

"After that?"

"Emerald Towers."

"Oh." Rod's eyebrows shot to the top of his forehead. "That place is high class. Did Perry pan them, too?"

I nodded in the affirmative. "He panned everyone but Union Bay Cabin."

Rod sighed heavily, then rubbed his chin. "I think I know what we're up against here."

I had no response to that, so I shot him a faint smile.

"Okay, go ahead," Rod said. "See ya."

I rose, collapsed the folding chair and replaced it behind the door, then slung my tote bag onto my shoulder. At the door, I turned. Rod stood with his hands in his pockets, his form framed by the window. Sunlight created an aura around his shoulders and face, obscuring his expression. I sensed it was sad by the droop of his posture.

"Hey, Rod," I said, squinting into the sunlight. "I just wanted to say, you know, I'm sorry. And also thanks, for letting me do the story. It means a lot to me."

Rod cocked his head, and the sun angled across one side of his face. It gave him a strong cheekbone and reflected flecks of yellow in his brown eyes. "I know you appreciate it, Harriet," he said, losing the grin. "But this is my family. Don't screw it up."

Chapter Fourteen

I pulled the door closed behind me and ran down the hallway. Torn between sheer joy at keeping the story, versus terror over messing up and disappointing Rod, with a layer of sadness that he thought I'd screw things up, I took the stairs in two leaps. At the bottom, I paused, took a big breath and a look around. The receptionist chair was vacant, Cherrie nowhere to be seen. In fact, the entire newsroom resembled a graveyard, computer monitors its nameless headstones. I shot a silent thanks to whoever answered my unspoken prayers and threw myself out the doors.

The Kia started up and I flew past three police cars, all filled with cops eating teriyaki out of white foam containers. One waved. I slowed down. Still, within five minutes I'd managed to put nearly five miles between Rod and myself. None too soon. I fidgeted in my seat for several moments sorting through my feelings.

How dare Rod tell me not to screw up? I've never screwed up a story in my life. I'd always done the very best I could with every lead he'd assigned me.

I stopped at the corner station to gas up. Tears welled as I swiped my card, unscrewed the cap, and stuck in the hose. Why did he choose me if he didn't have faith that I could do it well?

I pressed the button labeled "regular," then

squeezed and set the trigger. The pump whirred alongside my emotions. And what was with all those gushy feelings when he talked about his aunt? It was almost like we were…friends.

I shook my head and stamped the pre-numb cold from my feet. I shouldn't let him get to me. I couldn't spend time second guessing myself if I wanted to solve this murder.

The pump clicked, I holstered the hose, and the receipt spewed out. After pocketing the slip of paper, I sat tall behind the steering wheel. I was not going to let Rod decide who I was or what I could become. I would prove myself to Rod. To everyone. Even myself.

Tank full, I hopped back in and reviewed my options. I could start with Ulrich Alford over at the Emerald Towers first, then hit Laurette Roen at Bien. If there was still time before the big re-meet with Rod, I might even be able to squeeze in a visit to Green, the restaurant Dave and Debby Junette owned. All of the chefs had motive, and most importantly, all were board members of GAAS.

Foolproof plan? Not exactly, but a plan nonetheless.

I high-tailed up Yesler, took a left on Fourth, then drove north five blocks, parked, and trotted back to Emerald Towers. Housed in the pricey downtown district and surrounded by name-brand department stores, Emerald Towers had the distinction of being Seattle's only five-star hotel. I knew that not because I'd ever set foot in one of its rooms, or even the lobby, but because I'd read about it in the "Lifestyle" section of the Sunday *Daily Log*. Pausing a moment, I stared up at the hotel's two towers. The sparkling clean green-glass windows reflected the sun as it peeked through the clouds.

As I walked, I pulled out the Emerald Room review and read.

The Emerald Dining Room, No Jewel.

German chef Ulrich Alford, new to Seattle's fine dining scene, has carved the former Emerald Dining Room in the penthouse of our dear Emerald Towers into something gaudy and common: a heart-shaped Cubic Zirconia. To the unsophisticated, the cutesy shape may seem attractive. But when you grow up, and hopefully you will, you'll learn to appreciate the classic shapes: Marquise, Brilliant, and most importantly, Emerald.

Why would anyone pare the perfect Emerald into something else? I don't know. Ask the owners. My job is to report what Executive Chef Alford has done.

To begin, Chef Alford has hacked away at the menu. Instead of the fabulous prix fixe dinners created by the former executive chef, capturing the best the Northwest has to offer, Chef Alford has created a lead-heavy menu of gravies and sauces and red meat.

But that's not the worst of it. Chef Alford has carried the theme of rich and heady tastes well beyond the entrée list. Cleaved away is anything fresh, broiled, or steamed. Nearly every item on the hors d'oeuvres and accompaniment lists drips with oil and would drown a Seattleite's palate. The wine recommendations are another point of contention. Lemberger with Marinara. Zinfandel with poultry. Who is this guy? The wine Nazi? "You vill drink dis vine and you vill like it!"

Really, people. You can do better. Pass on the lab-grown emerald and go for the real thing.

About what I expected. Steaming smelly words served on a silver platter.

After stashing the printout in my bag, I strolled up the granite sidewalk, past the huge glass walls, and up to the oversized glass doors. A valet appeared out of nowhere and pulled on the huge brass handle. The door whispered open.

"Thanks."

I entered the lobby. A warm breeze, a tinkle of water and muted conversations greeted me. A ten-foot-tall fountain with gold-toned and gold-winged cherubs was the source of the water. It stood in the middle of the room. The munchkins held long-spouted cans that sprinkled water into a shallow pool. Pennies, at least enough to buy a latte, tiled the bottom. The surprised expression on the cherubs' faces may have been due not to the amount of money they'd collected, but to the realization that their privates hung out. Or maybe it was the fact that they'd exposed so much and received so little back.

Man, did I know that feeling.

On the floor was an ornate, Asian-influenced rug in shades of green, gold, and burgundy. Trios of chairs, one in each color, surrounded small dark wood tables. Each grouping acted as a satellite of the fountain, close enough to enjoy the view, but out of splash range. A gold bowl with ripe red apples inside topped each table.

From the ceiling hung a crystal chandelier, also edged in gold. It cast a million pinpoints of light around the room, winking out stars on the ceiling. Two half-circle staircases, one to the left and one to the right, met on the second floor. The hallway upstairs ran the perimeter of the lobby, and a brushed brass railing prevented anyone from falling. At various points along the hall were double doors in the same matching dark wood. One read "BALLROOM," another "ATRIUM." Nowhere did I see the words "EMERALD" or "ROOM."

Past the fountain lay the registration counter. Behind it stood a tall woman in a green blazer. I walked her way.

As I neared, I noted she was thin, had a crown of hair blacker than black, and boasted an ivory complexion. She reminded me of an anorexic Ice Queen after a hearty heave. Her head bowed as I approached, her attention focused on paperwork below the countertop. I strode up and parked myself on the opposite side of the counter.

Nothing. The Queen didn't even sniff my way.

"Hello," I said.

She looked up. The green blazer fit snugly, each brass button shining. Across one tiny breast, a gold nametag spelled out "Martique." She eyed me up and down, then spat out three words: "Just a moment."

She lowered her head again and shuffled some papers. After a moment, she moved to the other end of the counter where two briefcase-clutching men in business suits waited.

After punching at a keyboard, she slid two folders across the counter to the men and thanked them. The men grabbed the folders and headed for the attended elevator.

I waited two more minutes, but the Queen never returned to me.

I ambled down to her. "Hi," I said. "Can you tell me where the Emerald Dining Room is?"

She gave me a look usually reserved for people who should not be allowed to wander the streets alone. "It doesn't open until six o'clock for early supper."

"Oh, that's all right," I said, crossing my fingers below the counter. "I have an appointment with Ulrich. The chef." I'd gotten used to, if not good at, lying. I'm a quick study.

One eyebrow raised, but the steely look in her eyes didn't waver. "You have an appointment?"

I nodded. I didn't trust my mouth a second time.

She observed me a moment more, then picked up a telephone and punched in a few numbers. My heart raced. This is why I don't lie. I always get caught.

I considered sprinting, but before I could decide, a busy signal sounded through the receiver. I grinned.

The Queen re-dialed. Again, the line was busy.

I met her eyes. Before she could tell me to get lost, her gaze shifted to the lobby. A family had arrived: Mom, Dad, twin toddlers, and a baby who was shrieking loud enough to wake folks in Taiwan.

The Queen took a deep breath and placed the receiver to her ear one more time.

Still busy.

"Penthouse," she said to me, as the family got in line and the infant's wails reached what I hoped was its crescendo. She pointed one gold lacquered nail to the elevator.

I turned, gave the family behind me a smile, then made like a peasant and trudged my way across the lobby. Even if the restaurant wasn't open, someone was there tying up the phone line. And it made sense that someone would be Ulrich Alford.

As I neared the elevator, the gold doors opened. I

bounded in.

"Floor?" asked the attendant, a dark-skinned twenty-something male who rolled his R. His nametag read "Enrico."

"Penthouse," I said. "Emerald Dining Room."

"Penthouse," Enrico repeated, glancing toward the registration desk. I followed his eyes' trajectory. They ended at the Ice Queen, who nodded and returned her attention to the family now pawing at the counter. I had the firm impression that he knew to check with her before allowing me upstairs.

Enrico turned back to me, smiled, and pushed the top button. The doors closed and we were whisked upward in a momentum sickeningly reminiscent of the Space Needle yesterday, but with the bonus of Kenny G's clarinet solo piped into the eight-by-eight box.

At the top the same colors prevailed. Lush, dark-green carpeting, cream paint on the walls, gold doorknobs and gold lettering. Across the short hall a set of French doors stood closed, but at eye-level were the words "Emerald Dining Room."

I walked over, tried both the handles. Locked.

I knocked. No response.

I knocked again.

Nothing.

After ten seconds, I tried once more.

Still nothing.

What now? The directions in small print read: "Reservations can be made at the Front Desk in the Lobby." That wasn't an option, since I'd given said receptionist my appointment story. The problem with lying is it takes a lot of remembering.

Back to square one. I tried the handle again.

Definitely locked.

Damn.

I checked for additional entry points down the adjoining hall but saw nothing but green carpeting giving way to fire escape doors at each end.

I considered leaving. Then I thought about the six o'clock meeting with Rod. And his screw-up comment.

I hammered on the door with my fist.

A few seconds later came a voice. "*¿Hola?*" The door cracked open.

"Hi, I'm Jess Harriet." I spoke in an authoritative voice, directly into the crack. "I'm here to speak with Chef Ulrich Alford."

A slight shuffling ensued, then the door swung wide. Two brown eyes peered out. "*¿Hola?*"

"*¿Senor Ulrich?*"

"Yes," I said, "*Si, si. Ulrich.*" For the first time ever, I was glad I'd been raised in Eastern Washington. The Spanish I'd learned in school from the migrant workers' kids had finally paid off.

The face crinkled into a smile. Attached to it, a tiny woman with skin the color of browned butter, waved me in. She was approximately sixty years old and wore a maid's uniform. One hand held a dust rag. "Ulrich," she said. "*Si*, Ulrich."

She closed the door behind me, then raced off, presumably in Ulrich's direction.

I threw the latch, relocking the door. The echo scratched the silence of the spacious room. I scanned the area. At least two hundred tapestry-backed chairs surrounded fifty tables, each topped with a lace tablecloth and nestled against a wall or between ionic columns. At various intervals, golden ERs graced wall and column surfaces.

Despite the elegance, the mood was somber, quiet. Along the perimeter, heavy green drapes covered what I assumed were banks of windows. The room was dark, the only exception an aura of light created by brass and glass sconces affixed to the columns. Each released a soft amber glow of the same wattage as the matching centerpieces on the tables.

The smell of the room, however, could not have been homier. The scent of slow roasted turkey filled the air. I sniffed. Gravy. Something else. Pumpkin pie?

My stomach quaked, despite my heavy lunch. I couldn't help it. I love turkey and dressing. It reminds me of Thanksgiving. And home. Nostalgia took over, and a picture of Jenna formed in my mind. Hugely pregnant, she sat on the couch she and her husband Danny had unearthed from the barn when they moved into their own place a couple years back. She fanned herself with a newspaper folded accordion-style as two kids ran around like maniacs. She looked miserable.

A pang of something—apprehension, guilt, frustration—stabbed me in the heart. How could I not go home when she has the baby?

I made a mental note to reply to her e-mail.

A shuffle interrupted my thoughts. From the direction the maid had headed appeared the round white chef I recognized from Perry's memorial service. He strode toward me. "I am Executive Chef Ulrich Alford."

"Hi," I replied. "Jess Harriet." I stuck out my hand and smiled.

He took my hand but didn't return the grin. He still wore the chef whites, except the long sleeves had been rolled up, revealing hairy knuckles and forearms. I wondered if they made hairnets for parts of the body other than the head. This guy definitely needed some. Over his chef whites, Ulrich wore an apron. Smudges of red stretched like continents over a big globe of a belly, revealing that cranberries rounded out the menu for the evening.

He released my hand. "You do not haff an appointment."

Oops. The Queen must have gotten through. I wondered if she'd be sending a bouncer my way. Good thing I'd locked the door.

"No," I stammered. "You're right. It's just that the story I'm doing is so very important and, uh, timely."

"What is ze story for?" His accent chopped his words like a cleaver through bone.

"The *Sun*."

"I am sorry," he said. "We are not open. You vill leave."

"I only have a few questions," I interjected. "Do you think you could give me just a moment of your time? I'll be sure to mention how amazing it smells in here."

Ulrich eyed me. Publicity is its own language. "You vill say good things about ze Emerald Dining Room?"

I crossed my heart. "Promise."

He nodded. "Ja." He wrung his hands on a clean space of apron, then pulled out a chair. "You sit."

I sat. He pushed in my chair. Chivalry lives.

"I haff only five minutes." He held up one hand and splayed five beefy digits. Then he settled opposite me.

I decided not to mince words. "Did you know Perry Lowell was murdered?"

Ulrich's face went slack. The eyebrows drooped. His fingers froze.

I took that as a no and continued. "Poison. Chocoholic Ball." I'd perched on a logical limb that swayed in the breeze of reasonable doubt, but I didn't care.

Ulrich's cheek twitched. His jaw clenched.

I flipped open my notepad. "Were you there?" I asked. "At the Chocoholic Ball?"

"Ja." He bit off the word like a tough piece of jerky. "Of course."

I poised the pen above the paper and watched as Ulrich tracked my movements. "Did you see anything suspicious?"

"No."

"The cops think it was a chef." I put on my puzzled look. The limb became a twig. "Who do you think did it?"

Ulrich's eyes widened. He stared long enough to make me wonder if he ever planned on answering. Then he rose from his chair. "I cannot help you. My English not so good." He turned and began to walk away.

"I understand, being from Germany—" I said, pushing to my feet.

Ulrich pivoted on his heels. Impressive, given his size. He strode back to me. I faltered and took two steps back.

"I am not German." His voice, deep and guttural, belied his earlier statement of not knowing English well.

Who'd have thought being called German would

burn his brownie?

I stood my ground, but my knees started knocking. Fortunately, my slightly damp pants silenced the sound.

His face flamed red, and a slow tremble overtook his body. He exhaled, and a plume of spent coffee settled around my head like a thick fog.

I shifted my weight to my heels, away from the odor, and tried to look brave. My back found a column, and I pushed my spine against it. The raised "ER" dug into my shoulder blades.

He held my gaze but didn't move. Nor did he say a word.

I broke into a sweat and wondered if I peed my pants if it would look like rain when I returned outside. If I lived long enough to see the outside again.

The room, silent except for our breathing, expanded and contracted. In and out. In and out. He could have strangled me and no one would have heard. Where was that cleaning lady?

Just when I was about to call the whole thing off and return to Eastern Washington never to be a real journalist, Ulrich inhaled deeply and held. He closed his eyes a moment, then released the air like a slow leak. Color drained from his face.

"I am sorry for my burst-out," he said. "But I am not German. I am Austrian. There is a very big difference."

"Uh-hunh." I tapped my pen on the notepad, pretending at courage. "It must've really smarted, then, when Perry said you were a wine Nazi." Call me stupid. I deserve it.

Ulrich's eyes flared and his mouth worked, but no sound erupted. He was the worst kind of volcano. The quiet kind that gave no warning before exploding.

He raised his hand. I braced myself against the column and waited for his fist.

But instead of swinging, he placed it over his heart. "He did not need to be so cruel."

"He was cruel, wasn't he?" I said, easing away from the column. Ulrich didn't respond. "I mean, he really ripped into you and your friends."

Ulrich nodded once.

"So was anyone mad enough to kill him?"

Ulrich shook his head, his jowls flapping. "No. No one."

I changed tactics. "Tell me about the Chocoholic Ball. What did you bring?"

He didn't waver, but a near smile registered on his face. "Raspberry crème brulee," he said. "My specialty."

"What's in it?"

"Cream, fine sugar, eggs, but only the yolks." A drip of spit flew off the tip of his tongue.

"And raspberries?"

"Ja, of course the raspberries." His head bobbed repeatedly. "Raspberry liqueur in the custard, fresh raspberries on top. A little crème fraiche. A few chocolate shavings."

"No poison?" I winked.

"No." Ulrich glowered, but his expression shifted in an instant. "It is not on ze recipe."

I grinned at his attempt at humor.

"It would not matter, though," Ulrich continued. "He did not eat it."

"Why?"

Ulrich's face turned a shade of red I'd seen only

on, well, raspberries. "I do not know."

"Did you see him eat anything at all?" I asked. "Drink anything?"

He shook his head again, pulling his lips between his teeth so that the pink disappeared. He crossed his arms and tucked his hands next to his girth, his five-minute rule forgotten.

"You know," I said, concentrating to maintain my unfazed expression. "I've been wondering just how much a bad review can cost a restaurant. Or a chef. Seems Perry hurt a lot of people, both personally and professionally." I cocked my head. "How much did his review cost the Emerald Dining Room?"

"I have no idea."

"A lot?"

Ulrich didn't speak, but nodded once, eyes closed.

"Look, Ulrich. Even though you're innocent, the police questioning you will be a smudge on the Emerald Dining Room's reputation, not to mention the Emerald Towers. They might even lose one of their stars."

Ulrich grimaced.

"But I can help you. And you can help me," I said. "You and I both know the cops are going to ask the same questions. They can subpoena your sales figures and compare them to the dates of Perry's reviews."

"That is not part of my job," Ulrich said. "It is the manager's job." He focused on the far wall. As he stared, a drip of sweat rolled from his hairline, down his forehead, tangling in his shaggy eyebrows.

"C'mon. Help me now and avoid all that stress."

Ulrich appeared pained. "No. I cannot."

"Okay," I said. "Have it your way." I recapped my

pen and dropped it into my purse. "Just one more question."

Ulrich tilted his head and stared at me like a dog stares at another dog on the television. "*Ja?*"

"Tell me who was hurt the most, and I'll steer the cops away from you."

Ulrich tracked an imaginary fly as it buzzed through the room. Finally, just a little louder than a whisper, he said, "Junettes."

"Junettes?" I scratched my head. "The owners of Green?"

"Ja," Ulrich said. "The no-meat-eaters." He pulled a face I'd seen on Jody less than an hour before.

"How bad is it for them?" I asked.

Ulrich sighed, blowing two streams of hot air out his nostrils. Thankfully, he hadn't snorted the coffee, so the scent was bearable. "The bank has ruptured."

Chapter Fifteen

"The Junettes are bankrupt?"

Ulrich threw his hands in the air and began to shake them violently, as if there were spiders on every finger. I stared for a moment, confused by his gesture. A pounding on the door interrupted my thoughts and Ulrich's gestures. He dropped his palms to his sides and crossed the floor to the door. I followed. It was bound to be one of Martique's minions ready to offer me an escort back outside. Ulrich opened the door. Surprise. A large man in a tailor-made suit looked past him to me.

Definitely not a minion.

"This way, ma'am." He crooked a finger and nodded, revealing a landing strip pad of hair I'd seen only on active-duty Marines.

I didn't argue.

"See ya, Ulrich," I said, giving him a little wave as I crossed the threshold.

He raised a pudgy arm, flapped his hand my way, then turned and made for the kitchen as if it were on fire and he held the extinguisher. Bouncer man spoke into a portable receiver attached to the inside of his jacket. "I got her," he said.

He motioned me to lead. I walked straight to the elevator which had been held open by Enrico. The giant got in behind me.

"I can see myself out," I volunteered.

He smiled but didn't show any teeth. "No, ma'am. I'll escort you."

Enrico pushed the button marked "L," and down we went. I didn't bother with small talk. Instead, I pulled out my cell phone as though I had to check it every few minutes to keep up on all my messages. It was also to let the elevator occupants know someone would miss me if I disappeared.

The missed calls category read zero. I glanced Bouncer's way, but he wasn't paying any attention. I put it away and rode to the lobby in silence.

When the doors opened, Bouncer man took my elbow and steered me toward the great glass doors. Along the way, I snagged one of the apples from the gold bowls, a ballsy move for the new Jess. At the door, I grinned at the valet, who quickly turned away, then I strolled back to my car, munching the apple. As I neared the Kia, I took one last bite, munched it thoroughly, and chucked the apple into a trash can next to a sad looking tree growing in a square of dirt.

I jumped in and started the car, resting my hands at the ten-two position on the steering wheel, and closed my eyes. I breathed deeply for a few moments, reminding myself that the new Jess wouldn't need any recoup time after being thrown out of a hotel. When I opened my eyes, the clock flashed two thirty. I didn't have to get on the freeway to know that traffic would be congealing. After revving the engine, I hung a right and headed toward Bien.

The streets had dried, and there was nary an umbrella in sight. I tooled toward the French bistro and looked for the red, white, and blue banner Perry had mentioned in his review. It was, as he said, obvious.

I pulled into a parking lot and scanned Bien's review. Lowell had trashed Laurette Roen's award-winning dessert, called her "saucy," and summed up the entire dining experience with, "Boo to Bien." Par for Perry's course.

I sucked up the ten-dollar-an-hour parking ante and hiked up the street. Traffic had thickened slightly. People were making an early break for the suburbs. Not many seemed interested in hanging around downtown to grab a bite to eat. With fewer folks going out to dinner, and only a portion of the available diners making a break for the suburbs, a specialty restaurant like Bien must fight for customers, especially mid-afternoon ones. I made a mental note of that and crossed an alleyway. Directly in front of me stood Bien.

Below its bright awning, a realistic wall fresco of a Paris café scene appeared. Or at least what I expected a Paris café scene to look like appeared. An image of the Eiffel Tower rose a story and a half on the right side, the Arc De Triomphe spanned a solid fifteen feet on the left, and a mess of tables were sandwiched in between. Pastel people dined at bistro tables. All had been painted into confident, assertive poses, some with cigarettes, others with small poodles or parasols. The women all sported flowing, colorful scarves and hats. The men wore ties and gold watches. All look supremely, smugly happy.

Under the real exterior lights, posts had been painted, so that life and art blended in surreal fashion. Add to that Bien's bistro tables, enlarged replicas of those in the mural, and one live couple bundled in parkas and boots and sipping lattes, and passersby could almost believe they were in Europe. The outdoor coffee kiosk to the right of the door brewed a heavy, fresh ground coffee scent that spilled into the air, encouraging people to linger over a hot cup of java. I breezed past it all and into Bien.

Black lacquer and chrome shone in an ultra-chic, sophisticated ambience, albeit one circa 1980. A few steps in, and the smell of java gave way to baking bread.

"*Bon jour, Mademoiselle*. Welcome to Bien."

Behind the raised reception counter stood a youngish girl with hair streaked in shades of blonde and brown, a beret cocked to the right. Her eyelids were baby blue, and her lipstick the color of cotton candy. It seemed curiously out of place with the wide-collared white shirt and matching pinstripe vest and bowtie she wore. Even more out of place were the words coming out of her mouth. They were stilted, probably from on-the-job training.

"Would Mademoiselle desire a table for one?"

I crossed the distance to the podium and eyed her nametag. "Hi, Jennifer," I said. "Actually, I'm here for Laurette Roen."

Jennifer raised a finger to her lips in indecision. "Do you," she began, before shaking her head and trying again. "Does Mademoiselle have an appointment?"

"Not exactly." I handed her a business card. "But I bet she's expecting me."

Jennifer looked at my card and frowned.

"Is she here?" I prompted.

"Uh, yes. I mean, no. I mean, maybe," Jennifer said. She set the menu she'd intended for me atop the desk, then peeled a post-it from a dispenser. "Give me your name and I'll see if she's here."

Inwardly, I groaned. Jennifer was using the oldest trick in the book. I decided to play along. "Jess Harriet," I said. "Two s's, two r's, one t. I'm from the *Sun*."

Her eyebrows drew together as she wrote my name. I peered at the paper. She'd written *Jess Hariett*. She looked up. "Do you spell that S-O-N or S-U-N?"

Stifling a grunt, I explained. "Sun, like in the sky."

Jennifer smiled in understanding, poised her pen over the paper and thought a moment before scratching out "sun in the sky." She replaced the pen and straightened the loose tie at her neck. "Be right back."

With the note stuck to her right index finger, she made a beeline for the back. As she moved farther away, I saw that her menswear attire didn't go all the way down. She wore a tight mini-skirt in the same pinstripe pattern as the vest. Below the skirt were sheer black nylons, and below that, four-inch strappy heels. I wondered if she and Cherrie shopped at the same shoe store.

Once she'd swung through the kitchen door, I drummed my fingers on the desk and surveyed the foyer. Black vinyl bench seats lined both walls. A brass floor lamp stood at one end and an umbrella holder at the other. From my perspective, they were in perfect symmetry. I glanced out over the dining room. There, too, symmetry reigned. Black lacquered tables positioned parallel to the walls, bench seating on one side and black and chrome chairs on the other. Down the middle, two rows of four-person tables lay aligned so that each was directly in front of one and in back of another. Two chairs anchored each side. The entire room looked like a study in line and perspective.

I wondered if they marked the floor to indicate where everything went. Bending over, I studied the carpet. A floral pattern in green, cream, and raspberry formed perfect alignment with the back of the room. Positioned within each rose petal was a chair leg.

Aha. No need for masking tape when the carpeting provided the anchoring spots.

As I straightened, Laurette Roen emerged through the back door. I recognized her immediately from the memorial. Flaming red hair sprang from her head, and emerald eyes highlighted by green earrings could be seen even at this distance. She was crisply clean in a white chef's coat. But her shoes were the same as those she'd worn the day before. With those amazing red points, she could gut a person from navel to jugular if she kicked long and hard enough. I positioned myself a leg's length away from her.

"*Bon jour*," Laurette said.

"Hi. I'm Jess Harriet."

"There is no need to introduce yourself," Laurette said, smiling and extending her hand. "I am so glad you came to visit me, too."

So. My suspicions proved correct. Someone told her I'd been snooping around. But who? Probably not Jody. It had to be Ulrich.

We shook. She had a firm shake, but her skin felt colder than the room by at least ten degrees. When she withdrew her hand, my own felt chilled.

"Nice place," I said. "I like the entrance. It feels like you're in France."

"*Oui*," she said. "My friend created a lovely trompe l'oeil of all my favorite things in Paris."

"I've never been there," I said. "But I took two years of French in high school. I wouldn't mind visiting someday."

Laurette tipped her head slightly in response. "But of course."

She stepped back and motioned to the nearest table. After gliding one end of the table out to an angle, she held a palm my direction. I slid in. She reset the table and eyed the carpet. Table leg in petal. All was well.

I didn't have time to pull out my notepad before she spoke.

"Is so sad, yes?" She made a face. I didn't respond. "About Monsieur Perry?"

"Yes," I agreed. "Very sad. How'd you find out?"

Laurette brushed the question away with one hand. "Word travels like thunder."

She meant lightning. She also meant she wasn't going to tell me who told her. It had to be Ulrich, though.

I said, "Ulrich gave me five minutes. Can you do the same?"

Laurette clasped her hands atop the table, posture perfect. Her eyes didn't reveal her source, but they didn't deny it, either.

"What questions may I answer for you?" she asked.

"Were you at the Chocoholic Ball?"

"*Oui*." She closed her eyes and squinted as though the memory itself were painful.

"What did you bring?"

"I created my most famous dessert: Torte Chocolate avec Sauce des Framboise."

As she spoke, I watched her face. Not a twitch in sight.

"Did Perry like it?" I poised my pen over the paper as if to take notes.

Laurette's lips formed a pout and she shook her head. "He didn't eat any of it."

"Really?"

Laurette bowed her head. "Sadly."

"Why?"

A tiny flash of irritation crossed her face. "I cannot tell you."

More like wouldn't.

"Do you think it was because of the way he panned it on 'Perry's Prattle?' " I gave her my wide-eyed wondering look.

Laurette's smile froze in place. She eased back and crossed her legs. After pausing, fingertips to lips, eyes searching the room as if in deep thought, she answered. "No. I think he is simply too full." She held out her hands, miming a big tummy.

I jotted a note, hoping it would make her squirm. It didn't. If her eyes strayed, they returned to stare into mine before I raised my head. Laurette was one controlled woman.

"Did you know he was poisoned at the Chocoholic Ball?"

"*Oui*," she said, dipping her chin. "I was told."

"Who told you?"

She shrugged. "As I say, these things travel like windfire."

I ignored the butchered colloquialism. It had to be Ulrich at the top of the phone tree.

I asked, "Did you see him eat anything at all?"

Her eyes flashed. The look vanished a millisecond later. Was it anger? Irritation? Maybe I got to her. Or maybe it was just botox.

The muscles in her face released again, cementing into place before she spoke. "No, I am so sorry. I did not see him eat anything. Nor did he drink anything in my presence." She cocked her head. "If you are suggesting there is anyone from our little group who could be involved, you are making a very big mistake."

I felt a quiver at the tail end of my eyebrow. Who, I wonder, told her I knew about the group?

"You mean GA—" I began. "Gourmands And Artisans of Seattle?"

"*Oui.*" She dipped her chin again.

"That's strange. Everyone I've talked to thinks Perry was killed by one of the board members. They say everyone there hated him."

Laurette didn't move. "This is so silly," she said. "We are chefs, not murderers. You are barking up the wrong bush."

I stifled a giggle and continued the stare down. I would not be outdone by a person from a country that actually enjoys watching Jerry Lewis movies. "So who do you think killed Perry? You must have an idea, being the president of GAAS."

She shook her head. Not a red strand moved. "I have no idea. You would have to ask Monsieur Lowell."

I shook off the uneasy feeling her joke gave me. Suddenly, Laurette placed a hand on top of mine. I tried not to look afraid.

"*Mon amie,*" she said, patting slightly. "I think we have gotten off on the wrong feet with our little group. We never 'hated,' as you say, Perry. We didn't agree with him always, but that wasn't our job to do." She shook her head. "No, we respected his opinions when they were correct."

I nodded. My hands began to shake. Whether from the cold of Laurette's skin or her frosty words remained unclear. I wriggled free of her grasp.

"When was he correct?"

She smiled congenially and reclasped her hands in front of her. "I am so glad you came so we could clear up this misunderstanding," she said. "We at Gourmands And Artisans of Seattle have been planning a very special dinner to honor Perry this very evening. We'd like for you to come, too."

I didn't answer. Torn between fear and flattery, my brain refused to respond. An invitation to dinner?

"Mademoiselle Jessica?"

"Yes?"

Laurette clapped her hands. Somehow the gesture didn't seem so spontaneous. "So you will come?"

I shook my head. "No, I meant…"

She put on a sad face, a practiced pout. "That is too bad. There will be many members of the press there." She shook her head. "It would be a good opportunity for you to, uh, network, and get to know our group a bit better. You have the wrong impression of us now."

I couldn't respond. Was she playing me?

"We have invited all our press friends from Everett to Olympia," Laurette continued. "It will be a big party. A big celebration to honor the memory of Monsieur Lowell." She clapped her hands again.

I wavered. A party like that could make my career. I'd be crazy to miss an opportunity to network with so many newspaper people. Even if I didn't crack the story, maybe I could get an interview just by meeting and talking with other newspeople. It could be my big break. Something to fall back on if I didn't solve the murder and scoop the *Daily Log*.

"Say you will come." Laurette smiled.

I stared into her emerald-green orbs and asked myself if I truly thought she could be the killer. I found it hard to believe. She was poised, a businesswoman. She'd have so much to lose. And nothing to gain. Not really. Perry had already reviewed her.

"I would." I hesitated. "But I have a date."

"Oh, my darling," Laurette said, cool as a cucumber on a chilled salad plate. "Do bring him along."

I thought of Tom. If I brought him with me, it would solve two problems. One, it would prevent me from being alone with him. Two, he could protect me if things got weird at the dinner. And I'd still get the secret invitation list.

"How many people will be there?" I asked.

"Many, many people." Laurette said. "Writers, editors, publishers, even. And of course, Madam Lowell has been invited."

I breathed. Callie would be there? Maybe the party was on the up and up.

"What time?"

"Eight o'clock," she said, reaching out to pat my hand once again. "It is late, but we must first attend to our own kitchens." She paused a moment, making significant eye contact. "Say you will come."

Excitement filled me. As much as I hated to admit it, the idea of a free gourmet meal enticed me.

"That might work," I replied, calculating the time it would take to meet Tom at Mouse Hole, have a drink, then travel to Bien. "We may be a little late."

"Ah." Laurette shrugged. "Sometimes this cannot be helped." She put both her hands on the table, palms down. "So long as you come, we will count you on time." She smiled in a way I wanted to believe, then stood.

"We will see you as close to eight o'clock as you can come," she said, angling the table again to release me.

I rose and slung my bag over my shoulders. After I thanked her one last time, she showed me to the door.

It wasn't until the chill air outside shocked me that I questioned her motivation. Did she really want to prove the GAAS' members' innocence? Or had she wanted to charm me? Either way, it worked. And fast. What had it been, fifteen minutes? I ran to the car, started her up, and checked the clock. Three thirty. It had been less, maybe eight or nine minutes.

She was good.

Very good.

Or maybe she was very good at being bad.

Chapter Sixteen

If I took the back roads, I could still drop by Green on the way to the *Sun*. I hopped on old 99 and screamed up the highway. That would never have happened on I-5 at that time of the day, and if it weren't my own foot, pedal to the metal, I would never have believed it. I patted myself on the back for the good travel decision, then slowed as I wound my way around Green Lake.

As I puttered along the thick traffic, I reviewed what I knew. Each person I'd spoken to had given me something to go on. But I still hadn't found the proverbial smoking gun. Or in this case, the foaming toxin.

What bothered me the most, though, had to be every chef's reluctance to talk about it. They freely admitted to disliking Perry. All had good reason. So what were they doing at his memorial?

That would be a great question for Dave and Debby Junette.

Two miles of pondering later I spotted the gold marquee with green lettering. I pulled into the left turn lane and waited patiently as the opposing traffic passed. At the tail end of a line of cars, three helmeted cyclists sped by. I began to turn, but stopped short as a three-wheeled stroller, pushed by a shorts-clad mom, jogged into the crosswalk. I braked, straddling lanes. Following her were two Cocker Spaniels, one Dalmatian, and one

Greyhound, all on retractable leashes, all wagging their well-groomed tails. On the other end of the leashes were three youngish men, all sporting sunglasses, all on rollerblades.

I settled in to wait.

An older, classic BMW approached the intersection heading straight for me. He'd have to wait since I had his way blocked. I gave a quick sorry wave, fully expecting and deserving a one-fingered salute. Instead, the dreadlocked and bearded driver simply smiled and flashed me the peace sign. Green Lake was that kind of place.

When the parade had passed, I waved another thanks to Hippie Man, then pulled through the intersection and into a slot labeled "Green." I killed the engine and retrieved Green's review from my bag, then stretched my legs long as I read.

Green for a Reason

Green, located on Green Lake Boulevard, is the newest contribution to our culinary choices and a mixture of Californian ambition and food fads. All vegetarian, its menu boasts vegan selections on one side and lacto-ovo choices on the other. The best part, however, is that it comes complete with pictures. Like an aspiring Denny's.

But those are only the general reasons for avoiding this hue. Let's get down to specifics. Mushrooms are good, especially in a nice Bordeaux sauce. Lentils are okay when they add body to a soup or pilaf. I'll even go so far as to say bulgar can be dressed for a restaurant's plate. But they are not meals in themselves, as the Junettes refuse to understand. They are side dishes, or better yet, ingredients to a side dish. Repeat: They are not a meal.

And yet, patrons shell out good, hard-earned money for this former California duo to serve up a platter of green reeds and brown grains. Incredible. Have we lost our minds? Have we forgotten our roots in the earthy and pure forests, the abundant plains, rivers, and oceans of the Pacific Northwest?

Look, Seattleites, I can't tell you what to eat or how to eat it. But I can tell you where not to eat. That's at Green—that silly, trite, over-priced Wolfgang Muck's down the street.

Wolfgang Muck's? Oh, boy.

I replaced the review, climbed out, and headed for the entrance. Outside, the air breezed crisp and cold. The downpour had scrubbed Seattle clean of its city smell and in its place lingered a freshness that filled the lungs and warmed the heart. Spring was on its way.

As I rounded the corner, a skip in my step, I paused to stare across the street at the lake. Bluish-green and gorgeous, it issued invitations to all who lived nearby. Several people had RSVP'd and donned sweatshirts and below-the-knee shorts. They broke the surface in pedal boats, rowboats, and, occasionally, pairs of kayaks. Wrinkles of water formed perfect Vs behind them. Amazing. The rain had slowed to a slow leak in the clouds, and a cold sun played peek-a-boo, but the bohemians of Seattle had taken to the lake as though it were July in California. Gotta love that spirit.

I turned, dodged three moms with kids, one dad with a kid in matching red and black ladybug poncho and boots, and a couple of men with a tiny Chihuahua on yet another retractable leash before reaching Green's beveled glass doors. The set latched in the middle, resembling French doors, but were far more ornate with their wood and brass accents. Cold to the touch, but spotless and clear, they mimicked the day outside. I yanked the right door wide and stepped into warmth.

A reception counter sat in front of a self-contained waterfall that formed a liquid curtain between the entrance and dining room. The soft tinkling sounded like spring rain and muffled what little conversation existed in the room.

"I'll be right there." The voice came from a young female a few feet behind the waterfall.

I trained my eyes on the girl clearing the table. She appeared to be in her early twenties. Blonde and thin, she looked like a Los Angeles transplant with short, twin pigtails that stuck straight out from her head just above her ears. She piled the last of the small green plates atop larger green plates into a gray plastic container, then hefted the tray onto one shoulder and headed for the back of the restaurant, dodging chairs and tables with practiced movements of her hips.

She left behind three occupied tables nestled against the picture window that overlooked Green Lake. All diners, save one, focused on the street and lake beyond. The lone uninterested occupant, a toddler in a highchair that resembled wooden scaffolding, played a game of dunk the Cheerio-into-the-milk-then-fish-it-out-with-fingers. He noticed me, stuck a soggy O into his mouth, and grinned. I returned the favor.

"Sorry that took so long," the girl said, back from the kitchen. She wore cargo-style shorts that hung just a little below the green apron tied at her waist. Thick, heavy socks stuck out above well-worn, brown hiking boots, leaving only her rounded calf exposed. On top, she wore a white, sleeveless peasant blouse with a name badge: Gwen. As she stepped behind the reception counter, a cartoon bird tattoo on her right shoulder appeared. Under it was a caption. "Snookums."

She twisted with yoga-like ease for a menu in a plastic holder mounted to the wall. A jangling sounded as several sets of earring hoops clashed together.

"Would you like a table up front or a booth in the back?" Gwen swung her hand round the restaurant indicating the choices. Up front, I'd be seated next to the toddler, which would have been okay, but as we happened to look, he pitched a sloppy Cheerio at his dad's neck. It found its mark, stuck for a moment, then slid below Dad's shirt. Dad turned, gave the toddler a patient grin, then wiped the spot with his napkin. But when he attempted to extricate the Cheerio from somewhere near his navel, he gave up. He said something to Mom, who removed the remaining ammunition from the toddler's tray, then rose and headed toward the back of the restaurant.

Gwen turned back to me. "I'd suggest the back."

"Sounds good." I nodded, my eyes already set on a high stool that faced the open kitchen. There, even if the Junettes denied an interview, I could watch them at work.

We passed several square wooden tables before reaching a long, tall counter of dark wood. Its smooth, highly polished surface felt distinctly out of place. Probably a holdover from the last restaurant that graced the space.

Gwen pulled out a chair, the peasant blouse shifting just enough to reveal yet another tattoo on her left shoulder. This one, a sweet-faced possum with violet eyes, read "Cutie-Pie."

"Thanks," I said, taking the chair. She handed me a piece of 100-pound bond watercolor paper that had been edged with decorative cuts. At the top was written, "The Green Sheet."

"The Lavender Peach Soup is amazing," Gwen said, removing a set of silverware wrapped in a napkin from an apron pocket. "But so is the Grilled Portobello with Bernaise, you know, if you've got a bigger appetite." She smiled quickly, then said, "I'll be back." She bounded toward the front of the restaurant again.

I held the menu up to my face but peeked over the top to the kitchen. Not a sound, or a sight, of anyone in there. I glanced around but spotted no one who looked like a chef in the back.

Disappointed, I swung my gaze toward the front window. The three tables were still occupied, although the toddler and his family appeared more than ready to go. The dad angled the toddler's arms into a yellow coat with a duck bill and googly eyes on the attached hood. The mom dug through her purse. She pulled out two twenties, then dumped a handful of coins on the table.

Gwen delivered the ticket, collected the money, then caught my eye. After a stop at the register, she sprinted toward me. "Sorry that took so long," she chorused from eight feet away.

I wondered how many times in a day she said that. There didn't appear to be any other waitstaff, but at this time of day, a rush would be unexpected.

She reached my side, exhaled, and brought out a little notepad, almost exactly like the one I used for sleuthing.

"What'll it be?" she asked.

"Everything looks great." I grinned but kept my lips closed. Errant BBQ rib strands may have been stuck in my teeth, and I doubted that would go over very well at Green. "I think I'm just going to have iced tea. I'm actually here to see Dave and Debby."

Gwen's pen drooped and her mouth fell open. "Oh! You know Dave and Debby?"

I nodded.

Gwen bobbed her head a few times, making the pigtails flap like wings. "I just love them. I love working here at Green, too. I admire their talent. I wish I could cook like them. I can't even boil water." She laughed. "But as soon as me and my boyfriend save enough money we're going to move to California. He's in the food game, too. Black, Green, Passionfruit, or Mint?"

"What?"

Gwen slapped her forehead. "Sorry. I jumped tracks again. I always do that. The tea. Black, Green, Passionfruit, or Mint?"

"Mint."

"Grooviness," she said, scribbling a note on the pad. "So like I said, we gotta save up money. Then we can go for our dream. It's too bad some people won't let others pursue their dream. That's just not right. We should all be like Dave—computer whizzes, you know." She snapped her fingers. "I'll go get Dave and Debby."

"I didn't know Dave was into computers." I tried to mirror her energy but came up flat.

Gwen's eyes widened. "Oh, yeah. He was way up there down in Silicon Valley." She slapped her head.

"That sounds so funny—way *up* there *down* in Silicon Valley. Ha! Anyway, he did *Demolition Fest* for XBOX. That's the one where you choose a vehicle and go around trying to smash all your opponents' vehicles. There's a tractor, a tank, and a convertible. It sounds so fun."

She stared at me as though I should recognize the title or the description. I didn't.

"Anyway, he did *Hungry Hippo Hijinks*, too." Her eyebrows rose high on her forehead. "That's where he made all his money. It's a kids' game where a hungry hippo has to perform a bunch of tricks and solve puzzles to find food. It got made into a comic book and then a Saturday morning cartoon. They really sold a crapload of toys and stuff."

"Neat," I said.

"Yeah." Gwen sighed. "So that's how he opened up Green. And that's what me and my boyfriend are going to do, now that we're, uh, done up here."

"Cool."

Gwen cocked her head. "So you're not into computers?"

I shook my head. "I wish."

Gwen gave me an I-know-what-you-mean look. Almost immediately, her face fell and her eyebrows furrowed. "Oh. Are you from the bank?"

Abrupt, yes, but also in keeping with the rest of her conversation. Apparently, Ulrich was right about the rupturing.

"Happily, no."

"Whew." Gwen dragged the back of her hand across her forehead and wiped away imaginary sweat. "So do you know Dave and Debby from California?"

I grinned. If I'd known them in California, wouldn't I have known they were into computers?

"No, I'm here to do an interview," I explained. "I'm a writer."

"Oh!" Gwen pocketed her order-taking pad. "I'll go get them."

"No problem," I said. "I'll be right here."

Gwen giggled, then bounced through a swinging door into the kitchen. I heard her rubber soles slap against the tile floor of the kitchen, then the sound of metal scraping against metal and a door opening. "Dave? Debby?" Her voice was muffled.

Three minutes of near silence ensued as I waited. An occasional hissed whisper followed surprised exclamations. For a moment, I heard nothing.

Eventually, the male tiger-striped chef from the memorial strode through the swinging door. He padded my way. A moment later the female approached, also still wearing tiger stripes.

Quietly, Gwen sneaked out behind them, avoided eye contact with me, and made her way toward the front of the restaurant where two tables had emptied. "Just a minute," she called to the people waiting at the register. She picked up her pace.

"I'm Dave." He placed a tall, amber-filled glass in front of me, then wiped his hands on a white towel and folded it over one shoulder.

"Nice outfit," I said. "Different from other chefs."

Dave nodded. "We prefer prints to chefs' whites. Sort of a tribute to the animal kingdom. Plus, the pattern hides the spills." He forced a grin.

We shook. Afterward, he wrapped an arm around the female and pulled her forward. "This is my wife,

Debby."

Debby extended her hand. I took it and pumped it up and down slowly. They could have been twins. They were both dark blond and had piercing blue eyes. They were also both lean and tall. Perfect California specimens.

"I remember you from Perry's memorial yesterday," I said, taking a sip. Minty and refreshing. "This is good."

Dave perched on a stool adjacent to mine. Debby took a stool behind him and peered from behind Dave's shoulder. "What can we do for you?" he asked.

"I'm doing an article," I explained. "For the *Sun*. The *Seattle Sun*."

They stared at me, heads cocked. I repeated my we-only-come-out-with-the-sun joke. They smiled, but neither laughed.

"Nice restaurant," I said.

"Thanks," Dave said. "It's our pride and joy."

"Yeah, like our baby," agreed Debby, making like a bobble-head doll.

"Is business good?"

Dave's jaw tightened almost imperceptibly. "So what's the article about?"

"Perry Lowell," I said, cocky as hell. "And of course, his murder."

Debby's mouth dropped open. Dave continued to stare at me. It was a cheesy tactic—I knew that—but I didn't have time to fish around and see if they'd heard it wasn't a heart attack. I had a meeting with Rod in an hour and a half.

"Murder?"

"Yep. Poison."

"I thought it was a heart attack." Debby said, placing a hand on Dave's shoulder. He patted it once, then brushed it away.

"I don't get it," Dave said. "How can we help with that?"

"For starters, you can tell me who you think might have killed him." I took another drink and savored his confusion.

Dave shook his head. "Sorry, no can do. I have no idea who would want Perry dead."

"Puh-lease," I said. "Having listened to 'Perry's Prattle,' I can't imagine anyone wanting him alive."

Dave chuckled, his jaw relaxing. "I see your point."

Debby's eyes shifted to Dave, then me, and finally back to Dave again. She didn't speak.

"Why do you think so many people paid their respects to him yesterday morning?" I asked.

Dave shrugged, but the movement was too slow for nonchalance. "Professional courtesy?"

Ah, my favorite kind of answer. Politically correct, but unbelievable.

"Do you think Ulrich might have had something to do with it?" I asked, stirring the tea.

Dave frowned. "Ulrich Alford? I have absolutely no reason to believe that."

"That's funny. He said he thought you might know something." Bracing a sprig of mint against the side of the glass, I squeezed. "Actually, he made it sound like you might have done it." I shook my head as if the idea itself were ludicrous. "On account of the bankruptcy."

Their faces went whiter than a WASP in January.

I continued. "But I can't imagine a vegetarian

killing someone. Wouldn't that be worse than killing an animal?"

Dave kept quiet, clearly strategizing. Debby piped up. "Animals and people deserve the same rights." A flat silence stretched out as Dave gave her a look even I knew was a warning. Debby closed her mouth.

"So anyhoo," I continued, nonchalant as possible, "Ulrich thinks it's because of Lowell's review. I told him one little review couldn't hurt a restaurant that bad. Could it?"

Dave released a tight laugh. "I can't imagine Ulrich, or anyone else, for that matter, saying that. If he did, he's got quite an imagination. The idea is preposterous."

"We had nothing to do with it," Debby added. Dave looked at her. Debby clammed up again.

I leaned forward. "How much did his review cost you?"

Dave's baby blues turned to steel. "I have no idea. We can't track that for obvious reasons."

"Why not?" I asked. "What are the obvious reasons?"

Dave shrugged again, a little more convincingly, then nodded toward the entrance. "How do I know why people don't come through that door?"

I nodded. "Good point. So what did you bring to the Chocoholic Ball?"

Dave's eyebrows knitted together. "Why?"

"Just curious."

Dave did another half-turn but trained his gaze on a spot on the wall without meeting Debby's eyes. "What'd we bring, hon?"

"I made the Winterberry Torte," she said. "We use

sorghum and soy flour rather than wheat, and we top it with fresh Soy Crème Fraiche."

I scribbled some notes. "What are winter berries, anyway?"

Debby grinned. "It's actually a mélange of late harvest red and golden raspberries, and blackberries. They're all from hothouses."

"Sounds delicious," I said.

Debby pumped her chin up and down. "It really is."

I faced her for the next question. "So how'd Perry like it?"

Dave spoke. "He didn't try it."

Color me surprised. "Why not?"

"I have no idea." Dave shrugged his shoulders, but his face remained solemn. He rose and pushed his stool under the bar. "I wish we could have been more helpful to your story. But time and a lack of information will only prove your time's wasted with us." He took Debby's arm. "Feel free to finish your iced tea. It's on the house."

"Thanks." I waited until they had neared the swinging door that would take them back to the kitchen. Debby was in front, shepherded by Dave. "One more thing."

"Yes?" Dave's expression was friendly, his voice not.

"How do you know Perry didn't try your 'Winterberry Torte.' "

"Because I was serving, and he didn't come up to our table." Dave smiled, his alibi rock-solid in his own mind. "Walked right by us. In fact, I doubt he would've eaten anything from our kitchen. Ask anyone."

Dave grinned even broader, revealing his canines. Then he nudged Debby through the doors.

"Thanks for your time," I called out. To myself, I added, "And I will be asking around."

I took a long leisurely slurp of the tea before rising and gathering my things. It was nearly four thirty. I could head north to my office and pound out some words of the tribute story before meeting with Rod at six. I grabbed my bag, fished around for a dollar, and laid it next to the glass. Gwen deserved a bump. I headed for the counter and caught Gwen's eye. I crooked a finger.

Gwen's expression turned feral. She glanced once to the back where Dave and Debby had retreated, then toward me. She took a couple steps, then slowed. "Can I help you?"

I gave her a broad grin. "What's the special tonight?"

Gwen's shoulders visibly released, and a half-smile formed on her face. "Grilled Eggplant with Rosemary Lemon Sauce or Lentil Loaf with Carrot Sage Dressing."

"Mmmm," I said. "Sounds good." I turned and pushed open a door before swiveling back. "And what's the dessert?"

"Wheat-free Winterberry Torte with Soy Crème Fraiche." Gwen spoke with pride.

"Yummy," I said, making a rubbing motion on my stomach. "I should come back for dinner." Gwen frowned. I made a move toward the door again, then turned back. "Say, isn't that the same dessert they brought to the Chocoholic Ball?"

Gwen bobbed her head. "Everyone loved it."

"Everyone except Perry, right?"

Gwen's grin faded. "I don't know. I wasn't there."

I nodded and placed my hand on the door for the third time. When I swung round and faced Gwen, she didn't even look surprised.

I grinned, then caught sight of Dave storming through the kitchen door as fast as his plastic clogs would take him. It was a good time to say good-bye.

"Toodles," I called out before running down the sidewalk and jumping into the Kia.

In my haste to get out of Green Lake, I took the wrong turn and ended up circling the west side of the lake. I got caught in traffic and inched my way along back streets, crossing the Interstate at Northgate Way. It was five fifteen, straight up, when I parked in the *Sun*'s lot.

Thankfully, Cherrie was still absent from her desk, the flowers the only reminder that she'd ever existed. As I walked down the hall, goose bumps formed on my skin. The temperature in the space had cooled. I bundled my jacket closer and considered calling out "Hello," just to listen for an echo or response, but didn't. Instead, I reached the door to my office cave and stared.

The door was ajar, a large hole where the knob used to be.

Chapter Seventeen

My inner sleuth told me someone had been in my office while I was away.

For the first time ever, I missed Cherrie. The first floor felt desolate, and I was completely alone. Just eight hundred square feet of hallway, reception, and office caves, and all of it a potential crime scene. A cold shiver raced up my spine, ending in a distinct tingling in my fingers and toes. My head felt light. I leaned against the counter, considering my options, swinging my gaze from my office door to the front door, and listening carefully.

I could race back out the doors and hope that whoever had gotten into my office had already left and wouldn't grab me on my dash out. Or I could buck up and kick the door in, ready to rumble. I decided on the latter. At least I wouldn't go down without a fight.

I braced one foot against the door and pushed hard. The door jerked open. Right before it rebounded off the cement and 2 x 4 shelves and slammed into the frame again, I saw both bad and good news. The bad news: my office had been trashed. The good news: having destroyed everything, the intruder appeared to be long gone.

I sighed, an odd mixture of relief that I wouldn't be murdered any time soon and disappointment that I had to clean up my office. I waded through the books, papers, pens, and, gulp, unicorn poster on the floor. After setting my bag down on my desk, I stood back and surveyed the damage. Most everything in my office lay on the floor, including my chair that had been tipped over. The computer resided exactly where it always had. The dust ledge proved it. Whoever did this had been looking mighty hard for something. I wondered what it was and whether he, or she, had found it. Clearly, it wasn't my computer.

After a glance at my watch, I picked up the unicorn poster. It had torn away from the wall at the base of his horn. Now he was just a horse. A grunge rocker horse, but no unicorn. I repositioned it on the wall, matching up the horn with the top of the horse's head, then unearthed my roll of tape and fastened him to the wall. With that accomplished, the rest of the room seemed manageable.

It took me five minutes to pick up my small office equipment—pens, pencils, and erasers—and get them back into the tangled mess in the top drawer where they belonged, and another five to stack the papers that littered the floor. I separated them into two piles, ripped and unripped, then emptied my bag onto my desk. I closed the door, righted my chair, and sat down. Nothing seemed to be missing. My bag held all my story notes, so if the perp had been searching for those, he or she had come up empty-handed.

My frown turned into a grin. Keeping the story in my bag and my bag with me had curtailed being ripped off. I'd have to remember that for when I was an investigative journalist at the *Seattle Daily Log*.

A moment later, another thought stabbed my conscience. Maybe whoever broke in would come after me next. I swallowed hard, poked my head out the door, looked around, then closed my door again. I stacked a pile of books against it, then pulled out my notepad and read over my suspect list. Suddenly, it seemed all wrong. I crumpled the list and started fresh.

On the suspect side went all the names of the board members: Laurette, Ulrich, Dave and Debby, Doug, Tracy. Added to it were Jody, Mountain Man at KTLK, and for good measure, Will's boss. For fun I added Zit from Bayou Déjà vu, Jennifer from Bien, and Gwen from Green. A broken line went under the names, then I wrote Callie, Will, Rod. Immediately, I erased Rod's name. He would probably want to look at my list, and he wouldn't appreciate seeing his name there. Even if he could be a suspect.

Blame it on the break-in, but my mind started exploring least likely scenarios. What if Rod were involved? What if the reason he'd given me the story in the first place was because he thought I couldn't do it? Or that he could control how much information leaked out?

I checked over my shoulder, then got up and peeked through the doorknob hole. No one there and not a sound.

I returned to my desk. Why had Rod called me in for an after-hours meeting, anyway? No one would know I was there, so no one would know if I went missing.

My heart hammered in my chest as I listened for strange noises.

Forcing myself to calm down, I reviewed the facts. Rod stood to gain nothing by Lowell's death. He had plenty of money, plus a job, so he had no motive. He wasn't at the Chocoholic Ball, so he had no opportunity. Plus, he had offered up information about Lowell that only he had to help me solve the mystery. And why break in? He had a key and could have kept anything he'd found secret. No, it made no sense that Rod was involved.

I scratched my head. My imagination had run away with my reason. Probably because my quasi-investigation amounted to more names and fewer solid facts. I spent five minutes staring at my Skyline level drawing and improvising different versions of the poisoning before hearing the upstairs door bang open. That would be Rod using his private office door. I hoped.

I checked the time. Six o'clock straight up.

I scooped up my suspect list and my bag, swung through the door, and headed upstairs. Since I had no doorknob, I couldn't lock it. Whatever. Nothing of true value was in there anyway.

At Rod's door, I rapped twice, then entered without a summons. I took my seat in the high-back chair and braced my shoulders against the wooden carving. I opened my mouth to tell Rod about my office intruder but stopped short after examining Rod's face. He sat behind his desk, hands clasped behind his head. He looked sterner than usual, something I didn't think was humanly possible. His face, redder than normal, highlighted the circles under his eyes. They appeared a little darker, a little deeper. Compassion took over.

"How was the memorial?" I asked.

Rod frowned. "Not good. Aunt Callie's pretty much out of it. Will was beside himself." He grimaced. "The rest of us just tried to think of something to say to the two of them."

Rod paused, then grabbed a tissue from the container on his desk. "Excuse me." I nodded. He swiveled around and faced the outside window where he proceeded to blow his nose and, I suspect, dab his eyes. Totally old man behaviors, but it made him seem more real than he'd ever been before.

"Are you all right?" I asked, my words quiet.

Rod looked up. "I'm fine. It's Aunt Callie I'm worried about."

"I understand," I said. And I did. Gone was sensitive Rod. In his place sat Rod-the-editor. Maybe it was defense, maybe realization on my part. One thing was for certain, though. Death put things in perspective. I had a lot of what really counts: both parents, my perennially pregnant sister Jenna and her family, and my health. That's more than a lot of people had.

"Okay," Rod said. "Enough of the crybaby routine. What have you got?"

"Unfortunately, not a lot." I dug the legal pad and a pen from my bag. "But before I tell you about it, I need to tell you something else."

"What?"

"Someone's been in my office."

Rod cocked one eyebrow.

"Let me rephrase that. Someone broke into my office."

"Was anything stolen?" he asked.

"No," I said, frowning. "I don't think so. It was just trashed." I considered telling him about the damage done to my unicorn poster but decided against it. It seemed minor compared to what he dealt with earlier in the afternoon.

Rod pulled a pen from its stand and tapped on the doodle pad. "I don't want to alarm you, but I asked my dad about your, uh, encounter at the station. He said he hadn't had any new hires, and that description didn't fit anyone there."

"Oh." An image of Mountain Man rummaging through my office streamed through my head. It reminded me of Sammy's empty chair. "What about Sammy?" I asked. "Is she okay?"

Rod nodded. "Yes. Actually, Sammy called me to check on you."

"Thank goodness." I exhaled in relief. "Why'd she call to check on me?"

"She never saw you leave," Rod said. A puzzle worked its way across his face. "What happened between the two of you, anyway? Did you bond or something?"

I laughed. "Yeah, you could say that."

"What about?" He paused, then waved a hand in the air. "Never mind. I don't think I want to know."

"You don't," I agreed. "So who was the guy?"

"No one seems to know," he said. "I asked Sammy, but she said she never saw anyone. She'd been away from her desk only a few minutes. When she returned, she went to check on you and you were gone."

I gulped but said nothing as a strange little wiggle of worry wormed its way into my brain.

"So," he said. "Given the break-in, I think we ought to call the cops."

"Okay," I said. "But be sure to tell them that whatever he, or she, was after, it wasn't found. It's not worth their time."

Rod paused, tilted his chin down, and stared at me.

"It's just a story, Jess."

"I know," I said. "I just don't want to give up on finding Lowell's killer. Not yet."

Rod stared in response.

Softer, I asked, "Do you?"

Rod sighed. "No. I suppose the police will figure it out before we do, but that doesn't mean we can't try. So what have you got?"

I started with my notes on top. "It seems like most restaurant folks disliked him, but no one wants to implicate anyone else."

"No surprise."

I shook my head. "No, it's not. But I did find out about GAAS."

Rod raised an eyebrow. "Gas?"

"G-A-A-S." I outlined the group and ran down the list of board members' names.

"So what's your gut say?" Rod asked. "Who do you believe is capable, had motive, and seized the opportunity?"

I put my pencil down and settled into my chair, arms folded across my chest. I thought about the list a moment before responding. "My gut tells me it's one of them. Which one? I don't know. They were all on the list."

"List?"

"Yeah, so there's this super-secret list that everyone seems to know about."

"Sounds like Perry. Tell me more."

"Well, evidently, Lowell made a list of the most profitable restaurants in Seattle."

"Why'd he do that?" Rod frowned.

"Well," I stammered. I uncrossed, then re-crossed

my ankles. "Your uncle, Perry, was inviting people to advertise."

"Inviting?" Rod said. "As in extorting, right?"

I nodded meekly. "It sounds like it."

Rod slammed a palm on his desk. "That ass. I knew it." He was silent a moment. "Go on."

I cleared my throat. "It stands to reason that the next restaurant on the list was the restaurant on the index cards."

"Ah, criminy," Rod said. He hunched over his desk in contemplation, then snapped his fingers. "That reminds me." He dug in the pocket of the jacket hanging on the back of his chair and brought out a notepad and the index cards I'd given to him earlier. "First of all, I found out about the poison. He was killed by a combination of toxins: rat poison, nicotine, a form of ink normally used in newspaper, and a mushroom that contains the same ingredient as rocket fuel. It was a veritable poison cocktail."

"Or a toxic torte."

"Yep," Rod replied, scowling. "Could have been."

I paused a moment, thinking. "Rocket fuel?"

Rod's face scrunched in disbelief. "I can't imagine."

I shivered. "Wouldn't Perry taste it?"

"That's what I said. Apparently, you can cover anything with enough chocolate. If, in fact, that's how he ingested it."

"Wow." I stared at Rod.

"Yep. But it gets better. The forensics team says other substances were probably involved, but those four alone could do it in the time frame we're looking at."

"Wow," I repeated. "It almost sounds like

someone's making a statement."

"Or trying to be sure it takes." He tore off the top sheet of paper and the index cards and handed it to me. "Aunt Callie said it was definitely Perry's handwriting. She said she could make out the words, but they didn't have any meaning. She said they weren't in French, or English, but some combination of both."

I fanned the cards on the desk.

"I also asked her if she knew who he'd reviewed for Friday, but she didn't know. She said he always surprised her with the critiques for the week over lattes, muffins, and the Sunday *Daily Log*."

I thought it ironic that they'd be reading the family's competitor's newspaper but didn't comment on it. I looked at the index cards again. At the very bottom of the third card were the initials T. O.

"Wait a minute—" I scanned over my notes again. There it was: Tracy O'Sullivan, owner of Eirambique, a restaurant I couldn't even pronounce. "Could it have been eerie-am-bicky?"

Rod straightened, then laughed. "You mean Eirambique? Over in Belltown? It's pronounced Eye-ram-beak." He nodded. "I bet you're right. That's the place where the chef infuses Irish foods with African spices."

"He was also the caterer at yesterday morning's memorial," I said.

"Really?" Rod stared at me a moment, then pointed at the cards. "Let me see those again."

I handed them over. He looked at each one again. "These are all entrée items that have half English and half French pronunciations." When I frowned, he said, "A lot of Africans speak French, too."

"And Eirambique was the only Board Member restaurant not reviewed in the past two months," I said. "It's gotta be Tracy O'Sullivan."

Rod cocked his head. "I wonder why Aunt Callie hired him."

"Good question," I said. "Can you find out?"

"I can try," he said. He scratched his chin, then continued. "So what's your plan for later tonight?"

I checked the time. Six fifteen. "I'm going to head to Belltown and pay a visit to Tracy. Afterward, I'll meet up with Tom—"

"Who's Tom?"

"Oh, just a friend from college. He's my contact at the Space Needle who's going to get me the official list." I made a motion of zippering my lips. "Not a word. He could lose his job. Then we'll head over to the memorial dinner."

"What memorial dinner?"

"The one at Bien," I said. "Laurette Roen invited me to it when I was there earlier today. She said there'd be a lot of reporters and editors there." I stopped short of mentioning that it was also a networking opportunity.

Rod frowned. "I haven't heard anything about it."

"It may have been spur of the moment," I said. "But Callie's invited—she's coming too, according to the hostess."

"That's funny," Rod said. "She didn't mention anything about it at the family memorial. But knowing Callie, she'd go if she thought it would honor Perry. So where will it be held?"

"Bien."

"Good." He laughed. When I didn't respond, he

explained. "Get it? 'Bien' and 'good.' "

"Ha." I deadpanned.

Rod and I stared at each other a moment in uncomfortable silence. Finally, I spoke. "Well, I should get going if I'm going to stop by Eirambique on my way." I stood, gathering my pad and pen.

Rod watched. When I got to the door, he called out.

"Yeah?" I said.

"Be careful," Rod said. "Those people giving a dinner in Perry's honor is downright creepy."

"Maybe they're burying the hatchet?" I shrugged.

"That's what I'm afraid of," Rod said. "In the back of someone's head."

Chapter Eighteen

I scampered down the stairs and out the *Sun* doors without returning to my office with its missing doorknob. I'd call Tom from my car, alert him I'll be late, but that I'd make it up with a gourmet dinner at Bien. I didn't tell him anything about the break-in or the story. Didn't want anything to scare him off before I got that list of attendees at the Chocoholic Ball. After that, I'd scare him off myself.

Outside, the rain had picked up, and the teriyaki restaurant's vent spilled a delightful, spicy scent into the air. I took a deep breath, my stomach rumbled in response, and then I raced to the Kia once again.

Since Belltown was only a few blocks south of Mouse Hole, I figured I'd have no problem doing a quick interview with Tracy O'Sullivan, Eirambique's owner/chef—maybe even get a confession—before meeting with Tom.

I figured wrong.

The rain came down in sheets, rapidly filling the edges of the streets with rivers of water that splashed windshields and slowed traffic. Cars, trucks, taxis—all were on a slow march out of the city. I didn't get to Belltown until six forty-five, and it took me another five minutes to find a parking space.

I hopped out and began running in the general direction of Eirambique, using my bag as an ineffective makeshift umbrella. The rain fell at a slant, so no matter how big the shield, some part of each pedestrian got wet. In my case, my pants got the brunt of it. Many folks ducked inside a building or peered out from below awnings to wait out the deluge. At least one guy said, "Noah, build an ark."

I ignored him and made for the multi-colored Eirambique in the sky.

As I neared, I saw that each letter in the Eirambique marquee sported an African pattern or print. The "E" held zebra-like stripes in black and white, the "i" pimpled like ostrich skin, the "r" a spotted hyena. The green background reflected the other half of Eirambique—the Irish part, I assumed.

I lengthened my stride and upon reaching the entrance grabbed the wooden door handle that had been carved into the shape of an elephant's trunk and swung the door wide. Deep beats of a drum, and heady airborne spices welcomed me into a long narrow dining space. A wall of windows at the far end gave the illusion that the room continued right out to the water. At least twenty-five light and dark wood tables graced the dining room. Surrounding each table, four alternating chairs, two light, two dark, stood like herds of antelope around watering holes. About half the tables were occupied, all on the far side of the room. It appeared the seating had begun at the far end, near the windows and worked its way forward. The tables near the front door were empty.

A moment later, a waitress emerged from a swinging door and eyed me. "I'll be right there," she called out. I nodded, surprised at her casual blue jeans and camouflage tummy shirt in tones of blue that revealed a blue stone dripping from her navel. I didn't know what I expected—Zulu or leprechaun, but not that.

I focused on Eirambique's decor again. The dark and light pattern continued on the floor. Blond wood from the tables and nearly ebony accent woods formed blocky geometric patterns like a heavily outlined maze. Wall paintings depicting the Irish countryside interspersed with African tapestries and line drawings. The unique juxtaposition of quaint, thatch-roofed cottages and angular storks in hues of brown completed the jumbled effect.

But it worked. Although the scenes seemed the opposite of one another—water and greenery versus desert and browns, each suggested the same theme: home.

A pang shot through me. Home. Jenna. Maybe she really needed me.

Or did I need her?

The guilt at not responding to her e-mail was sudden, immediate, and overwhelming.

"Table for one, or meeting someone?" the waitress asked, interrupting my train of thought. Young, Black, and pretty, she wore a smile that twinkled like the gem in her belly button.

"Actually neither," I said. "I'm here for Tracy O'Sullivan."

She frowned. "It's pretty busy right now," she said. "Tracy doesn't like to be bothered when it's busy. Is it important?"

"Very," I replied. "It will only take a minute. He might even be expecting me." Given the GAAS phone tree, anything was possible. "If not, I can come back."

"Okay, cool." She turned and headed for the kitchen.

A long moment later, Tracy O'Sullivan, hottie caterer from the morning memorial, stepped out. Again, I was struck by the notion that he could be mistaken for a young Denzel Washington, given the right distance and lighting. And the distance and lighting were just about perfect.

Hubba, hubba.

He walked my way wearing a cautious smile. A few steps from me, he wrung his hands on a white dish towel, then tucked the rag into a bright yellow apron wrapped around his middle. Atop and below the apron was a tan camouflage duo of T-shirt and pant, highlighting his creamy mocha skin.

I swallowed hard and willed my heart to beat a little slower. The guy could be a killer, I reminded myself. This was no time to wonder how long it would take to untie his apron.

"Can I help you?" he asked, his brogue thick with Irish charm.

My pulse jumped. "Do you have a minute?" Gone was ballsy Jess from Green. Replacing her was meek, please-like-me Jessica. Why do some men do that to me?

"What's it about?"

"Perry Lowell."

"I don't know anything," he said. But he didn't move away. I took it as an invitation to ask more questions.

I shot him a broad grin. "But you'd know if he reviewed your restaurant, right?"

Tracy's head cocked to one side. "Yes." The word

was slow, deliberate.

"Did he?" I bundled my jacket closer and shivered.

"No," he said. Indecision crossed his face, and he scanned the room. "I mean, yes."

I followed his gaze. As we watched, the waitress burst out of the kitchen with four steaming plates, two on each arm.

Tracy turned back.

"I know you're very busy," I said, my words hurried. "Could you come back out when you have a couple minutes and talk to me?"

He shook his head no.

"I'm trying really hard to clear all the board members' names," I said, crossing my fingers behind my back. "And since Perry's most recent review, yours, disappeared, you're going to be the first one they look at."

Tracy's eyes grew wide, but his mouth formed a straight line. I was right. He knew it.

"Who's they?" he asked.

"The cops."

He sighed. "I don't see how I can help you. I don't know anything."

"Just answer a few questions," I said. "When you have time."

He glanced back to the tables. The waitress mouthed *help*. He nodded toward her. "It might be a while."

"No problem." I parked myself at the nearest table and watched his tight rear as he strode toward the kitchen. As soon as he swung through the door, I glanced at my watch. Seven o'clock straight up. Crap. Tom and I would have to skip the drink and head straight to Bien for the memorial dinner.

Then it struck me. As a GAAS board member, Tracy would be at the dinner, too. Shouldn't he be heading over there now? Or even be there already?

Within a moment, he reappeared, bearing a round-bellied clay teapot and two cups. "I have five minutes to share a pot of tea with you."

Surprised, I rubbed my icy fingers together. Apparently, Tracy had decided to play nice. "Sure. What kind is it?"

"Cinnamon. I get the cinnamon fresh from Madagascar. I blend the tea meself." Tracy tipped the pot forward. Steaming rich, reddish-brown liquid filled my cup. With mine filled, he poured for himself. He sat and raised his cup to his lips.

I did the same. The heady aroma embraced me. It smelled like Sunday morning at home in bed with cream cheese-topped cinnamon rolls and the Sunday *Daily Log*.

"This smells amazing." I tested the temperature with my lower lip.

"So what have you on your mind?" He took a sip, eyeing me over the rim.

Watching him there, in the curious collection of light and dark, I could almost forget he was a suspect. His keen sense of style and warm good looks made him a player, not a killer.

"Run of the mill stuff," I said. "Like whom do you think hated Perry Lowell enough to want to kill him?"

Tracy squeezed his eyes shut and centered his cup in his saucer before releasing his hold on it. "I know of no one."

"Really?" I blew across the surface of the tea. A

tiny wake formed, splashing the edges, but not flowing over. Bravely, I took a small sip.

Delicious. The tea, dense as syrup, flowed over my throat in a warm river. The cinnamon was naturally pungent, but not unbearably so, and whatever had been used to sweeten the tea felt lighter than sugar and somehow more natural. And with that much cinnamon, I wouldn't need a breath mint for a week. On the off chance that someone might want to kiss me. I raised my eyes to Tracy again.

" 'Tis. I don't know nothing," he replied, sipping again. "I was hired to cater the memorial. That's all."

"Who hired you?"

Tracy glanced to the diners near the window. All had been served. "The wife."

"When did she contact you?"

"Saturday morning." Tracy's eyes shifted to the door as a trio of bedraggled urbanites flounced in. He scanned the area, made eye contact with the waitress as she emerged from the kitchen, then returned his gaze to me.

"Wow," I said. "That was fast work."

"Yes," he said, pausing to watch the waitress greet the group and seat them near the windows at the far end. "But I only had to oversee the production and service. It was not a problem."

He didn't cook? "Is that the way it always works?" I asked. "Do you ever cater your own food?"

"Yes, but not always." He twirled a spoon through his tea. "It depends on what my customer wants. I always please my customer."

I stopped myself before saying *I bet.* Instead I asked, "Why'd she choose you?"

Tracy searched the ceiling. "I dunno. Didn't ask."

I furrowed my eyebrows. "Didn't you have any reservations, given the situation?"

Tracy harrumphed. "I need the money."

I nodded. His answers didn't tell me anything I didn't already know. I tried another tactic. "So how'd it go when Lowell ate here?"

I watched carefully as he phrased his response. If Tracy had been startled by my abruptness, he didn't show it. First, he took another sip of tea, then he placed the cup carefully back on the table. "He was fine. Look, I really don't know anything." He started to rise.

I was torn. Was Tracy being evasive deliberately, or did he not realize how serious the situation was?

"Look, Tracy," I said, my words hurried. "What you may not know is that I have his index cards from your review."

Tracy's face fell, but he picked it up immediately. He leaned back in his chair, crossed his legs at the knees, and tilted his head.

I continued. "As usual, he had nothing good to say. He had planned to air his opinion on Eirambique last Friday, but something stopped him. I don't know what it was, but the moment the cops get the index cards, they're going to assume that something was someone. And that someone was you."

Tracy uncrossed his legs and leaned forward. "He promised me while he was here that he was open to my brand of infusion. He said that direct to my face. Later he said his review would be headlined 'Infusion Confusion.' Can you believe it?"

"Wait a minute," I said. "How do you know that?"

"He called me." Tracy glowered. "Last Thursday."

"He called you Thursday to tell you the title?"

"That's not all, though," Tracy said, his eyes wide, angry. "He read me the review."

"He read you the review?"

Tracy rubbed the back of his neck. "Yes."

I stared, a dozen questions bouncing around in my brain. "Why?"

Tracy's mouth opened, then closed. He shook his head.

"Tracy," I said. "This could mean the difference of whether you're arrested or not. Think about it."

He slapped the table. "But I didn't do anything."

My gut told me he was telling the truth. "How can you prove that, if you were at the Chocoholic Ball?"

He ignored my question. "I'm married to my art," he said. "Married! But does he understand that? Not at all. He just writes about us and makes people stay away. He said, 'Eirambique is culture shock…Eirambique tinkered with the master plan of keeping Ireland and Africa far apart.' "

Tracy scraped his chair away from the table. He crossed his legs and arms and ground his teeth. "Infusion confusion, my arse."

"Wow," I said. "That's crappy."

"It is that."

I gave him a minute to unwind before asking, "So why'd he call you? Was it just to taunt you?"

Tracy mulled over his answer in silence. "He wanted me to advertise," he said finally, his voice low. "If I did, he would pull the review."

When I spoke, my words were soft. "Did you pay?"

Tracy nodded. "Yes."

"You paid?"

"Aye, I paid."

"Are you the only one who paid?"

"I am." He hung his head and avoided my eyes.

I thought back to Jody's words. The GAAS had been angry at Tracy. "Is that why the board's mad at you?"

"They aren't happy," he said. "They say it weakens their fight. Like I am a traitor. But they'll get over it now that he's dead. I think."

That explained why he wasn't already at Bien. He hadn't been invited. He probably didn't even know about the press dinner.

I stared, unsure if I believed him or not. The waitress approached, cupped Tracy's ear and whispered something. In response, Tracy got up, untied his apron and retied it snugger than before.

"You'll have to excuse me," he said. "I need to get back to me kitchen."

"Of course," I said. "Thanks for the tea. And the answers."

He nodded and turned to leave.

I waited for him to walk three steps, then called his name.

"Yes?" Tracy turned and faced me.

"What'd you bring to the Chocoholic Ball?"

"My Chocolate Cinnamon Soufflé," he said. "I use the same cinnamon as in the tea. But you won't find a trace of it in Mr. Lowell's gut."

"Why not?"

"Because he wouldn't eat any of it."

Chapter Nineteen

I gave up my parking spot to an ancient Yugo and sped north parallel to the waterfront. Tracy had given me not ten, but five minutes, so I figured I'd reach Mouse Hole by seven thirty. Once there, I'd tell Tom about the dinner invitation to Bien. I hoped he'd agree, since it was free.

Fortunately, I hit several green lights, so by the time I found parking across from Pier 52, I had time to check my cell for messages. There weren't any, but the battery icon flashed low. I muted the cell and hightailed toward Mouse Hole.

When I reached the brown stucco façade, Tom was nowhere to be seen. I scurried through the front door and down a coved corridor, past the hostess station and several burrowed-out dining areas with circular bench seating. As expected, Tom was at the bar, a half empty drink in front of him. I plopped onto the red vinyl stool next to his, and asked, "Whatcha drinkin'?"

"Hey." He leaned in and gave me a peck on the cheek.

I wanted to be horrified, even repulsed, but my body didn't react that way. Maybe I was still worked up over Tracy O'Sullivan. That man was a god. He couldn't be the killer.

I pointed to Tom's frosty glass. "What's that?"

"Caipirinha," Tom said, leaning in and raising his

voice. The arrival of a very young, very loud group ratcheted the volume up several notches. "You've gotta try one. It's made from Prata…an alcohol from Brazil made of sugar cane. Sweet." He chuckled at his own joke.

"Okay," I said. "But only one. I've got a proposition."

Tom waggled his eyebrows, then caught the eye of one of the five bartenders milling about behind the bar. The young man nosed over. He wore a white shirt, red suspenders, and black shorts. In one shorts pocket, he'd tucked the end of a very long black tail. A black felt hat with protruding ears perched atop his head, but in place of his name, "Mouse Hole" had been stitched in red thread.

Tom ordered, and the bartender turned and squeezed past a woman wearing a similar outfit. The only difference was her fishnet stockings and black high heels. In addition, she'd darkened her nose and drawn whiskers on her face.

For the second time in one day, tracking a killer didn't seem like such a bad job. In fact, it seemed pretty chic compared to slinging drinks in cartoon garb. I turned back to Tom. Gone was the outer space-themed vest and in its place was a light-blue denim button-up shirt and a pair of clean, wrinkle-free black jeans. The shirt also appeared clean. Good. He'd fit right in at Bien.

"I put our name on the list about half an hour ago," Tom said. "So our table should be just about ready."

"Hey, about that," I said. "I got invited to a memorial dinner tonight. I can bring a date, I mean guest, along. What do you think?"

His grin faded. "Memorial?"

"Oh, the guy's being honored, that's all," I said, grinning. Behind us, a woman squealed. I raised my voice. "Don't worry. There won't be any dead bodies."

"I don't know," Tom said. "I was really in the mood for Wharf Rat Feast. That's all seafood, served platter style. Scallops, prawns, crab…"

I interrupted him. "The dinner's free."

As he considered this the bartender returned and set a tall glass of clear liquid in front of me. "Eighteen," he said.

Eighteen dollars? That was a lot of scratch for a drink.

Tom whipped out two tens and handed them over. The bartender thanked him, grabbed the end of his tail, looped it twice, then stuck it into his front right pocket. Sighing, he headed to the other end of the bar.

I took a sip. Sweetened lime juice slid down my throat. "This is great." I sipped again.

Tom grinned. "I always have one when I come here."

I took a long drink. "It doesn't taste like there's any alcohol in it."

His eyebrows rose. "Careful," he said. "There is." He drained his drink without slurping.

"So what do you think?" I placed my elbows between two sets of claw marks on the counter. "About the free food."

He pondered my suggestion, gazing at a tall lamp in the corner of the room. Its shade resembled Swiss cheese with a couple bites taken out. "Do you want to go?"

"Yeah," I said. "There's going to be all kinds of

food people and newspaper people there. We can both make some contacts."

"That's a good point," Tom agreed. "I'll be looking for a sommelier job in about six months."

"Cool." I took another swig, reducing the fluid another inch. "It starts at eight o'clock, but Laurette Roen, that's the owner—"

"It's at Bien?" Tom's eyes widened and he set his glass down.

I swallowed. "Yeah."

"Oh, we're going." He pushed his glass forward and twisted on his stool to face me. "She's like one of the best chefs in Seattle."

"Cool." I took another long swig, ending in a slurp. I pulled the straw out, fought down some ice cubes and reinserted it. "If we leave right away, we'll make it there by eight fifteen."

Tom rose. "I'll go cancel the table. You finish your drink."

I obliged willingly. The drink was sweet and good. And he'd paid eighteen dollars for it. I don't believe in wasting money.

Almost immediately, Tom's stool got nabbed. I would've complained, but by the time he canceled the table, I'd be done. A big gulp later, I grabbed my bag and met Tom in the foyer. He was still waiting for the hostess.

"Let's go," he said. "When we don't respond, they'll give the table away."

I nodded, bracing myself for the frozen air outside. We slipped out the door.

"Let's take my car." Tom hunched his shoulders up around his ears. "Parking's a bitch downtown."

I nodded again, unwilling to open my mouth and allow the chill factor in. The temperature seemed to have dropped ten degrees in the past half hour, and the raindrops were copulating in hopes of making sleet. We crossed the street, walked a block north, then stopped in front of a blue Honda. After fishing out his keys, he flashed the lights and opened my door.

"After you," he said.

I got in, set my bag on my lap, and buckled up.

Tom shut my door, walked around, and got behind the driver's wheel. "It'll be warm in a minute," he said.

"I'm fine." And I was fine. Maybe the drink had had booze in it after all. I touched my nose with the tip of my finger—my surefire method of determining my level of tipsy. If my nose felt tingly, I'd had enough. Unfortunately, both my finger and my nose were numb. Whether it was from the cold or the Prata I couldn't tell.

He wound round the parking lot and exited onto the main street. "Bien's a great place. Great reputation. They've got an awesome wine list."

"Um-hmm." I rubbed my hands together and exhaled onto them.

"So who all will be at the dinner?" He looked at me. His startling blue eyes had mellowed to a softer gray-blue, and he'd shaven. Maybe he wasn't so bad. Or maybe it was the booze doing the thinking.

"Some chefs, Perry's wife, newspaper people." I paused. "Did I tell you Perry was my boss's uncle?"

Tom shook his head. "Who's Perry?"

"The guy they're doing the memorial dinner for."

He stared at the road, a scowl on his face. "What's Perry's last name?"

"Lowell."

He turned to view me. "Perry Lowell the restaurant critic?"

"Yes."

"Oh, man!" Tom said. "He's dead? When'd that happen?"

"Yep. Last Thursday night."

"How'd I miss that?"

I shrugged.

He stared at me a moment, then turned his gaze forward. "And Laurette Roen's giving him a memorial dinner?"

"Yep," I said. "She and a bunch of her chef buddies."

Silence filled the car, and Tom's face pulled into a frown. "I don't get that."

"Why?"

"Because those folks hated Perry Lowell," he said. "Rumor has it Doug threatened Lowell after the Space Needle review."

"What?"

Tom nodded. "Oh, yeah. Shit hit the fan. I wasn't there, but I guess Doug called him from the kitchen phone. Really laid into him."

"Wow."

"Yeah. People said Doug screamed so loud, they could hear him in the lobby." He laughed at the idea. "They said he was screaming things like extortion and destroying reputations. The one thing everyone heard, though, was him saying Perry had better watch his back."

"He said that?"

His eyebrows rose high on his forehead. "That's what a couple people told me."

"Wow."

"That's why Douggie wasn't invited to the Chocoholic Ball."

"Really?"

"Yeah. He made a bunch of noise like he didn't mean what he said as a threat. But it didn't matter. The Space Needle big guys wouldn't let him attend." Tom shifted into a higher gear. "He's lucky he kept his job, from what I heard."

"Wow. I had no idea."

His profile twisted into a question. "So how'd you get invited to it?"

"The article." I realized too late I'd kept the real reason for the article to myself. Blame it on the Caipirinhia.

"The article on the Chocoholic Ball?"

"Yes," I said slowly. "They're connected."

Tom's eyebrows furrowed. "How are Lowell's death and the Ball connected?"

I thought quickly. If I told him what I really believed, that Perry had been poisoned there, he might get angry that I lied to him. He might even turn around and refuse to go with me to the dinner. That wouldn't do. I needed him for protection—another human being who knew I was there and would know if I went missing.

"I don't know for sure." That wasn't exactly a lie. "I don't have anything I can prove. But I'm hoping I'll learn something tonight."

He frowned and thought a moment. "Then you'll probably be needing this. He unfastened the glove box and retrieved a folded piece of paper. He set it on my lap, then closed the box again.

"What's this?"

"The invitation list."

"Oh," I said. "Great."

"Remember," he said, winking, "you didn't get it from me."

"No problem." I unfolded the paper and scanned the chef list, looking for names of the key players in this poison game. L. Roen, check. U. Alford, check. D. and D. Junette, check, check. T. O'Sullivan, check. J. Lish, check. Absent, as expected, was D. DuBois. None of the other names rang a bell. At the bottom of the list, under "Independent," G. Smith had been written.

Independent?

G. Smith?

"Tom?"

"What?"

"What's an independent?"

"Oh, a caterer or someone like that."

The car hit a pothole and my stomach threatened to toss up the day's foods. Too much of a coincidence.

"Who is G. Smith?" I asked.

Tom successfully parallel parked a block south of Bien, then turned to me. "Who?"

"G. Smith?" I said. "An independent. Do you remember?"

"Some chick—" he said. "I mean, a woman. I don't know her, but she's with a catering company called Double D's." He killed the engine. "Let's go."

He jumped out of the car. A second later he was at my side, opening my door. "It's half a block away," he said. "It should take only a few minutes."

After shoving the list in my bag, I got out and glanced up the block. Bien's façade shone red, white, and blue in the distance. I stuck my hands into my blazer pockets, found the gloves I'd stuffed there the morning of the memorial, and pulled them out. They were still damp but warmed from body heat. I wiggled into them.

"If you get cold, I'll give you my coat." Tom shut the door, linked my arm in his, and pulled me forward. Together, we assumed the stooped posture of folks walking uphill against a polar wind.

"What'd she look like?" I asked, raising my face long enough to be pelted by freezing raindrops. They stung my lips and cheeks. I bowed my head again. Something about the name bothered me.

"Who?"

I trudged a few more steps, then inhaled a cold gust of air. "The G. Smith?"

Tom raised his chin above his jacket collar. "Sweet," he said before tucking his chin back down.

We walked a few more steps. "Describe her," I said. The wind bit at my skin and tears edged out of the corners of both eyes.

"Blonde," Tom replied. "Why the interest?"

"I don't know." That was the truth. Something was bothering me, more than just the unknown. But I couldn't put a finger on it.

We quickened our pace. A few more steps and we'd be under Bien's awning.

"She's a flower-child type," he added.

Tom pulled Bien's door open and ushered me in. He stepped in behind me and closed the door again. I shivered and stamped my feet.

"Works at a vegetarian place." Tom stared at the black and chrome décor.

My voice caught. I swallowed, then said, "In Green Lake?"

Tom shrugged. "Dunno."

I stopped mid-stride and turned to him. "Tom," I said, my voice catching, but not from the cold. "Is her name Gwen?"

Tom made eye contact with someone at the back of the restaurant and gave a small wave.

"*Bon jour*," Laurette called out. She locked eyes with me and strolled toward us.

I tugged on Tom's sleeve. "Is her name Gwen?" My words took on a harsh whisper quality.

He tilted his head and stared at me. "What?"

"Gwen." I forced the words through my teeth. "Is her name Gwen?"

His eyes focused on a spot on the wall, his eyebrows pulling together a moment. When he returned his gaze to me, he smiled. "That's it," he said. "How'd you know?"

Chapter Twenty

G. Smith was Gwen from Green?

The knot in my belly tightened. She didn't own a catering company. She'd said she wasn't even at the Chocoholic Ball. And yet, there's only one reason anyone lies.

They're guilty of something.

My stomach lurched, and not from hunger.

But if Gwen had killed Perry, the obvious question was why? I couldn't see it. It made no sense. And then I realized that she couldn't have acted alone. Dave and Debby were probably in on the plot to poison Perry, too.

And if the Junettes were involved, wouldn't it seem even more likely that Laurette and the entire Gourmands And Artisans of Seattle group were, too?

Before I could shudder, however, Laurette called out.

"*Mes amies*." She'd changed into an emerald-green silk shirt and slacks combination that shimmered in the scant light. She'd also exchanged her blood-red pumps for rhinestone-studded slides. The toes narrowed to the same knife-sharp point.

She embraced me first, her collarbone jutting into my neck twice as she air-kissed both sides of my face. Afterward, she turned to Tom. "And you must be Jessica's friend."

Tom held out his hand and a broad grin formed across his face. "I'm Tom."

Laurette released a tsking noise. "In my house, *mon ami*, we embrace as we would in Paris." She clasped Tom by the shoulders and bussed both cheeks.

Tom started stuttering, saying how much of a pleasure it was to meet her, that he'd heard all about her Chocolate Torte with Red Raspberry Sauce, and that he was studying to be a sommelier.

Laurette acknowledged each statement with a sound more like a purr than a word.

"Sorry we're late," he concluded.

"Not at all," Laurette responded, eyeing me again. "We are all in the very back room. Follow me, *s'il vous plait.*"

Laurette locked the front door behind us, then took off, walking a fine line toward the back of the restaurant. We followed. She bypassed the swinging door to the kitchen, where the scents of onions and garlic hovered. I glanced inside. Not a single person tended the stove. Odd, I thought, but my stomach vetoed any concern. Instead, it gurgled in appreciation and happy anticipation. Not only had I solved the murder, I'd done it in time to enjoy a free dinner with myriad networking opportunities. I'd just have to keep what I knew under my beret, so to speak.

We continued down a dimly lit corridor painted red. Along the walls, candle-shaped sconces gave off a muted light. Laurette's shoes caught and reflected the rays, displaying dazzling prisms and flecks on all surfaces. It was like a bloody disco without music.

At the end of the hall, Laurette turned sharply left. Six feet ahead, the corridor opened up to a room roughly fifteen-by-fifteen. It, too, was red, but brighter and louder with the voices of many people. Ruby carpeting covered the floor, and rich velvet drapes hung on all walls, save the one we entered through. The tabletop had been trimmed out with red linens and white china. The two-toned silverware in gold and silver framed each setting, each knife a full inch longer than the fork and spoon that rested to the side. Roses centered the table in a maroon crescent, and a white spray of baby's breath helped define the thorns' jagged edges. Even the chair coverings, a tapestry depicting a fox hunting scene, contained multiple hues of burgundy. The walnut dining table broke the color scheme, peeking through the tablecloth and the slivers of baseboard along the wall's edges.

"*Mesdames et messieurs*," Laurette said. "I believe you all know Jessica. So may I introduce her friend, Tom?"

Murmurs of hellos greeted us. I surveyed the arrangement. Twelve chairs surrounded the long rectangular table, five to a side and one at each end. I recognized all but one of the occupants. To our left sat Ulrich Alford smack in the middle of the row, his girth forcing him to sit sixteen inches from the table. Still his belly rubbed against it. On the right were Dave and Debby Junette. At the far right Gwen Smith held the hand of a red-headed thirty-something man who anchored the end of the table. He wore chef whites and an intense, almost surprised expression. I had never seen him before.

An uneasiness settled over me. Where were the newspaper people? Where were the editors? Where was Callie? Most importantly, where would they all sit when they got there?

Tom spoke, interrupting my thoughts. "Hey, Doug."

The man with red hair at the end straightened in his chair. His expression had gone from surprise to shock. He exchanged a quick look with Gwen who dropped his hand and frowned in response. Doug stood.

My mouth went dry.

In a whoosh of thought, I got it. I knew not only who had poisoned Lowell, I knew why. And I also knew when. Unfortunately, they probably knew I knew.

That was the most frightening thought.

Blood rushed to my face, and I eyed the door. Laurette closed it firmly.

Tom grabbed my hand and escorted me to the end of the table. He and Dave shook hands. Then Tom said, "Jess, this is the famous Doug DuBois I told you about."

Any hope to plead ignorance slipped away. I had no choice but to play along and then bolt when the time was right. I forced my hand out in greeting and my mouth to form the word "hi."

Doug's face fell as his brown eyes narrowed. He gave a slight nod, then gestured to his right. At that setting, a tiny placard with my name on it held my place. Tom's placard, next to Ulrich, read "Guest." We exchanged placards, and Tom sat next to Doug. That left me wedged between Tom and Ulrich, and far from the exit.

I began plotting my escape at that very moment.

Quiet conversation started up again. Laurette poured water that bobbed with ice from a crystal pitcher into each of our glasses. She made a second round, setting hunks of sourdough bread onto each small plate. When she reached me, I asked, "Where's Callie Lowell?"

I shouldn't have been surprised when she shot me a gracious smile and responded, "She is running a bit late. But not to worry. She'll be here *tout suite*."

I wanted to believe her but couldn't.

I took a drink to moisten my parched throat, my pulse racing. I counted the seats remaining. After Laurette sat, there would be only four chairs left. A glimmer of hope sparkled like the chandelier overhead. Maybe other guests were coming? Maybe Callie, or an editor. But why weren't they here yet? I crossed my fingers that everyone was running late, and that my imagination had worked overtime.

I swung my gaze to Laurette seated at the head of the table, nearest the door. She locked eyes with me and raised her glass. I broke contact and began a slow, counterclockwise sweep of the other side of the room. I couldn't read any additional placards. Worse yet, each person—Dave, Debby, Gwen—avoided my eyes. I felt like a mouse at a cat picnic. One wrong move, and their nonchalance could become a collective pounce.

And that's when I knew for sure.

The others weren't coming.

They'd never even been invited. This dinner party was for me.

I picked up my glass and took several gulps of icy water in an attempt to wake myself from this bad dream.

There were six suspects seated at the table. And me. And Tom. And no other witnesses.

I fought the urge to panic. Maybe we could bolt for

the exit. Tom could lead the way and I'd run in his wake. But to put that plan in action, I'd have to clue him into what was really going on. And I couldn't let the others know I was on to them. The only chance I had was to wait for their guards to drop, then I could make a break for it. Correction. We'd make a break for it. I had to take Tom with me. After all, I'd gotten him into this.

After another drink of water, I attempted to get Tom's attention. He was deep into a conversation about Pinot Grigio. Doug listened with an impassive expression.

"Attention," Laurette said. Conversation fell off. "We will begin by toasting Monsieur Lowell."

Dave set his glass down and picked up the placard to his left. He flipped it around. *Perry Lowell*. They'd saved a place for Perry.

An icy liquid shiver coursed down my spine.

We had to get out of here.

Chapter Twenty-One

After a solid three minutes of mental self-flagellation, I realized not only had Laurette played us, but we could truly be in danger. What made matters worse was that I, in turn, had played Tom. Gone was my Prata buzz. In its place were guilt, remorse, and more than a twinge of fear. I'd placed myself, and Tom, at a dinner party in a room full of suspects, no witnesses, and undoubtedly, an array of poisons.

Somehow, I didn't think Diane Sawyer started out this way.

In a flash, I saw my sister Jenna. This time, she sat at her computer, composing an e-mail to me. In the Re: box she'd written "Where are you, Jess?"

In my head, I answered: "In trouble."

I did a quick calculation of my options. I could run out of here, leaving Tom behind to fend for himself. That wouldn't be fair, even if they were after only me, which I sincerely believed was the case. Plus, I'd have to climb over Ulrich and Laurette to get to the door. I didn't think they would move aside willingly.

The other option was to grab Tom's attention, explain, and enlist his help in getting us the hell out of here. But it would take some doing. I couldn't say it out loud, so it would have to be in code. The problem was, Tom and I didn't have a code.

My best bet would be to stay quiet, eating and

drinking nothing suspicious until I had an opportunity to clue Tom in.

Longingly, I glanced to the door. Laurette caught and held my gaze again, which would become her pattern. It was as if she already sensed my plan. She paused a moment, then spoke to the group. "Dave will do the honors first with champagne cocktails."

Dave rose, retrieved a large circular platter with wine glasses atop and placed it on the table. I did a quick count. Eight glasses.

I struggled with playing the innocent. If I pretended not to notice that there would be no more guests, they might figure out that I was on to them. But if I asked where the other guests were, they'd know for sure. I frowned. It hadn't been only Doug and Gwen on a self-righteous streak of vengeance who'd murdered Perry. They'd all conspired his execution—family style. All of them. Maybe Gwen fed him the poison, but they'd all schemed in on it from the beginning, all agreed it had to be done.

That explained Jody's absence. She was no longer a board member. She'd even said she didn't like the way things were going. And Tracy O'Sullivan? He was out of it, too, having paid off Lowell to the chagrin of the others.

But one thing still bothered me. The timing of Tracy O'Sullivan's pulled review.

I thought about it a moment as Dave began his speech. Tracy must have been framed. The rest of the group were angry at him for paying Perry off—maybe they'd had an agreement that no one from GAAS would pay, a kind of economic sanction to silence Perry. But they didn't know Perry's wife owned the station and that he couldn't be stopped.

So in the end, the board had decided to kill two birds with one stone: Perry would be poisoned and Tracy sent to jail for the murder.

It all made perfect, logical, cold-blooded sense.

Unfortunately, I'd figured it out a little too late.

Fear wound in my gut like a snake.

The chefs had to know I was close to figuring things out. Maybe they'd even guessed that Tracy had told me about the extortion. One thing was fairly certain, though. They planned to poison me the way they'd poisoned Perry. And they weren't going to leave anything to chance.

I already felt sick. Sweat beaded on the nape of my neck and a trickle coursed down my spine.

As Dave set out a bottle of bitters and a crystal bowl filled with brown, irregularly-shaped sugar cubes, I tugged on Tom's sleeve. In response, Tom reached below the table and squeezed my knee. I turned to glare at him but was met with a smug smile. My eyes narrowed of their own accord.

Tom didn't notice. He returned his focus to Dave who made chit chat as he gathered his ingredients. Tom's hand, however, remained firmly on my leg.

I scooted away. Tom retracted his hand. Dave plucked sugar cubes from the bowl and dropped one into each glass. They plinked as they hit the edges and spiraled to the bottom. "Sometimes," he said, picking up a glass and drizzling brown bitters onto each cube, "sweet and bitter go well together. They sharpen our taste buds, make us more aware of both ends of the palate."

He set the glass down and repeated the process.

"But drown the cube in bitters, and it becomes nothing more than brown goo."

Murmurs of agreement followed.

"Fortunately, we're too smart to allow that to happen," Dave said. He poured champagne into each glass from a napkin-wrapped bottle. Immediately, the cubes began releasing air into the champagne, doubling the effervescence. Fizzing evolved into a sharp hiss that moved like a snake as glasses passed from hand to hand around the table. Reluctantly, I accepted mine.

With the glasses distributed, Laurette tapped the edge of her own with her knife. "*Bon soir*, ladies and gentlemen. Thank you again for joining me here this evening as we celebrate the life of a man who probably would not appreciate the meal we are about to enjoy." She raised her glass toward the group.

"To Monsieur Lowell's life." Laurette tipped her glass once toward the empty chair before drinking.

Ulrich stood and raised his glass in confirmation. "To his life," he repeated.

Nods followed, then the tipping of glasses, and at least two sighs.

I did a quick risk analysis. The champagne and bitters had come from one source. The drink didn't bother anyone else. If I didn't drink, they'd know I was on to them. I had to play the ignorance card for as long as I could in the hopes that they'd slip up, and I could slip out.

I sipped the champagne.

People glanced at me, then away.

Guests drank again, guessing the vineyard of the grapes and the label on the bottle. Tom chimed in, drinking like it was his last day on earth. How ironic.

When he righted his glass, the champagne reached only to the halfway mark. "Great champagne." He winked at me.

This was not going well. The last thing I needed was a horny, two-hundred-pound drunk man out who couldn't walk on his own.

I tried to get his attention. He needed to know we were most likely in the company of Lowell's killer and to ease up on the alcohol consumption. I couldn't very well carry him out of here. And I wasn't leaving without him. I was the one who got him into this mess.

Dull pangs of guilt coursed through my belly, like a tape worm after a heavy Thanksgiving. I'd really screwed things up this time.

I waited for a lull in the debate over the merits of champagne between Tom and Doug, then nudged Tom with my elbow.

He didn't face me. Instead he grazed my thigh with his fingertips.

Oh, sweet Jesus. He thought I was flirting. I looked away.

Finally, Tom stopped talking, Doug responded, and the conversation concluded. Tom turned, his hand now resting midway between my knee and hip. "What?" he said, his eyelids lazy.

I met his gaze, and Doug's stare behind him. I couldn't tell him anything with Doug eavesdropping. Tom slid his hand up and down my leg a couple times, dangerously near my crotch. His mouth formed a sly, slow grin.

Indignation replaced guilt.

Maybe I would leave him there.

Then I realized that the best chance I had was to

play along. It might make him hurry through dinner in an effort to get me back to my apartment and away from whatever plot these chefs were cooking up.

I forced a sweet smile. "So what does the future sommelier say about the champagne?"

"Very nice," he said, his voice husky. He drank again and set his glass down. Two-thirds empty. Tom wasted no time with the booze.

Debby Junette rose and lifted a large ceramic duck with a stake in its neck from the serving cart. "We made a sweet potato soup for the first course," she said, setting the duck on the table. She lifted the head from the body and pulled the stake out. It turned out to be a ladle. "Sweet potatoes and yellow Finns in a creamy, spicy broth. On top are shaved ginger curls, crystallized with brown sugar, then baked 'til crispy."

The group applauded as she stirred the soup and began ladling portions into bowls.

"The important thing about this dish is that every ingredient is respected, every flavor allowed to stand out."

I barely registered her words. I was too busy noting the communal serving bowl. Tom and I were safe for another course. I exhaled. I'd have a little more time to figure out our escape.

With the bowls distributed, Debby sat down again. Dave rose. "I've paired the soup with a Chardonnay," he said. "Scoot your wine stems my way and I'll fill 'em up."

One by one he poured two-ounce portions into each glass, then randomly distributed them again. "*Salut*," he said.

We raised our glasses, drank, and turned our

attention to the soup. Spoons lifted, mine included. But first, I sniffed. The scent, both sublime and spicy, elicited a rumble from my belly. If I ate a little, I'd be keeping up my strength, I reasoned. When I made a break for the door, my legs would be ready and strong.

I tasted. Outstanding. I scooped several spoonfuls into my mouth, munching the candy-like ginger curls at the end.

Dave began to speak again, discussing the process of candying ginger curls.

"That was really good," Tom whispered in my ear as I pushed my bowl forward.

"Yeah," I replied. I cast a gaze around the room. Every chef's attention was on Dave's explanation. I leaned toward Tom and spoke under my breath. "We need to get out of here."

Tom waggled his eyebrows again. "Yeah, I know."

I shook my head. "That's not what I mean."

Tom's expression grew confused. I leaned closer and hissed, "It's not safe."

Tom cocked his head, a puzzled expression forming. It gave way to a grin as he said, "Oh," and patted his breast pocket. "I've got it covered."

It took only a nanosecond for me to figure out what was in his pocket.

A ginger curl snaked its way back up my throat. I swallowed hard and turned away. One more comment like that and I'd poison him myself.

A heavy hand came to rest on my shoulder. I faced the owner. Ulrich.

He leaned toward me, his mouth oily at the edges. "Pace yourself," he said, drawing a napkin across his lips. "We have many more courses."

I shuddered. Simple suggestion or fair warning?

I whipped my head toward Tom and gave him my most meaningful glare. He took another guzzle of Chardonnay, then drained his champagne. "What's the matter?"

How I wish I could have told him.

Doug DuBois stood next. "Hello, everyone," he said. "I was asked to put together a little salad course. Now where I come from, salads are special. They're treated with respect and not dismissed."

He moved his chair aside and in its place thrust a serving cart. It slammed against the table. I jumped. He wasn't talking about salad. In fact, I realized, as I gazed around the table, no one had been talking about food in their dramatic little soliloquies.

Quickly, he regained his composure. Atop the cart were two foil-wrapped bowls. He removed the foil from each and picked up salad tongs lying adjacent.

"I decided to combine the heat of the south with the crisp and juicy flavors of the north. I call it Rainier. Hope you like it."

He fanned four purple leaves into a semi-circle atop each of eight salad plates, then fluffed ingredients in a frosty bowl. Afterward, he scooped salad onto the leaves, forming mini-mountains of shredded green and purple cabbage. At the top, he poked a small crater and placed three rounds of jalapenos inside.

I strained to keep my anxiety in check as the plates settled around the table. One more safe course. But how long would this last?

Laurette topped off wine glasses, setting an ice-cold hand on my shoulder as she passed me. When she'd returned to the head of the table, she raised her fork, and we commenced our salad course.

I poked around the vegetables like a kid at Thanksgiving, barely tasting the few cabbage strands that found their way into my mouth.

Instead, I watched the others. They were drinking and eating, commenting on the delicious food. A pinch of hope entered my stew of emotions. Maybe, just maybe, they'd get drunk or distracted or both, and I could find a way out of this mess.

Five minutes later, Ulrich hoisted himself up. At once, everyone silenced and focused on him. The air shifted in the room. Something had changed, but I didn't know what. My pulse jumped.

Ulrich crooked a finger toward Laurette. "You will help me do the honors?"

Laurette bowed her head at an angle. The two exited the room. In their absence, the group quieted. Tension grew every second the silence continued. I glanced around the room, but not a single chef met my eyes. Uh-oh. My heart leapt into overdrive and stayed there as the existential question of fight or flight kicked into supersonic speed. I should grab Tom's hand and lunge for the door. But I didn't know how the group would respond. Would they stab me with a butter knife? Could they stab me with a butter knife?

Before I could answer, Laurette and Ulrich returned, carrying platters with four silver domes atop. They split off at the head of the table, Ulrich on our side, and set a domed plate in front of each of us. When everyone had been served, they made another sweep through, collecting the domes and placing them on the platters, revealing our entrees. I stared at my plate: a hunk of red fish flesh topped with rice and mushroom sauce that looked like brown gravy, next to asparagus spears topped with more mushroom sauce.

Ulrich spoke. "I have created a dish especially for this evening. Salmon. And in my 'Nazi-like' way, I paired it with a red wine. Pinot Noir." He paused, looked to Laurette. She nodded, held a bottle for all to see, then began circling the table and pouring the rich hue into our glasses.

Ulrich continued. "The salmon has been steamed, then poached in own juices with caper, tomato, garlic, shallot. Then is turned in the frying pan with lemon and olive oil. Then, is topped with black and white sesame seeds. Jasmine and black rice with pecan and walnut over the fish, Morel sauce on top. Steamed asparagus with lemon and rose water, blanketed with beet and heart of palm sauce."

A quiver of fear pierced me between the ribs, pinning me to the chair. The dishes might look alike, but they'd been prepared separately. This was how they planned to poison me. I knew it as certain as I knew Seattle would rain again tomorrow. If I lived to see tomorrow.

Ulrich spoke. "Although some may disagree…" he stared at Lowell's chair, "many tastes are good. And sticking together makes them stronger, especially when defeating an enemy."

We'd officially exited metaphor lane and were smack in the middle of rationalization avenue. I stared at my plate in dismay. Not only was Ulrich acknowledging the murder of Perry at the Chocoholic Ball and the upcoming murder of me, he'd reminded everyone they were in on it together.

I glanced at Tom. A flash of confusion crossed his

face, but it disappeared almost as quickly.

I poised my fork along with the rest of them. I swear I saw a smirk pass from Laurette to Ulrich.

That was all I needed.

Now or never.

With one swoop, I nudged my water glass one way and my red wine goblet the other. They went over in a smooth motion, sending a flood of diluted wine in a rapidly expanding circle. Old tactic, yes, but it grabbed people's attention.

"Oh," Laurette exclaimed. She and everyone else, save Ulrich, jumped from their chairs, lifted their plates, and mopped below with their napkins. Ulrich simply set his plate in the middle of the table and stood. "I will get towels," he said, hustling out of the room. This time, Laurette failed to lock the door.

"I'm so sorry," I said.

No one responded. They were too intent on swabbing the red out of the white lace.

In a flash, an idea formed in my head. Without considering the consequences, I picked up my plate, set it in the middle of the table next to Ulrich's, then dabbed at his and my place setting. Finished, I replaced the plates—his in front of me, and mine in front of him.

"I'm so sorry," I repeated. I sat down again and quickly surveyed the group. No one appeared to have noticed the swapping of plates. I forced myself to breathe normally.

"No matter," Laurette said, flipping her napkin over and giving the lace another pat. "I will soak it later this evening."

Ulrich returned, exchanged clean towels for Laurette's dirty ones, then hurried off again. Laurette gave a final wipe with a fresh towel, as the others tucked folded napkins to the sides of their plates. She then poured new wine and water and set both glasses a few inches from my plate. No doubt she didn't want any more spills. Ulrich sat down beside me.

Laurette resumed her station at the head of the table. She lifted her glass and said, "*Mangez*. Please." She stared at me, a glint in her eyes.

I stared at my plate, sweat beading at my hairline now. As Ulrich began shoveling food into his pie-hole, I managed a few bites. The food had to be okay, or Ulrich wouldn't have eaten his...or rather, mine. As I chewed, I struggled with my conscience. One seat over, Ulrich ingested poison intended for me. My musical plate action would be the end of him.

Actually, I realized, his actions were the end of him. Somewhat consoled, I turned my attention to Tom. "Hurry," I said. "We have to leave."

He shot a toothy grin my way, then burped discreetly into his napkin. "Excuse me." He put a fist to his chest and thumped. "I must be eating too fast."

"Are you enjoying yourself, Miss Harriet?" Ulrich wiped a napkin across his brow.

I nodded, noticing that the pupils of his eyes had dilated. He returned to his food.

Without facing Tom, I muttered, "We have to go. Wait for my cue."

"Before dessert?" He took several large gulps of water, then grimaced. He turned back to me. "Oh, I get it," he said. "You're dessert."

I bared my teeth, hoping Tom would mistake it for a grin.

He did. "Just give me the sign, babe," he said.

Babe?

He did *not* just call me *babe*.

I glowered and gulped at my water.

Tom leaned in. "I wish I had more of an appetite," he whispered, his face registering pain. "I guess I filled up on everything else."

"Good," I said to him. I took another drink of water, then began to cough. The cough turned into a wretch. Several of the guests set their forks down and watched as my face grew red from the exertion. No one made a move to help me. In fact, Laurette took a sip of wine, her eyes zeroing in on my jerky movements. No doubt they all thought it was the beginning of my end.

"Excuse me." I coughed, clutched my stomach with one hand and Tom's shoulder with the other. We stood.

He folded his napkin atop the table and said, "Please excuse us."

All eyes fixed on us as we squeezed past Ulrich, then Laurette. Rounding the corner, I grabbed Tom's hand and broke into a run. I led him down the red hall, through Bien's dining room and onto the street.

Headlights appeared everywhere. I took a moment to get my bearings, then pulled Tom left. We were halfway down the block before he slowed. I dropped his hand and stopped.

He bent over and set his hands on his knees. He took several hard breaths.

"Come on," I said, looking back toward Bien's entrance. "We have to go." I had no idea what the group was capable of but wanted to put as much distance between us and them as humanly possible.

He turned a splotchy face upward. "Hold on," he

said, his eyes squinting. "Something's wrong." Tom took another breath, wretched, and out came a colorful combination of salmon, white rice, jalapeno peppers, purple cabbage, and green asparagus.

Oh, my God.

How could I have been so stupid?

They couldn't leave Tom as a witness. They had poisoned his food, too.

Chapter Twenty-Two

I whipped out my cell phone, turned it on, and punched 9-1-1. When the operator answered, I gave her our location and said, "My date's been poisoned."

"What are his symptoms?" she asked.

"Puking, fever, chills," I said. "Just get here." I gave her the address again and pocketed the phone.

I maneuvered a frothing Tom against the building. I didn't know how long it would take Laurette and the others to figure out we'd left the restaurant, and I wanted to make sure we were out of sight if they came after us. Fortunately, the night had grown dark, which helped, but our outlines were clearly visible by streetlight.

After glancing up and down the street, I turned to Tom. "Stay conscious," I said. "Please."

Tom gurgled a response, but his eyes closed to a slit. He clawed at his stomach and bent over, vomiting green bile laced with thin streaks of red. Blood.

I scanned the block for ambulance lights and tuned my ear for sirens. Nothing. I cursed out loud, but my words were drowned out by Tom's retching. I kneeled next to Tom and patted his back. "They'll be here soon."

Tom's eyes had closed completely. He dropped his hands. His body went slack against mine.

Mingled with the most intense despair I'd ever

known was the knowledge that this was all my fault. If I hadn't felt so guilty, the fear would have caused me to wet my pants.

I struggled to hold him up as long as I could, then eased his body to the sidewalk, avoiding the larger vomit splotches. Squatting beside him, I took his wrist in my hand and felt for a pulse. I'd taken First Aid in high school but hadn't paid a lot of attention. My teacher told me I'd be sorry someday. He was right. I half-expected someone with a gun to ask me a tricky algebra question next.

Tom's pulse weakened under my fingertips. "Shit!" I pressed harder. "Tom," I screamed. "Don't go to sleep, Tom."

Tom's mouth twitched and his pulse jumped once under my fingertips.

"Thank God."

The sudden scream of a siren overpowered my voice.

I jumped up, flagged the ambulance in, then watched as they loaded a limp Tom into the back. A small crowd had stopped and stared, but I ignored them.

A paramedic jumped back out. "Whoa! He's a sick one. What kind of drug did he take?"

I shook my head. "No drugs. Poison." I tried to climb into the back of the ambulance, but the medic blocked my path. "You'll be in the way," he said. "Meet us at Harborview."

I turned and ran toward Tom's car, then pivoted on one heel and raced back. I hopped into the back of the ambulance. Tom lay naked, save for green boxers, socks and shoes, on the gurney, his chest and abdomen a pale gray sprinkled with fat red welts. At that moment, a second paramedic jammed a long white tube down his throat. Tom's body became rigid and he gagged. Just as quickly, he went slack again.

The first medic swiveled his head and yelled at me. "Please. Let us help your friend." He pointed out the back.

"I need his keys!"

He grabbed Tom's shirt and jacket and threw them at me. I leaped out of the back and shook the jacket until keys jangled to the ground. As I bent to pick them up, a sharp screech rose from one of the machines inside the ambulance.

I looked up but saw only a flurry of blue activity. Tom's feet appeared, splayed open. On the bottom of one shoe, a four-leaf clover had been drawn. Suddenly, shame sank to a new level. There was so much I didn't know about Tom.

The second paramedic slapped the partition between him and the driver and shouted, "Go!" He met my eyes, then slammed the back doors closed. The ambulance squealed away, narrowly missing a Mercedes parked at the next light.

I sprinted to Tom's car, started it up, and floored the accelerator.

As I passed Bien, Laurette ran out. I flipped her off, but she didn't see me. Instead, she ran onto the wet, black pavement, her hair mussed, her gaze darting up and down the street. I didn't wait to see what she'd do next.

I ran a yellow light, then screamed up James Street. After hanging a right at Harborview, I double-parked, then ran into the ER. Tom was nowhere to be seen, but the paramedic who'd kicked me out of the back of the ambulance stood at the counter, chatting up a nurse.

I dashed over to him. "Where's Tom?" His blank expression reminded me he didn't know Tom's name. "The poison patient?" I said. "Where is he?"

His eyebrows rose. "Oh. He's inside. But they're not going to let you back there unless you can tell them what he took." He stared at me a moment. "He is one sick puppy."

"I do! I do!" My voice broke and tears threatened.

"You do what?"

"Know what he took!" My voice turned shrill.

He glanced once to the nurse, who began shuffling files. "Follow me," he said.

He swung through a large door, me trailing. We passed a reception area, three gurneys, one of which was covered in blood, and then jogged down a short hall. At the end, a doctor, two paramedics, and three nurses hovered over a bed. Tom's bed.

"This one knows something," the medic said.

A nurse broke free. Without lowering her mask, she asked, "What drug? How much?"

I shook my head. Why did everyone think he took drugs? "Not drugs," I said. "I think it's the same stuff they gave Lowell."

The nurse remained calm. She was most likely used to dealing with crazies like me. "I don't know Lowell," she said, her words slow and exact. "Tell me specifically what he took."

I couldn't recall everything Rod had told me, so I said what I remembered. "Newspaper ink, nicotine, rat poison, and, um, rocket fuel," I said. "The kind that comes from mushrooms."

The nurse's brows knitted together. She shook her

head, then her eyes grew wide. "Take her away," she told the paramedic.

The paramedic grasped my elbow and guided me down the hall. When I turned to glance over my shoulder, the nurse ran to the doctor, lowered her mask and spoke directly into his ear. The doctor hollered a bunch of Latin, Tom's feet jumped, and the little shamrock dissolved into a green blur.

"Is he going to be okay?" I asked the paramedic.

"They're doing all they can." He wrapped an arm around my shoulders and steered me down the corridor, away from Tom. "Your friend's got a great team working on him."

We turned the corner and exited through the swinging doors. The paramedic released me. I turned and peered through the doors' eye-level window. He got between me and the doors, blocking my path. No way was he going to let me back in there.

I met his eyes, my lip trembling.

"Ya gonna be all right?" he asked.

Had he not asked, I would have been fine. I would have gone to a chair and sat like the other ER waiters, twiddled my thumbs, bit back tears, and been wracked with guilt pangs. But when he spoke, I sobbed.

He reached out, pulled me against his chest, and held me like he saw this all the time and he knew what I was going to do next.

He didn't have to wait long.

A split second later, tears flowed from my eyes and snot flew from my nose. I'm pretty sure I drooled on his nice blue uniform, too.

Chapter Twenty-Three

"Is he going to be all right?" I asked the ER receptionist for the fiftieth time. It was after midnight. I'd told the cops everything I knew, but no one had given me an update since ten p.m. I'd promised myself I wouldn't pester the nurses and had decided on a two-hour interval update request. I plopped my elbows on the high counter, rested my chin on my hands, and stared at the nurse.

She tapped a few buttons on her keyboard, stared at the monitor, then closed the page and shook her head. "I'll let you know as soon as we know something." She blinked twice, then patted my shoulder. "I know where you are."

I dragged my arms off the counter and my feet back to the waiting room. Four people had been my companions in that room since the cops left. All of them had fallen asleep, despite a blaring television set, the strong odor of antiseptic, and the constant cycle of anguished patients who came in, talked their way through triage, and were escorted to a room.

I sat heavily in a green vinyl chair and lifted my feet to rest on a hassock. This was all my fault, I thought, for the hundredth time. If I hadn't been so aggressive. If I hadn't ignored Rod. If I hadn't included Tom. If I hadn't...The list went on and on and on in my head. Wearily, I loosened the laces on my shoes and wiggled my numb toes.

Eventually, I, too, dozed off, only to be wakened by a tiny earthquake rocking my bag. I opened my eyes and clutched the armrests. That was no earthquake. It was my cell phone on vibrate mode.

I plunged one hand deep in my bag, rooted around, and pulled it out. It pulsated once more. I stared at the number on the screen.

Rod.

I groaned, scooted higher in the chair, and checked the wall clock. Two o'clock in the morning, although it could have been two o'clock in the afternoon for all I knew. Nothing changes in the windowless ER waiting room. I flipped open the phone and pushed my spine flat against the chair, wincing at a muscle spasm.

"Hello," I croaked, my mouth a playground of bad tastes.

"Jess?" Rod's voice sounded anxious.

"Yeah."

"Thank God." He exhaled, loud in my ear. "I've been trying to reach you all night. Don't you ever check your messages?"

"I…" I began, but logic and words failed me.

"Are you all right?" Rod asked. "Where are you?"

I fought back tears as the realization of what had happened washed over me. "I'm at the hospital."

Rod gasped. "I knew it. Okay, I'm coming over. Which one?"

I told him, adding, "But I'm okay."

Silence filled the phone line. "Then what are you doing there?"

"My date." I stopped as my breath caught and I paused to get my emotions under control. After clearing my throat, I continued. "Tom was poisoned."

"Who's Tom?"

I swallowed against a lump that had positioned itself in the vicinity of my Adam's apple. "My friend in high places."

"Oh, right. The guy from the Space Needle," Rod said, his words slow, thoughtful. "Is he going to be okay?"

"I don't know," I said. Tears escaped my eyes. "They won't tell me anything."

"Okay," Rod said. "I'm coming. Just give me a half hour."

I wanted to tell him he didn't have to. I even wanted to tell him I didn't want him here. But the truth was, I needed the company. Even if it came from someone sure to remind me he'd told me so.

We hung up. I pocketed the phone, then stared at the television set. It had been muted at some point, so instead of a story, I saw random images of a late-night crime show, the close-ups revealing nothing of the plot. I looked away and focused on my thoughts.

Why had Rod been trying to reach me all night?

He'd never called me at two o'clock in the morning before. Six, yes; two, no. He'd always been aloof—the quintessential boss. Then again, we'd never had a murder scoop before, either.

Without a firm answer, I shoved myself off the chair. After weaving past a couple and stepping over a teenager who'd camped out on the floor, I wandered to the vending machines. I bought a soda and a bag of peanuts, then slowly walked past the nurse's station. Seeing me, she checked her screen again and shook her head. I mumbled a thanks and returned to the waiting room.

I settled down, chewing the peanuts one at a time and sipping the soda. People came in, others left, but I didn't keep track. By the time Rod showed, I had convinced myself I was lower than pond scum for allowing the whole incident to happen. He strode in, wearing a purple University of Washington sweatshirt, the mascot peeling at the edges, black jeans, and a frown.

I wasn't sure which seemed more odd. The fact that he wasn't wearing a tie or that I noticed.

He saw me and waved, zigzagging past a toddler somersaulting across the floor and two people spooned on a makeshift bed made of four chairs scooted next to one another. Without a word, he pulled me to my feet and threw his arms around me.

"Thank God you're all right," he said.

"Me?" I laid my head against his shoulder. It occurred to me that aside from a handshake at my interview, we'd never touched, let alone hugged. Again, odd. But so was everything else in the past twenty-four hours.

The canoodling was also very comfortable. About what I expected it would be, so long ago when I'd fantasized about it. He was the perfect height, and the groove between shoulder and collarbone cradled my skull perfectly.

"How's Tom?" he asked, his words near my ear.

"I don't know," I said, closing my eyes. "I'm still waiting."

He pulled back. "So what happened?"

I shrugged, avoiding his gaze. "Poisoned."

If ever there was a look that said "I told you so,"

that was the look Rod gave me. "Have you called the police?"

"Didn't have to. The hospital did, just after we got here." I pulled away and sat down. Rod sat next to me. "I knew what had happened as soon as he started, uh, throwing up."

Rod grimaced.

I gave him the gory details. "Have you ever smelled recently ingested salmon?"

"No, and I don't intend to." He grimaced.

"Nasty." I shook my head. After a moment, I turned to face him again. "Go ahead and say it."

Rod shot me a crooked smile. "No way. You already know I told you so."

I punched him in the arm, frustration giving way to curiosity. "So why'd you call?"

Rod heaved a sigh. "You're not going to believe this."

I was numb already. "Try me."

Rod kicked off his flip-flops and extended his legs. His toenails were cut short, and his feet were clean. He closed his eyes a moment and rubbed them slowly. When he reopened his eyes, they were red. "I'm going to start from the beginning."

"Shoot."

"After we talked, I called Aunt Callie. I wanted to know why she'd hired Tracy O'Sullivan for the memorial. It didn't make sense." Rod exhaled gustily. "She told me the police had called her—her name's on record as the *Sun*'s owner."

"What?" I wasn't sure if Rod was talking gibberish or if the combination of the late night and strange events prevented me from following his train of thought.

"Okay," Rod said, his words slower. "I talked to Callie. She knew about Tracy paying off Perry. That's why she hired him. She wanted to pay him back. She was embarrassed."

I nodded. Okay. That made sense. And Tracy, needing money, took the job. They may even have discussed why she wanted to hire him. Maybe she'd offered an apology.

"So what about the police?" I asked.

"They caught him."

"They caught who?"

"The guy from KTLK. The big guy," Rod said. "The cops knew who he was, knew he'd show up at your office eventually. Sure enough, when neither of us was there, he showed."

That's why it had been so cold inside the office when I'd arrived for the five thirty meeting with Rod. I shivered at the memory as well as the realization of the close call. The cops had probably held all the doors open. And that's why there were so many of them at the teriyaki place next door when I left. Then I thought about the only other person who could have been there.

"But who was he?"

Rod raised an eyebrow. "Cops didn't say, but from the way they talked, I think he knew Laurette and the rest of the gang."

"Where's Cherrie?" I asked, my heart jumping into my throat. "Was she there when he got there? Is she all right?"

"She's fine," he said, his tone abrupt. A shadow of a frown crossed his face. "Don't worry about her."

"Good," I said, truly relieved. Tom's poisoning

was enough guilt for one night. If I'd caused Cherrie to be hurt, I'd never atone, not in a lifetime of Sundays in the first pew in a Lutheran church.

I frowned. "So how'd they know it was the right guy?"

Rod shrugged. "Apparently, only so many people fit your description who are local thugs."

"Local thugs?" My mouth dropped open. It was easy enough to believe, but I didn't want to.

Rod nodded, removed his glasses, and cleaned the lenses on his sweatshirt. When he reset them, he continued. "He's got a mile-long record, as they say. Mostly petty stuff."

Goosebumps raised on my skin, and I had an eerie sensation someone was behind me. Before I could turn around and check, the hospital doors burst open. An extremely pregnant woman leaking a clear fluid limped in. She screamed, "I'm having a baby," which to me seemed unnecessary.

The nurse eased out from behind the desk and set the momma-to-be into a wheelchair, then pushed her down the hall toward the elevator. The woman whimpered as a huge, hulking man, her husband most likely, twitched and jumped. When the elevator door slid open, an orderly stepped out, turned on his heel, then wheeled her in. The doors closed and her moans muffled, then faded away.

The nurse walked past. I made eye contact. She smiled, held up a finger, and said, "I'll check again."

I glanced at the clock. After three a.m. I yawned, despite my anxiety, covering my mouth midway through.

"So then I asked Callie if she was going to the

press dinner," Rod continued.

I shook my head. "She wasn't invited. It was all a big set-up."

Rod nodded. "That's when I started calling you." He closed his eyes and sighed. "But I couldn't get through."

I thought back. I'd turned the cell phone off as we went into the restaurant, then on again when I'd called the hospital. The vibration hadn't registered with me probably due to all the commotion.

"When I couldn't get a hold of you, I drove down to the restaurant. No one was there."

"Shocker," I said.

"There's more bad news, Jess." Rod laid his hand atop mine.

I stared at him, then at his hand covering mine. I didn't move a muscle. I was almost afraid to ask. "What?"

"The…" Rod began, but stopped as the reception desk nurse came in.

She stood in front of me and said, "Your boyfriend can see you now. He's groggy, but it might help both of you." She pointed to a door. "Just tell the attending nurse who you're here for." She turned on her heel, leaving Rod and me alone again.

"He's your boyfriend?" Rod cocked his head.

"No." I shook my head and stood. "I had to tell them that so they'd let me see him."

Rod nodded, but frowned.

I slung my bag over my shoulder. "Will you be here awhile longer?" I asked, hoping he would, but not wanting him to know I cared.

"Yep," Rod said, sitting again. "When you get back, I'll tell you the rest. We haven't put this to bed yet."

Chapter Twenty-Four

I edged over to the bed.

Tom stared at me, his face less gray than before. The breathing tube had been removed, and his lips were chapped and flaky. The red hives on his forearms, just below the hospital gown, painted his skin in shades of mottled pink.

"I'm so glad you're okay," I said.

Tom lifted one hand. Attached to his middle finger, a clamp with a red light in the center flashed. Its cord connected him to a machine on my right that recorded data in digital numerals. I frowned.

"I'm sorry about all this," he said, his voice hoarse.

I shook my head and sat in the chair next to the bed. "Why are you sorry?" I took his hand.

Tom swallowed, squeezing his eyes shut as his Adam's apple bobbed. "Because I ruined our date." His voice squeaked.

Guilt overwhelmed me. I squeezed his hand tighter. Tears threatened again. He had no idea what really happened. He thought it was all his fault. I couldn't let him think that. Not when I was to blame.

I had to tell him. There was no other way I could live with myself otherwise.

"Uh, Tom," I said, my shoulders hunching forward. "What all do you remember?"

Tom raised one hand six inches off the bed before

allowing it to drop again. "I think I combined too many spices with too much alcohol." He grimaced again before continuing. "Too many kinds of alcohol."

I hedged, chewing on my lower lip. I felt the same way I did when I was six and had used my dad's fishing line as a Barbie clothesline, tangling the entire spool forever. It could have been any one of us kids, or even the dog. But it wasn't. It was me and he hadn't known. I could have walked away and hoped he wouldn't find out. But I couldn't do that then. And I can't do that to Tom now.

Tom cocked his head, his eyes dilated. "Do you think we could go out again sometime?"

I stared at his swollen face and shook my head. "Tom," I said. "Before I answer that, there's something you need to know."

"What?" His brow furrowed slightly, as if a complete frown would be too much effort.

I took a deep breath and leaned on the metal railing of his bed. "It's not your fault. It's mine."

Tom laid his head on the pillow and stared at me. "What are you talking about? You didn't make me eat and drink so much."

I relayed the events of the evening, telling the whole truth this time. I even told him about Mountain Man and the cops in my office and Rod showing up here. At the end, I said, "So Tom, I want you to know, I'm really sorry."

Tom wrestled his hand away, breaking a sweat as he did so. He tried to speak but shook his head instead. Then he fell asleep.

I waited a moment to see if he'd wake again. When he didn't, I walked back to the waiting room. The clock on the wall read three thirty. I rubbed my eyes and glanced around. Rod had held to his promise. He was still there, sacked out in a chair.

"Hey," I said, settling in next to him.

"How'd it go?"

"I don't know."

He frowned. "You don't know?"

I shrugged one shoulder. "He thought he'd drunk too much. But I told him the truth. He looked pissed, but he fell asleep before he could say anything."

"Oh." Rod's eyebrows rose. "What are you going to do now?"

I chewed a nail in indecision. "I think I'd better wait until he's up again," I said. "But you don't have to wait. I can do this on my own."

Rod shook his head. "No, I'll wait with you."

I stared at him. Rod's words held too much compassion. Especially from him. "Why?"

Rod put an arm around my shoulders. I didn't know if he meant it like a brother or not, but at the moment, I didn't care. I needed someone to lean on. "Don't think about that now. I just don't want you to be alone."

I murmured my thanks. The next thing I knew, the night nurse was tapping me on my shoulder. "He wants to see you," she said.

I disentangled myself from Rod's arms and jumped to my feet. Over two hours had passed since I'd fallen asleep. I had to pee but didn't stop moving until I reached Tom's room. When I arrived, his eyes were open. He glared at me.

Uh-oh.

With obvious exertion, he heaved himself to a

sitting position.

"Hi," I said, my voice meek. I sank into the chair next to his bed. I tried to take his hand, but he slid it under the cover. And I was not about to follow it. I'd seen the yellow tubes.

"Let me get this straight," he said, bringing a hand to his forehead, his words far stronger than before. "You knew there would be suspects from Perry Lowell's murder at this dinner?"

"Yes," I admitted.

He gave me the best scowl a man who was lucky to be alive could give. I apologized again, just for good measure, but he turned away.

It was anticlimactic. I wanted him to yell at me, get even for what I'd done. But he didn't. Instead, his eyes softened, and he spoke.

"So how come you're not sick?" he asked.

I stared at my shoes. "I switched plates with Ulrich."

Tom's eyes rolled to the ceiling. "Oh, God," he said. "That's it."

"What's it?" I asked.

He faced me again, strength in his glare, but voice weak. "I ate from your plate."

"What?" I leaned in. "Did you say you ate from my plate?"

"Yep," he said. "Before you spilled your water."

My mouth dropped open. "Why? How?" I asked. "You had your own. And when?"

"Yours had more mushrooms. Didn't you notice?" He formed a fist and thumped his chest. A foul-smelling belch erupted. "And the minute your plate was set down. You were focused on everything but the plate. I guess I know why now."

"Do you think your plate was poisoned, too?"

"I have no idea. I don't know if we'll ever know."

We sat in silence a moment, Tom's face flushing more intensely with each passing second.

Finally, he spoke. "How could you do that?" he asked. "I mean, if you want to put yourself in danger, I get all that. But why me, too? I didn't even know what was going on."

I didn't have a good answer. "I'm sorry, Tom." I shook my head. "I didn't know what to do. I didn't realize who the killers were until we all sat down and I knew Laurette had lied to me. And maybe it was only in my food. Not that it makes it any better. Maybe they didn't mean to poison you."

Tom slouched down and rolled away from me. I would have mentioned that his hind end showed, maybe advised him to get a nurse who knew how to wipe without leaving stripes, but I didn't want to embarrass him. I fixed my eyes on the side of his face that showed and ignored his hairy behind. It was the least I could do.

I waited a moment in indecision. Should I leave? Should I stay? Maybe he'd fallen asleep again.

A nurse entered the room, silent on white-soled rubber shoes, and solved my quandary. "You are one lucky man," he said, pulling the curtain closed around us.

Tom rolled onto his back again and said hello to the nurse. He didn't even acknowledge my presence.

The nurse checked Tom's vitals—his pulse, heartbeat, blood pressure, IV bags, and a disgusting gray bin under his bed that the yellow tube dripped into. All of it served to make me feel even more miserable about what I had done. Or not done. I didn't even know the difference anymore.

"How the hell am I so lucky?" Tom asked.

"Well, you're alive," the nurse continued, his eyes flickering to Tom and then me. He removed the stethoscope from his ears. "The other guy wasn't so lucky, you know."

Tom tracked the nurse with his eyes, but his head remained motionless. "What other guy?"

"The chef." The nurse checked the contents of a plastic pitcher on the table next to the bed. He removed the lid and filled it with cold water at the sink.

"The chef?" Tom's eyebrows furrowed and his eyes narrowed.

"Yeah." The nurse set the pitcher on the table.

He had to mean Ulrich. My mouth dropped open and my heart sank. I'd forgotten about him. "Is he…is he dead?" I asked.

"Unfortunately, yes. He got the same stuff you did, only way more and waited longer to come in. His friends were pretty tight-lipped, too. That didn't help." The nurse recorded notes on a clipboard that hung at the end of the bed.

I put my head in my hands. It was like a bad dream. I could be lying where Tom lay now. Or, three floors below, in the morgue, where Ulrich lay.

"Poor Ulrich," I said.

"Yeah." The nurse replaced the clipboard and shook a finger at me. "That's the one. The chef there got it bad. He puked blood for a full two hours before going into shock. By the time we got him here, he was convulsing so bad, it took three orderlies to hold him down so the doc could aim a tube down his throat. He slipped out of consciousness just as we figured out what to do. Less than an hour later, he was gone."

Tom met my eyes, glared, then turned away again.

The nurse continued. "It's rare to get two poisonings so severe in one night. But if you were at the same party and ate the same food, I guess it makes sense." He shrugged and placed the call button next to Tom's hand. "Give me a ring if you need me," he said.

Tom nodded.

When the nurse left, I repeated myself. "Tom, I am so, so sorry."

Tom gave me a wary look in return. He opened his mouth to speak. I perched on the edge of the chair and leaned forward, eager to take my punishment.

A stream of obscenities followed, all directed at me. His face bloomed in exertion. Every so often, one of his words would be punctuated by a loud fart. He didn't seem to notice, and I didn't point it out. Hospital courtesy.

"God damn it." Poot. "Such a bitch." Pwut. "You had no damn right." Bwuuupt.

After three solid minutes of chewing me out, his voice weakened to a rasp and his bowels had deflated. "Just get out of here," he said.

I rose, apologized yet again, and retreated to the hallway. As soon as I was out of sight, I raced out. There wasn't anything left for me to do—I couldn't screw this up any more than I already had. A few feet away, Rod waited, shoulder against the wall.

I stopped. "Did you hear?"

Rod nodded. "You got an earful." He gave me a half grin. "Not to mention enough methane to power a garbage truck."

I released an exhale and rubbed my forehead. A wicked headache had developed. All I could think of was sleep. "Don't make me laugh," I said, walking toward him. "I don't deserve it."

"Okay," he said.

Then I let him drape an arm around my shoulders and walk me out. At the nurse's station, I dropped off Tom's keys and told the nurse where I'd parked Tom's car. She didn't seem judgmental, but I figured everyone had heard the story of my deception, Tom's illness, and Ulrich's death. If the situation were reversed, I wouldn't have thought highly of me, either.

"Thanks for all your help," I said to her.

The nurse gave me a patient smile, then bowed her head over paperwork.

"Forget about it," Rod said as the sliding doors whisked open and we faced freezing temperatures outside. "I'll drive you home."

"That's okay," I said. "I'll call a taxi. I need to get my car, anyway."

"That can wait," Rod said. "I'm not letting you out of my sight until they catch the hired gun."

I stopped, frozen, my legs heavy. "You mean Mountain Man? I thought you said they caught him."

Rod hustled me along. "I also told you there was more to the story."

I scratched the back of my head. "Can it wait until my brain's awake?"

"Not really." We reached his car, and he opened the door. "The guy escaped. Ran right over the detective questioning him. Like a linebacker, the detective said."

I got in, stuck my hands under my thighs for

warmth, and waited for him to settle in the driver's seat. "Why wasn't he handcuffed?"

He locked the doors, turned the key in the ignition, then turned to me. "He was."

"Oh." My body sank like lead into the seat cushion. If he hadn't been afraid of the police, he certainly wouldn't be afraid of confronting me. I sighed. How did this situation get so out of hand so quickly?

Rod shifted into drive. "Just sit back in the seat. I'll drive you home."

I dozed, each pothole abruptly jarring me awake, until we reached my apartment. Just before tucking me in, shortly before eight in the morning, Rod said, "I'll be in the living room."

I had a strong desire to pull him into bed with me and curl around him. I was in such need of human compassion…and perhaps a little forgiveness. But that only happens in the movies. Instead, I passed out.

Chapter Twenty-Five

I padded into my living room in sweats and a T-shirt. Murky light fought its way through a dirty window into the living room/kitchen combination. Rod sat on my worn, fold-out couch. He'd removed his University of Washington sweatshirt and now wore a black polo shirt that hung a few inches over the waistband of his black jeans. Next to him, a stack of books rested atop an old pizza box.

"Good morning." It was Rod's voice. "Or should I say afternoon?"

I grimaced. If I'd known company was coming, I might have cleaned. And then again, I might not have. "Sorry about the mess," I said. "I've been busy."

Rod waved my comment away, then held out a twenty-ounce cup with a familiar logo. The sippy hole held a chocolate-covered espresso bean.

"Is that for me?" I asked, mouth watering in Pavlovian response.

Rod grinned and handed it over. I plucked out the bean and popped it in my mouth, then wrapped both hands around the cup so only the mermaid peeked out as I chomped through the chocolate to the caffeine-filled bean. With just the grit in my teeth, I touched my tongue to the opening on the lid and tested the temperature. Ah. Just right. I drank four big gulps, then sprawled in my brown fake-leather recliner across from

Rod.

"What time is it, anyway?" I asked.

Rod glanced at his watch. "Two o'clock."

I groaned and took another drink of the coffee.

Rod set his cup on the side table and pulled a folded *Daily Log* out from under his sweatshirt.

I frowned. "Is that today's?"

"Yep."

"How'd you get it so early?" I asked. "It doesn't smack against my door until six at night."

Rod grinned. "I have a friend in high places."

"Very funny," I said, sipping again. "So who's your friend?"

"My dad."

My jaw dropped. "Your dad works at the *Daily Log*?"

Rod raised an eyebrow. It didn't seem so threatening anymore. "Sort of."

"Oh, I suppose he owns that, too." I slurped my coffee.

"Actually, yes."

I sputtered, coughed, then spoke. "Your family owns the *Daily Log* and the *Sun*?"

Rod nodded and set the paper in his lap. "Okay, we need to have a little talk."

I wedged the cup between my knees and folded my arms. It felt a little eerie seeing Rod on my couch, drinking coffee and reading the paper. It was odd and overwhelming. But I liked it, which only confused me more.

"What?" I said.

"Well, you know how I gave you the story and not Cherrie?"

I smiled at the memory. "Yeah."

"Cherrie didn't exactly take herself off the story."

"What?" Visions of Cherrie writing my story and selling to the *Daily Log* filled my head. Granted, it had been my plan all along, but when I thought Cherrie might have scooped me, anger coursed through my body. My gaze leapt to the paper in front of him, and my heart jumped to double-time, and not because of the caffeine in my system. "Oh, no."

"Oh, yes." Rod frowned. "I know this is going to hurt like hell, Jess."

I nodded. "Don't tell me," I said. "Cherrie scooped my story, sold it to the Daily Log, and is reaping the glory."

Rod shuffled through the *Daily Log* stack until he found the front page. After backfolding it, he read, "Murder a l'allemande."

"Murder a l'allemande?" I said. "What does that mean?"

"She means murder by German or murder attributed to a German," Rod said. "But it's not a perfect translation." He sipped, then set the cup on my table and held up the paper. "Ready?"

Resigned, I leaned back and kicked out the footrest. "Ready as I'll ever be."

"Here goes." He glanced once my way, then focused on the paper.

"Murder a l'allemande, by Cherrie Belle."

Rod peered over the paper at me. I gritted my teeth and dug the nails of one hand into the arm of the recliner.

"Passion. People can feel passionate about anything: their lover, their beliefs, even their food.

Passion can create. Passion can destroy. For recently deceased Perry Lowell, host of Seattle's favorite restaurant review radio show, 'Perry's Prattle,' passion inflamed his quest for the perfect meal. And for German Chef Ulrich Alford, who served the highly toxic mushroom mixture to the critic, it was passion that drove him to kill."

"But that's not right," I said. "It was all of them."

Rod nodded. "I know. But since Ulrich's dead, and it was his meal that held the poison, the other chefs are going to let him take the rap for it. They may even get away with it."

I held my forehead in my hands. "I can't believe it."

"It's a damn shame. They'll walk. They'll all walk. Unless there's a way to prove they all knew." Rod paused, staring at me. "Did they say anything at the dinner that would prove anything?"

I thought a moment, the lack of sleep from the night before clouding my thoughts. "Does it matter?" I asked. "It would be my word against theirs. I didn't use a tape recorder."

Rod rubbed a hand over his face and sighed. "Maybe Tom would remember something?"

I shook my head. "They were all talking in platitudes: 'One for all and all for one.' Like they were Musketeers. I doubt Tom would take any of it the way I pieced it together. And I sure don't want to ask him for any favors right now."

"Yeah," Rod said. "You're probably right."

"Unless," I said, remembering the invitation list.

"Unless what?"

I jumped out of the recliner and bounded down the

hall. The last time I'd seen the invitation list it had been in my bag. I dumped the contents onto the floor and dug through the junk. At the bottom lay the list.

"I got it!" I called out.

"What?" Rod stood at the end of the hall. I ran toward him, extending the folded-over paper. Rod took it and stared. "What's this?"

"The elusive Chocoholic Ball invitation list."

Rod scanned over the names, raising his eyebrows a few times. When he finished, he folded it again and handed it to me. "Sorry, Jess. This doesn't mean anything."

I frowned. "Why?"

"Because they were all there." Rod rubbed the back of his head. "Ulrich included. And unless we find all the toxins in someone else's kitchen…" Rod shook his head. "Which they would have cleared completely by now…"

I stared at the list. "This really pisses me off," I said.

Rod snorted. "They sure covered their tracks."

"Yep," I said. "Except I think the person they were trying to frame was Tracy O'Sullivan."

Rod stared at the ceiling a moment. "Because he paid?"

I nodded. "Yeah. Probably." I was silent a beat before continuing. "I'm glad they didn't succeed. Tracy seems like an okay guy. I still can't believe they're going to get away with it. There's got to be something we can do."

"I can't believe it either." He shook his head. "Someone should go to jail for my uncle's murder."

I put a hand on Rod's arm. His skin was warm

against my fingertips. "I'm really sorry."

He wrapped his hand atop mine and squeezed. Adrenalin shot through my system. "Thanks, but I feel a lot sorrier for Aunt Callie."

I nodded in agreement. "And Will, too."

Rod hooked an arm through mine, and we walked back to the living room. This time, we both sat on the couch. He picked up the newspaper. "Want me to continue?"

"Nah. I get the idea," I said. "Why don't we go see Callie and tell her the real truth?"

Rod's eyes brightened. "Yeah. There will be time to discuss the possibility of a new—and improved—story later," he said. "Let's go see Aunt Callie."

I showered, dressed, and dried my hair in twenty minutes flat. By the time Rod and I got into his car, the sun was shining. I hadn't noticed what kind of car it was last night. I was too zonked. But in the daylight, the Acura MDX's black exterior and smooth lines were impressive.

"Some car," I said.

Rod pressed a button on his key fob and released the lock on my door. "Yeah. I bought it for its reliability." He pressed another button that started the engine. "But it's pretty cool, too."

We got in. I ran a hand over the tan leather seats and the dashboard that resembled a cockpit more than a car.

He turned to me, a question knitting his brows together. "So where's your car?"

I put a hand to my forehead, remembering my Kia sitting overnight on Seattle's streets. "Probably at the impound," I said. "I left it at Mouse Hole."

"Mouse Hole?"

"Yeah." I shrugged. "That's where Tom and I met."

"Mouse Hole." Rod laughed. "I haven't been there in years." He faced me. "Do they still dress like mice in there?"

I rolled my eyes. "Yeah."

Rod snorted. "I'll take you over there as soon as we get back from Aunt Callie's."

I didn't see what difference it would make, now or later. If it had a twenty-four hour grace, I still had plenty of time before it'd be taken away. If it didn't have overnight grace, it was already gone.

"Sounds good," I said.

Rod merged onto Interstate 5. Despite being mid-day, traffic thickened like winter snot as we neared the Interstate 90 bridge. I looked out over Lake Washington and breathed deeply. Sailboats dotted the blue surface in tiny triangles of red, yellow, and blue. They moved by bursts, the cloth semi-circles billowing in and out. Salted air poured through the car vents, filling my nose and lungs. As we exited the freeway, the outside noise quieted to a suburb-appropriate hum.

I relaxed in my seat and enjoyed the ride. I'd only been to Mercer Island once, but never stopped to relish the view.

Rod headed for Roanoke, the northernmost tip of Mercer Island. Big-ass, expensive homes lined the roads, wrought-iron gates denying our entrance. Eventually, the freeway noise only a memory, we came to Zinnia Lane, a private road. After turning left, Rod slowed to a crawl on a gravel one-car path. After two hundred yards, yet another black, wrought-iron gate awaited. It had to be Callie's. Rod braked, rolled down the window, and pushed the intercom button.

A moment later, a woman's voice channeled through the speaker. "Yes?" Slightly tinny, it could have been Callie, a maid, or a visitor.

"Hi, Aunt Callie. It's me, Rod."

"Oh, Roddie," she said, her words brighter. "We're in the back. Just come round."

A click followed as the intercom cut out. The hinge pinged, and the gate shuddered, then jolted open.

Rod rolled up the car window and turned to me. "Okay, she calls me Roddie. Don't laugh."

I pulled my lips in and suppressed a giggle. "What makes you think I'd laugh at you?"

Rod lifted an eyebrow as he eased through the gate. He drove down an old cobblestone drive, steering clear of copious amounts of shrubbery on the right. After about a hundred feet, the mansion came into view. Perfectly symmetrical, the main body of the house had been painted yellow and trimmed in white with plenty of framed windows that arched at the top. Flanking the mid-section, two half-houses formed points above circular windows. Matching white brick chimneys stood like bookends at either end, and a large white arbor, covered with deep-green ivy, covered the walkway to the front door.

I whistled low and even. "Some house."

"Yeah," Rod said. "Been in the family since the turn of the century."

He parked to one side, next to a huge rose bush. We got out and crossed to the other side of the house, our footsteps clumsy on the cobblestones. Rod took my elbow.

I let him have it. It was nice to be with him. Comfortable. Just like at the hospital. And again in my apartment.

When we neared the end, the cobblestones gave way to a cement path, obviously a newer addition. He released my elbow. He'd only been trying to keep me from falling, I realized.

I surprised myself by feeling disappointed.

"Let's head around the corner to the back," Rod said.

I nodded and focused on the walkway. Its width spanned two feet, too narrow for a sidewalk. Bordered by two stories of nearly windowless house on the right and a perfectly manicured hedge that must have been ten feet tall on the other, it extended approximately fifty feet. Above the hedge to the left, the top half of the second story of the house next door rose high, also windowless.

At the end of the path, Lake Washington appeared. The same sailboats I'd seen from the freeway were magnified by proximity, the colorful dots sharpened into bulbous sails, and framed by aqua water and blue-gray sky. I peered up. Today had been sunny and rain-free so far, but the wind was cool. It had to be frigid on the water.

Nothing had deterred the sailors, though. What had looked from the road to be a small group turned into a primary-colored fleet cutting across a glass lake with the aid of the wind. Squinting, I made out orange life vests and sailors leaning out over the water to balance the boat. It could have been my imagination playing tricks, but I thought I saw determined looks on their faces, as well. They'd have to be brave to court the

February wind and water.

We rounded the corner. In front of us lay a brick-laid courtyard. In the center, a rectangular pool sparkled clear and blue. Surrounding the pool, heavy wooden outdoor loungers pointed toward the lake. Callie reclined on one, bundled in what appeared to be a heavy Chenille robe, boots on her feet. On the matching table next to her were a pack of cigarettes, a lighter, and an amber-filled glass. Will sat across from her, bundled in a wool jacket and jeans, his focus on the marine view.

Rod stiffened beside me but greeted them both. "Good afternoon, Aunt Callie," he said. "Hello, Will."

A few steps closer and I noticed three pink-stained butts lay crushed in a crystal ashtray. Callie turned, exposing a lavender velour jogging suit with matching leg warmers beneath the robe. She looked snug and cozy.

"Beautiful, isn't it, Roddie?" Callie said. She held out her arms for Rod.

Rod walked over and hugged his aunt. "Are you smoking?"

Callie looked embarrassed but nodded. "It's been stressful," she said.

Rod turned toward me. "You remember Jess?"

Callie smiled at me. "Of course," she said. "How are you? Did you read the *Daily Log*?"

I returned her smile. "I'm fine," I said. "And yes, I've read part of the story." I looked to Will. "Hey, Will."

Will wagged a hand our direction, then returned his gaze to the lake. I waited for Rod to explain our visit.

Callie settled her gaze to the scene before us.

"Have a seat," she said, her voice low, relaxed.

We moved forward. Rod sat crosswise on a lounger next to Callie. I sat a respectful distance from the trio. Rod took her hand. "Aunt Callie," he said. "We came because we want to talk to you about the *Daily Log* piece."

Callie's eyes never wavered. When she spoke, her words were low and even. "This is bad news, isn't it?"

Will turned to stare at Rod, his eyes dark and somber.

Rod frowned and lowered his eyes. "Yes. Sorry, Aunt Callie."

Callie picked up the sweaty glass and drained the fluid inside, wincing as she gulped. "It wasn't Chef Alford, was it?"

Rod shook his head. "Yes and no."

She and Will stared at Rod.

"It's a long story, and I'd like Jess to tell you if she doesn't mind." He looked to me. "She did the research."

Callie and Will turned to me then, their eyes rimmed with tears. "What did you find out, Jessica?" Callie's words were soft, so I didn't even mind that she used the name my mother uses.

"Well," I stammered. I wasn't sure I wanted to be the bearer of such devastating news. "It was Ulrich, but not only Ulrich."

Callie dipped her chin once. "Go on."

"I think he was involved, but I'm pretty sure the others were, too."

"Who are the others?" Her gaze shifted back to the boats on Lake Washington.

"It was the group," Will said, cocking an eyebrow.

"Wasn't it?"

"What group?" Callie asked. She glanced at Will and then to me. I was silent. Will should answer that one.

"The Gourmands And Artisans of Seattle," he said. "I told you about them, remember?"

Callie turned toward me. "Is that right, Jessica?"

I nodded, frowning. Will had been right from the beginning.

Her face turned to stone. "What are their names?"

Will blew his nose into a tissue and waved a hand my direction.

I picked up where he left off. "Laurette Roen, Dave and Debby Junette, Doug DuBois—"

Callie swung to face me. "Doug DuBois?" She met Rod's eyes. "He's the one who threatened my Perry."

Rod nodded. "Afraid so."

Callie's mouth dropped open. "But he wasn't at the Ball," Callie said. "They wouldn't let him participate. How'd he get in?"

I shook my head. "He wasn't there," I said. "But his girlfriend was."

"His girlfriend?"

"Yes. Her name's Gwen Smith. She's a waitress at Green." I paused, allowing Callie time to absorb each part of the story. "That's the restaurant owned by Dave and Debby Junette. They're board members, too. Rumor has it they're bankrupt. Gwen told them she was a caterer and they let her in."

"But the paper said it was Chef Alford."

I looked to Rod, unsure what to say.

"That's right," he said. "That's who'll go down in history as having killed Perry."

Callie's eyes drooped a bit, and she wriggled a tissue from the pocket of her robe. She dabbed at her face, then spoke. "They're going to get away with it then?"

Rod frowned. "Maybe, Aunt Callie." He looked to me. "Unless we can prove they were involved."

Torn between the utter sadness I saw in Callie's and Will's eyes, and the odd joy at having Rod refer to him and me as "we," I met his gaze. When I returned my attention to Will and Callie, they had reached across the table and now held hands. Soon, they began crying.

Chapter Twenty-Six

I waited until Rod merged onto the freeway before I asked the question that had been nagging me since that morning. "So why are you working at the *Sun* if your family owns the *Daily Log*?"

Rod shrugged. "My turn."

"What do you mean 'your turn'?"

Emotions tugged at his expression. "Sometimes in a family business, you pull straws." He accelerated as we approached the bridge over Lake Washington. "I pulled the short straw a year ago last Christmas."

"Your family pulls straws?" I found it hard to believe that a business mogul would resort to a childhood decision-making strategy.

"Metaphoric straws," he said. "Sometimes. But sometimes we choose our assignment."

I stared at the water that looked blue against the gray sky. The sun had risen as high as it was going to, but it hadn't had much success warming the air.

"So if you could choose your assignment, what would it be?" I asked, shivering. I folded my arms and held tight.

"Easy. I'd be on assignment in the Middle East." Rod flipped a switch on the center console. "That'll warm your seat."

"Good God! Why?" I'd never pictured Rod anywhere but behind a desk.

"I'd like to do the real news. News that really matters." Rod's words were quiet.

I paused as my seat began to warm. I'd never thought of Rod as being anything other than a desk jockey. "Maybe you should tell your family that."

Rod nodded. "Yeah. I was going to, but then Perry died. It doesn't seem right to tell them now." He braked as we eased off the bridge. Traffic slowed due to new construction near the Arboretum.

I reflected on that a moment. Maybe everyone has family that pushes them in different directions. I thought about change, and family, and Jenna. I still hadn't replied to her e-mail. The fact was, I didn't want to go back home. I didn't want to admit it, either, even to myself. But it was what I needed to do. I sighed.

"Why the heavy sigh?" Rod asked.

I paused, trying to put it all into words as we merged onto Interstate 5. Rod accelerated, then moved into the right lane to exit into downtown Seattle.

"I don't know how to say this," I said. "But I'm going to need to take some time off."

"When?" Rod pulled to a stop behind a long line of cars. He turned to me.

"August, or thereabouts."

"You planning a vacation?" Rod glanced at the light, then back to me.

"Not really," I said. "It's a family thing."

The line inched forward. Rod released the brake and began navigating toward downtown Seattle.

He laughed. "Is she pregnant again?" I'd told him my Jenna story when I interviewed a year and a half ago. I felt I had to explain the blank spot on my resume and the lack of a degree. At the time, I hadn't thought he'd paid any attention. Evidently, he had.

"Yep," I said.

He laughed. "Okay."

I stared at him. He'd never been that nice about time off. Not even a long weekend. "Well…" The truth was, I didn't know how long I'd need. I waited until we were two blocks from my car, then asked, "Wait a minute. How come you're being so nice?"

Rod laughed, made a right turn, spotted my car, and drove toward it. He pulled to a stop and shifted into park. He turned toward me, resting an arm on the steering wheel. "I guess this whole thing with Perry has affected me, you know? I'd never really thought about all that stuff. I've never been married, don't have any kids. But I'm wondering if there's more to life than what I've seen so far." He shifted his gaze to the front window again and was silent a moment.

"I mean, look at Callie and Perry," he said, his words wistful. "They'd been together for a decade. When they got together, everyone thought he was in it for Callie's money. But the longer they were together, the more obvious it was that they really loved each other."

Rod shook his head, then continued. "And then there was the whole Will thing." He faced me. "I never really knew how much they all loved each other until this morning," he said. "They were there, comforting each other, over the loss of a mutual love. Like they were a big family. I don't have to understand it to see that it worked for them. You know?"

I nodded. I did know. It's the reason I had to go back home.

I stared at the Kia. I didn't see a ticket, or a boot,

but I did notice red splinters on the ground behind my car. Probably a broken taillight.

"How long can I have?" I asked.

"How long do you need?"

I raised an eyebrow at him before he could raise one toward me. He smirked.

"I don't know," I said.

Rod rubbed a spot off the top of the steering wheel with his thumb. "I'm not telling you what to do," he said. "But if it were me, I'd book a round-trip ticket."

"Why?" I asked.

"Because you need to come back," he said. "You need to keep chasing your dream."

"Look who's talking." I met his gaze and held it.

Rod ran an imaginary knife through his heart. "Touché," he said. "So what is Jess's big dream, anyway? Besides solving a murder mystery and reporting it."

I couldn't tell him. He was my boss. He might fire me. Then I'd be further away from reporting for the *Daily Log* than ever before.

"C'mon," Rod said. "I showed you mine."

I rolled my eyes. "Okay, fine," I said. "I want to cover real news. But not in the Middle East. Seattle's dangerous enough for me."

Rod looked surprised. "How come you never told me?"

"How come you never told me your family owned the *Daily Log*?"

"Never came up." Rod looked pained. "Do you want me to talk to my dad? We can get you on down there—especially after the detective work you did for Callie."

I thought about it. Seriously considered it for at least a minute. But I couldn't say yes. "I really need to do it on my own," I said. "I'm not ready yet. I need to go back to school, work my way up."

"I know what you mean," Rod said.

"I can't believe I nearly got myself, and Tom, killed on this story." I shook my head at the memory of Tom puking out his guts on a dark street. "There's probably a lot I don't know."

"We all can learn more," Rod said. "But it's not fair to blame yourself completely. There was no way to predict how the story was going to go."

"But you knew," I said. "You knew there was something fishy about that dinner."

Rod nodded.

"How'd you know?"

"Because I didn't need the story as bad as you."

"What do you mean?"

"I mean I was able to be objective because I wasn't so close, even though it was my family." He shrugged. "You were too close. You wanted it too much."

"Oh." He was right. What I needed was a chance to do real stories and focus on the story, not the result.

"So how long will you be gone?" Rod asked.

I thought about that a moment. If I did as Rod suggested and bought a round-trip ticket, I could return in time for classes at the University of Washington in September. I'd still be helping out Jenna, but I'd also do what I needed to do for me.

I met Rod's gaze. "Six weeks. I'll be back in mid-September."

"Good."

That settled, I reached for the door handle.

"Because I'd miss you if you didn't come back."

The statement registered only halfway. Sure, he'd miss me. He'd probably have to take over for the personal ad takers while I was gone. I pulled on the handle, heard the catch, and swung the door open.

"Jess?"

I set one foot on the street outside the car, then turned to face Rod. His eyebrows pulled together in confusion.

"What?"

Rod swallowed. "I said I'd miss you." His smile was faint.

My mouth dropped open. I stared. Was that a twitch in Rod's cheek? I'd never seen that before. It tweaked something inside of me.

Or maybe I'd been tweaking all along.

Or maybe I was emotionally and physically exhausted from chasing a story I'll never get credit for.

I got back in the car and closed the door. His grin broadened and the twitch stopped.

"Why are you telling me this now?" I asked.

"Like I said, Perry's murder got to me." Rod placed his forearm on the steering wheel. "I don't want to waste any more time."

I stared at him, waiting for the punch line.

"Okay," he said. "I'll say it: I like you."

When I didn't respond, he added, "I think you like me, too."

I grinned despite myself. "Maybe."

Rod checked his watch. "Tell you what, let's take the rest of the day off, then meet up later for a beer."

Uneasiness spread through my body. "Date my boss?" I said, shaking my head. "I don't know." What would happen if we broke up? What would happen if we didn't?

"It's just a beer," Rod said. "Look, I'll be down at Pier Forty-nine at seven o'clock. If you show, we'll have a beer. If not, I'll have a beer by myself."

"Okay." I jumped out of Rod's car and into my own as quickly as I could. I'd bought a few hours to go to the office, reply to Jenna's e-mail, and head home for a nap. Then maybe things would get right in my head again. And I'd know if I should show up at the pier and for a beer.

I made my way to the *Sun* offices, waving at the delivery guy practicing his moves behind the teriyaki restaurant. He did a little jump that ended with a kick, then put his hands in prayer position in front of his chest. After a quick upper-body bow, he broke character, grinned wide, and waved with both hands.

I parked and walked through the *Sun* doors. In an instant, I was reminded of why I'd fought so hard to solve Perry's murder. There, in front of me, stood Cherrie Belle behind the old receptionist desk. She wore a white shirt that frilled at the collar and wrists, and her hair had been slicked back into a neat ponytail. An expensive black briefcase lay open atop the desk. As soon as she saw me, she stopped rummaging through the drawers and threw a couple diskettes into the briefcase. She straightened and leveled her gaze. In a flash, I knew she knew I knew.

"Did you hear the good news?" she said, her words breathy. "They caught him again. The guy from KTLK. He went to a friend's house to get the handcuffs off. Turns out, the friend wasn't a friend, you know?"

I raised an eyebrow and stared directly at her. What

I wanted to say was, *Like you?* Instead, I said, "Yeah, I know."

Her eyes hooded, and she broke eye contact. She snapped the briefcase closed and dialed the brass combination locks at either end. "Once the cops told him he'd be charged with murder, he gave up the names. All of them."

I had a choice. I could tell her off and ask who she had to blow to get the info. Or I could be a lady. Before I decided which way to go, Cherrie continued.

"Laurette Roen, Dave and Debby Junette, Gwen Smith, and Doug DuBois," she said. "I just finished up the story." Her gaze rose just enough to meet my jaw line.

I released the strained muscles in my cheeks and said, "Congratulations, Cherrie."

Cherrie appeared startled at first, then narrowed her eyes. She walked around the desk, briefcase in hand. I opened the door for her.

"Nice story," I said, realizing that something good would come out of all of this. It was probably the last time Cherrie would ever steal a story from me. "Enjoy your new job."

Cherrie paused, staring at me. Then she opened her perfect ruby-red mouth and uttered, "Thanks, Harriet." Her eyes held mine a moment more, then she took one last look around the office, turned on her heel, and walked out the door.

I closed and locked it after her. As I made my way down to my cave, I caught a whiff of fresh flowers. I looked around, then down. The pink tulips that had been on the desk had been tossed in the round file. A shame. They hadn't even lost their scent, and the blooms were still intact.

Shrugging, I continued down the hall and pushed my knobless door open. After waving the door a few times to release the musty scent, I stepped in, punched the computer on, and settled in my chair. I took a few minutes to listen to the hum and acknowledge the grungicorn poster. Was it me, or was he proud of the way I had handled Cherrie?

The computer beeped, and I logged on. I opened up my e-mail and replied to Jenna. I told her I'd be home in early August, and that I'd be staying until September fifteenth. I told her I couldn't stay any longer because I was going to go back to school, but that while I would be there I was on diaper-duty. Then I signed my name and added: "P.S. I really, truly love you."

I closed down the computer again, ran out the front door, and locked it behind me. As I neared the Kia, I began to hum. I started the engine, tuned the radio, and headed for the southbound ramp of I-5. But instead of taking the Bothell exit toward home, I exited onto Southcenter Mall Boulevard.

I drove straight to Macy's and parked, singing along to the radio until the song finished, then killed the engine. After a quick glance in the overhead mirror, and an equally quick check of my teeth, I bounded up to the front doors and asked the nearest salesperson where they kept their little black dresses.

"As in date dresses?" she asked, a waggle in her well-shaped brows and a grin on her ruby-red lips.

I thought only a moment before responding. "Yeah."

She pointed toward the escalator leading to the second floor. "One flight up," she said. "And have fun."

"Yeah," I said, and hopped on.

A word about the author...

Lori Pollard-Johnson is a retired educator and current wife, mama and grandma. She writes from her homes in Washington and Arizona, and has been published in fiction, nonfiction and poetry, in publications as diverse as Vegetarian Journal, Seattle, Black Belt, Bridal Connections and The Binnacle, in addition to five novels. When she's not writing, she's playing with her grandbabies, braiding rugs, perfecting her shavasana, swimming, hiking, practicing her releves, renovating fixer-uppers, reading, or watching javelinas dance through her backyard.